a different hurricane

a different hurricane

a novel

H. NIGEL THOMAS

DUNDURN
PRESS

All characters in this work are fictitious. Any resemblance to real persons, living or dead, is purely coincidental.

Publisher: Meghan Macdonald | Acquiring editor: Kwame Scott Fraser | Editor: Russell Smith
Cover designer: Laura Boyle
Cover image: Meteorological map: istock.com/Yuliya Shavyra; upper drop: Adobe Images/Microgen; middle drop: Adobe Images/Faizan; lower drop: Adobe Images/Sheviakova

Library and Archives Canada Cataloguing in Publication

Title: A different hurricane : a novel / H. Nigel Thomas.
Names: Thomas, H. Nigel, 1947- author.
Identifiers: Canadiana (print) 20240340329 | Canadiana (ebook) 20240340345 | ISBN 9781459754065 (softcover) | ISBN 9781459754072 (PDF) | ISBN 9781459754089 (EPUB)
Subjects: LCGFT: Gay fiction. | LCGFT: Novels.
Classification: LCC PS8589.H4578 D54 2025 | DDC C813/.54—dc23

We acknowledge the support of the Canada Council for the Arts and the Ontario Arts Council for our publishing program. We also acknowledge the financial support of the Government of Ontario, through the Ontario Book Publishing Tax Credit and Ontario Creates, and the Government of Canada.

Care has been taken to trace the ownership of copyright material used in this book. The author and the publisher welcome any information enabling them to rectify any references or credits in subsequent editions.

The publisher is not responsible for websites or their content unless they are owned by the publisher.

Printed and bound in Canada.

Dundurn Press
1382 Queen Street East
Toronto, Ontario, Canada M4L 1C9
dundurn.com, @dundurnpress

For the Richards family in Riley, St Vincent, especially
Agatha Richards, "Tant Alice," where I found the
quiet haven I needed during the last four years —
1964–1968 — before I immigrated to Canada.

Chapter 1

A MUG OF COFFEE IN HIS LEFT HAND, GORDON WALKS from the living room onto the front porch. He disturbs a grey grackle searching for crumbs under the patio table. It flies left, to the fence separating his property from Austin's, and fluffs its feathers. *Protesting my presence*, Gordon thinks.

It's past eleven. He's still in his pajamas. He wonders what Allan would say if he finds out that for more than a week, he hasn't done the prescribed morning walk out to the highway at Sion Hill. "Exercise is imperative, Gordon. We're descended from hunter-gatherers." *Imperative.* He chuckles at Allan's bookish language. His has become bookish too. Maureen's influence. Exercise. He sighs. Allan, who lifts nothing heavier than a stethoscope, castigates him for not exercising. Has a gym downstairs. Never uses it, his wife, Beth, says.

He turns left and limps to the seaward end of the side porch, the other arm of its reversed *L*; it runs the width of the house. The short arm is at the front. He leans against the porch railing, holds on to the mug, and stares down the cliff at the Grenadines Wharf and the cruise ship berth. No cruise ship in the harbour today. Six cars are lined up to enter the hold of *Admiral I*. It should have departed for Bequia fifteen minutes ago. In the few square feet of mostly bare space between the Grenadines Wharf and the cruise ship berth, someone's afterthought for a park, a man sits on the lone picnic bench eating from a container perched on his lap. Near the shore, the sea is emerald with patches of turquoise. Farther out, it's azure with linear patches of brown sargassum, less now than in 2015, when it was fouling beaches all over the Caribbean and causing tourist cancellations and panic in hotel owners and workers. Calm everywhere. Just the occasional car horn and the rhythmic slosh of the waves against the quays. No hint of a breeze, even. To his right the red and green corrugated roofs of Kingstown extend all the way out and up to Edinboro, where Allan lives. The air is humid and heavy.

◆

What will Frida ask him when she arrives today? In his nightmare two nights ago, she wagged the flash drive containing Maureen's journal in his face and shouted, "Murderer! Murderer!" He awakened, relieved. Frida wouldn't read that journal for another twenty-four years. Usually it's Maggie, his mother-in-law, who accuses him.

His legs feel tired. He should sit. He turns and glances at the patio table and its four chairs. Rust shows in the wrought-iron frames. Six years ago, he'd have promptly sanded and repainted them. In the last six years, he couldn't convince Maureen to sit here, even with the light turned off.

There's a stabbing pain in his neck. He holds the railing firmly with his free hand and rotates his head eight times to relax the neck muscles. Sometimes this works. He's had these neck pains for the last six years. At first, they came with a tremor and chills, even on the hottest of days. The muscle relaxant Allan prescribed helps; the piercing jab with each heartbeat is gone, and the tremor and chills are now rare.

He can resist his legs no longer. He hobbles to the table and sits.

Since Maureen's death a year ago, he has had more trouble sleeping. He awakens instinctively to curtail the nightmares. Maureen wags her finger at him and threatens to expose him. Sometimes it's Medusa Maggie turning him to stone as he tries to run from her, but can't move. He awakens and spends hours thinking about the nightmares and how to stop them.

He couldn't fall asleep last night. Two hours before going to bed, he learned of Dexter Pottinger's death on Facebook. Dexter's face, painted in the colours of the rainbow, haunted him. He'd thought Dexter courageous for being the public face of last year's Jamaica Gay Pride. Dexter's neighbours heard him calling for help and didn't respond.

After lying awake for more than five hours, Gordon had got out of bed around 5:00 a.m., went to the liquor cabinet, and poured himself a double Scotch. Allan must not know he does this regularly. He prescribed melatonin for him to take in the early evening. "Gordon, you must sleep for eight hours." Said with the usual unctuousness. *My dear Allan, you must know I cannot command sleep any more than you can medicate against nightmares. Bet you have nightmares too. Might explain your recent interest in psychiatry. Guilty like me. But lucky. Damn lucky.*

He took the Scotch into the living room, sat on the recliner bought for Maureen's comfort eighteen months before her death, and watched BBC World to get the latest on Irma, now a Category 4 hurricane and projected to return to a Category 5. It was predicted to hit northern Cuba and Florida. In the evening, Allan had phoned him from Union Island, worried about the damage Irma might do to Cuba. He'd spent a year there studying Cuban methods for treating psychiatric illnesses, and had visited Baraguá, where the descendants of English-speaking West Indians, including some of Allan's relatives, still live.

Together, three years ago, they watched Gloria Rolando's documentary *Los hijos de Baraguá*, and Allan pointed to a few of his cousins among a group of women doing the maypole dance. Some of them might well have been Gordon's cousins too. One of his father's uncles had moved to Cuba after work on the Panama Canal ended. The Baraguá houses are like the wooden houses of Gordon's childhood: unpainted, perched on metre-high cement pillars, and roofed with rusting sheet metal. In 2004 Ivan, a Category 3, devastated Grenada. He shudders at what a Category 5 might do to Baraguá. "And while we're following the devastation Irma is causing," said the BBC newscaster — a South Asian woman in a skintight royal blue dress, her accent like Maggie Thatcher's — "José has become a Category 4 hurricane and is following the same path as Irma. Barbuda and the Virgin Islands might again be struck."

His mind swarms with pictures of the devastation in Barbuda and St. Martin; Harvey in Texas; the monsoon floods in India, Nepal, and Bangladesh; the five hundred thousand Rohingya escapees from Myanmar now huddled in camps in Bangladesh.

The horn signalling the departure of the Bequia ferry brings him back to the present. The pain in his neck has lessened. Now, with his elbows on the table and his hands supporting his chin, he recalls the two hurricanes he experienced: Allen in Barbados in 1980, and Tomas here in 2011. In 1980 he was on his way home from Montreal the first Saturday in August, having just completed the first year of an economics degree at Concordia University. He'd had to change planes in Barbados for the flight to St Vincent, and had decided to spend the rest of the weekend there to visit his two paternal aunts and to fulfill a promise he'd made to May to find out what had become of Albert, their half-brother who'd lived with them in St Vincent briefly. His plan had been to leave Barbados on the Monday morning. But two days before, his cousin Mark had picked him up at the airport and said that Hurricane Allen was heading for the island. It struck the next night. His aunt's recently built one-storey wooden house withstood the thunder, lightning, rain, and wind. He thinks the worst of the terror lasted about two hours. Next day Mark took him on a drive from Bagatelle to Speightstown. They saw very little damage — fallen trees for the most part. Later he learned that five hundred homes had been damaged. But in mountainous St Vincent, the hurricane had knocked out all radio communications. The first sight that greeted him as he landed in St Vincent three days later — the airport had been inaccessible before then — was the large number of houses in Arnos Vale and Villa that had lost their roofs. At the time he and Maureen lived in a rented house in Kingstown Park. It wasn't damaged. But in Riley, it left their neighbour Mrs. Beach's house a pile of rubble. Visiting May and his mother ten days after the hurricane, he found the trunk of a breadfruit tree still blocking the road.

Six years ago, Tomas blew off several roofs, including Austin's and May's, and left water damage all over the island. A glancing blow. The micro rainstorms, atmospheric rivers, hitting St Vincent in the last ten years have been deadlier than the hurricanes. Some of the graves the last one unearthed are still open. Disasters that kept him working late into the night, costing the damage and providing the figures the PM needed to bolster his pleas for overseas assistance.

◆

In Montreal there had been accusatory nightmares too. He'd been tempted to divorce Maureen and stay in Montreal. But there were the tens of thousands of dollars he'd have had to repay the St

Vincent government for the scholarship he'd received. He'd signed a contract to work for a minimum of seven years following graduation. Most of all there was Frida. But in Montreal he'd felt free. For the first time he didn't fear prosecution, persecution, or disgrace. Were it not for Frida, he might have remained, the money notwithstanding. André would have helped him repay it. How would that have affected their relationship? In his dreams about André there's always an element of betrayal. Would he have been the one to look after André when he became ill? Would the relationship have lasted that long?

That scholarship. God and governments work in mysterious ways. A month before Frida was born, a scholarship that he had been promised for three years was suddenly available. He was informed about it in mid-July, and Frida was born on August 13. She was four days old when he left for Montreal. In his four years at Concordia he made one trip back to St Vincent — that August when Allen pounded Barbados, St Vincent, and St. Lucia — to celebrate Frida's first birthday. When he saw her, already walking and saying her first words, he knew he had to return to St Vincent to raise her, a fact he remembered each time he was tempted to remain in Montreal.

◆

He stands, swings his arms a dozen times, then returns to the front. Above him on the steep incline to his left, Theo, Austin's son, is dribbling a basketball, reminding Gordon that it's Saturday. On weekdays Theo attends community college. Gordon stares up the incline. Behind the fence of white plastic laths, only Theo's head and extended arms are visible. He shakes his long hair out of his face each time he's about to throw the ball. The ball bounces off the rim of the basket or misses altogether.

Austin Nichols is White, sixty-two, a widower, and the heavy equipment manager at what was once Cable and Wireless. "Without a university education," he sometimes brags. He irritates Gordon with his never-ending complaint that St Vincent is no longer a British colony. "We had things good-good and then that damn fool Cato went and got independence and fucked things up. Then Mitchell, he fuck it up some more. Now under Gonsalves ... man, all I can say is, we totally fucked. I want to be in a country where my son have a future. You know, Gord, in 1998, I had a chance to work in Tortola. Right after Francine and I got married. But she had her job as a pharmacist here. No way she wouldo' find that kindo' job in that one-horse place ... Theo wouldo' been born in Tortola, though. Today he would be a British citizen and have a future." He paused a long time and stared at Gordon across the patio table. It was just the two of them sitting on Gordon's side porch. Austin never speaks about Theo when Beth, Allan, and Percival Grant (Freckles), the neighbour to Gordon's right, are present. Maureen was already dead. "You know, Gord-boy, you lucky to hell and you don't know it. Your Frida born the right time. Look how that girl take off like a jet plane! We did just move here when she get that scholarship to study in Jamaica and her picture was in the papers. And now she have a big job with a drug company. You must be proud as hell."

"Theo will turn out all right. You're too pessimistic. There are still opportunities here, only harder to find."

"Man, them opportunities is for the brightest o' the bright. Or the ones with connections. I ain't got no connections with them higher-ups. And my boy ain't scholarship material. I know he does study hard. He does work his ass off. But he not like your Frida, nuh ... his name not going be in the papers. He barely passing his courses. Them opportunities you mention, they's not for him."

"But his name *was* in the papers."

"You mean for that painting!" He shook his head. "That don't mean nothing. You don't see all them Rasta fellows on Bay Street and outside the market with their art? You ever see anybody buying?" At the arts and culture fair held at Easter, Theo had won first prize in the painting category for his thirty-by-forty-inch canvas of *Kingstown Seen from Cane Garden*. A picture of the painting was in *Searchlight*.

"Austin, cut the boy some slack. Look at the millions paintings going for these days? Peter Doig, a Trinidadian that dropped out o' high school, sells paintings for millions."

"You pulling me leg or what? He is a exception. Most o' them paintings is by dead men. I hear them painters starve to rass when they been alive. Some had to bull to eat."

"A few did well. Andy Warhol died a millionaire. Theo's work is better than his. Peter Doig is still alive. Austin, loosen up; let the boy follow his dream."

He pouted and shook his head skeptically.

Austin is worried about more than Theo's intelligence. At eighteen, he's a bit overweight, and his voice is as high-pitched as a keskidee's chirp. His beautiful hairless face (minus his jowls), dark hair reaching midway down his back — sometimes in a ponytail — mincing walk, swinging hips, and rippling *boley*-size buttocks — draw attention. "*Une demoiselle*," Beth once remarked and quickly added, "I don't mean anything. He can't help how he is."

Theo's fat comes from Austin, who has quite a beer gut and heavy jowls. The swinging hips too. But not the buttocks. Flatter than Gordon's. Austin's trousers hang there like pleated curtains. Theo got his from his mother, Francine. Every couple of years, Theo's maternal cousins come from Mayreau to visit. The paternal relatives live mostly in Bequia. They never visit. Austin rarely mentions them.

Theo no longer accompanies Austin when he visits Gordon. Never did more than eat and play games on his tablet when he used to come. Probably a recluse. Gordon has never seen him bring friends to the house or interact with the neighbourhood kids. For good reason. Freckles the neighbour tells his sons, loud enough for half of Cane Garden to hear, to keep away from "that *sissy* up there."

Freckles thinks that Flossy, Austin's housekeeper, does more than cook and clean. "Gord, you ain't see she in that house some-times past eight o'clock of a night and then he driving she home? Can't say I blame he, nuh. She a sweet little thing." He swallowed and licked his manicou chops. "See that ass on she?" He whistled, passed one hand over his clean pate, and placed the other on his crotch. "You and Austin is buddies. Ask him for me, nuh? I want to make a move on she, but I don' want to trespass, yes."

Freckles's wife, Christine, was still around then. She is childless. A pediatric nurse. For a while, she took Freckles's beatings in stride, including one he gave her the day after they celebrated their tenth wedding anniversary. Until she left him, she got beaten on average once per week. One time she ran out the house and called the police to escort her back home.

"Maybe she thinks there's nothing better out there. Better the devil you know," Maureen said while she and Gordon stared at the police and Christine entering Freckles's gate. (The steep downhill curve in the road gives a full view of about a third of Freckles's house.) She had already told Maureen that she was afraid to leave him.

Austin had a different explanation for Christine's staying. "You see that thing he showing off in them tight jeans. That's the secret. It have women who go endure fire and brimstone for that."

Maureen gave him a frowning stare. That time it was just the three of them sitting on Austin's porch. Francine had taken Theo to visit relatives in Mayreau. "Where do you *men* get your infor-mation? The *things* you feel empowered to say!"

"I only repeating what I hear you-all women say."

"Penis size isn't what a woman looks for in a good man." She sounded disgusted.

"Just repeating what I hear you all say," Austin said with raised palms and bulging blue-grey eyes.

"No, you're repeating the misogyny that male calypsonians promote."

Gordon was silent but felt like saying that some females promoted it too.

Freckles has four sons living with him. They and Gordon have quarrelled about their Rottweiler defecating and peeing on his lawn. Still, he greets them when he sees them in their yard or on their porch. Sometimes they don't answer. Everett, one of the nineteen-year-olds, who recently dropped out of community college, seems to be every bit a cocksman as Freckles. He'll be a father in a couple o' months. "Chip off the old block," a chuckling Freckles told Gordon. The pregnant girl comes to cook and clean almost every day, now that Christine's no longer there to do it.

Freckles is fifty-two. Looks forty. No signs of wrinkles in his honey-coloured, freckled face. As soon as he gets out of his grey uniform, a jumpsuit with the logo — a purple car — and Grant's Car Rental, the name of his company (staffed mostly by Everett and Bentley, and financed, it's said, with money Freckles made from transiting drugs when he was a baggage handler at the airport), he dons tank tops, T-shirts a size too small, and tight jeans that display his well-developed thighs and his penis arranged to the right. Even on cloudy days, his eyes are hidden behind Ray-Ban sunglasses. When he wears a cap, the brim's turned backward. He has the most pointed lips Gordon has ever seen on a human being. Rhinestones glisten in both of his ears, and a thick gold chain comes down to just below his sternum. He's about five foot three. Stands a full head below Gordon and almost two heads below Austin. He stomps the earth when he walks. Beth calls him that "pestle that thinks the earth is a mortar." What he lacks in height he makes up for in voice, which his immediate neighbours distinctly hear when he's calm, and half of Cane Garden, when he's enraged. He goes to the gym early every morning, and brags about his adventures with women who, he says, constantly waylay him. "That's 'cause you's like a sandwich board," Austin once told him, chuckling.

When Freckles moved next door, Gordon was the junior economist at the ministry of finance. Guffawing, his boss said, "Gord, you keeping a watchful eye on Maureen, I hope?"

"Should I?"

"Ain't Freckles just move next door?"

"Freckles? You mean Percival?"

"He name Percival? I always know he as Freckles. I mean the manicou-mouth fellow with them donkey teeth and bug shit all over he face." He gave a cackling laugh. "Uglier than sin but he ain't no fool. Didn' waste the money he got working for them drugs kingpins ... aa, aa, you looking at me like if you think I lying. Man, when the cartel blow up, and everybody been trying to save their skin, he threaten to name the higher-ups in the police and government. He lucky they didn' kill him. They give him good money to keep his mouth shut ... get serious, Gord. Where you think a' airport baggage handler, poor like church mice and pulling down the bloomers off every young woman, she mother, she sister, and she aunty, going get money to set up a car rental company?"

The quarrel about the Rottweiler notwithstanding, Gordon feels duty bound to invite Freckles for a drink once in a while — especially now that Christine has left him. He rarely accepts. Christine, unless she was on duty, never missed an opportunity to socialize with them when Beth and Allan, and Maureen's friends — Claudia, Joel, and Gloria — were present.

♦

Flossy is indeed attractive. She came, a shy girl of around seventeen, to work with Francine and Austin in 1997, a year after they bought the house on Gordon's left, and it's a good thing she stayed with them. Almost six years ago, Francine, at age forty-two, suffered a brain aneurysm and collapsed in a pew of the Anglican cathedral one Sunday morning. She was pronounced dead when the ambulance arrived at casualty. Two blows to the family in two months. Tomas blew the roof off their house in October, and death took Francine in December, the same week the repairs on their house were completed.

No fun losing your mother at twelve. But Theo has known Flossy since birth, and Austin is a caring father. Gordon has never heard him shout at Theo. He sees them high-fiving sometimes. When Austin travels, and it's feasible, he takes along Theo. Maybe he pressures him to overperform. The vice of Caribbean parents — all parents for that matter — who want brilliant children to brag about.

In Gordon's time in elementary and secondary school, boys who looked androgynous were mocked and called woman-man, antipympym, and buller, and rarely got selected to play football or cricket. He sighs. Parents can't help worrying about their children. Tortola is under the regimen of British laws, which ostensibly protect LGBTQI people from persecution. It makes sense that Austin wishes Theo had been born there.

He never had to worry unduly about Frida's future. Austin's right about that. Frida, Maureen, and he are lucky too — in more ways than educational and employment opportunities. Elizabeth, one of Maureen's colleagues, has a son with spina bifida. Joy, a girl Gordon dated back when he was in the Methodist Youth Fellowship, had to suspend her nursing career to take care of a son born with Alexander disease (dysmyelinogenic leukodystrophy).

◆

How well, Gordon wonders, does Austin know himself? How well do people know themselves? Austin spewed his usual anti-independence rant on a Saturday evening when Beth, Allan, and, exceptionally, Freckles and Christine were present. Francine was still alive, but was at home with Theo. They were on Gordon's porch, drinking beer and eating popcorn. A beautiful evening, and Allan had remarked on it. A full moon in a cloudless sky tinted the harbour silver, and a gentle breeze rustled the leaves of the flamboyants, acacias, and figs growing on the ledges of the cliff below them. It was interrupted by Austin's anti-independence rant. They didn't know what had provoked it. They glanced uncomfortably at one another. Maureen responded, "Austin, you're just longing for the good old days when Whites had the first pick of everything good, followed by Browns, with trash left for Blacks."

Under the porch light, Austin's face reddened, and his blue-grey eyes flashed. "I ain't racist. You blind or what! Francine black ... blacker than every one o' you. When me family said, what you marrying that pitch-black woman for, I told them to go jump into the fucking sea."

Gordon tapped Maureen gently on the thigh and with a slight headshake signalled that she drop the subject. Maureen hated losing arguments and would have cited statistics about the number of Caribbean Whites who'd immigrated to Australia and South Africa to avoid living under post-independence Black governments.

Chapter 2

THE SOUNDS OF THE DRIBBLING BALL HAVE STOPPED. Gordon looks at his watch. Ten past noon. Frida hasn't called or texted. Means her flight from Toronto is on time. He picks up the coffee mug, stares at the black liquid inside, eases himself up, hobbles to the porch railing, and pours the coffee onto the ixora blooms a few feet below. For a moment he's captivated by the line of red florescence they create the length of the house, interrupted only by the stairs and the carport. They bloom all year long. Maureen wanted them to form a red-and-green fence around the entire house. At the front, between the ixora and the lawn, she kept a space four feet wide in which she grew gerberas, zinnias, and asters. The rest of the yard — from the garden to the chain-link fence that separates the property from the road, the slivers of space separating his house from Austin's and Freckles's, as well as the five yards of sloping ground at the back — is all lawn, now emerald green because of the recent abundant rain. His neighbours have been more pragmatic. They scatter individual ixoras, hibiscuses, and bougainvilleas here and there across their lawns and avoid the sweaty, back-breaking work — the constant weeding and fertilizing that gerberas and asters require — that took up Maureen's weekends and vacations.

For the last three years of her illness, to please her, Gordon got a gardener to come once, occasionally twice, per month. During his travels to CARICOM meetings and other summits, after he became the senior economist in the ministry of finance, she hounded him to bring back seeds of any new flowers that he saw.

He never did. Couldn't risk being caught with agricultural products. In the last six years of his career, he'd had to be careful. Not just from colleagues who craved his job. The henchmen of both political parties wanted to know which party he voted for. He sometimes eavesdropped on the general office staff telling their wily-Wiley jokes. Not even Maureen knew which party he voted for. Sometimes she yapped too much.

He stares at two gerberas not yet strangled by the weeds two feet above them. He hasn't asked the gardener to come since Maureen's death. Frida will upbraid him for letting weeds take over Maureen's garden. Maybe he should keep the ixoras and seed the rest with lawn grass. It would be simpler. Anything to simplify his life.

●

In two days, it will be September 11, a memorable day. Not just for Americans, Iraqis, and Afghans. For him too. It's the anniversary of Maureen's death. He swallows. The house feels empty. Before her illness, their relationship had morphed into one of companionship. Lukewarm sex three or four times a year. Sometimes after he returned from Trinidad. Before disease melted her, she was still very attractive. The races mixed well in her: from Maggie, Eurafrican; from Clem, Afro-Indian. She kept her semi-straight hair long. By age fifty it was mostly grey. Her flesh was still firm.

The crow's feet came with her first illness. When cancer compli-cated it, she became unrecognizable and began looking more and more like an Egyptian mummy.

Day after tomorrow, he must carry a big bunch of ixora when he and Frida visit her grave. He turns his head to the right and glances across Kingstown at the cemetery and the Milton Cato Memorial Hospital below it.

How will his week with Frida go? He hasn't seen her in a year. She flew back to Toronto five days after Maureen's funeral. She offered to pay his passage to Toronto so he'd spend the anniver-sary there, away from surroundings that would remind him of Maureen's death. He said no, that he wanted to be near Maureen on that day and to visit her grave.

"Well then, I'm coming home, and we'll visit Mom's grave together."

"But, Frida, you made me schedule my cataract surgery for the end of January. You promised you would come then ..."

"And who says I won't?"

"I'm saying you shouldn't. Two trips in a few months. Be realis-tic. Let it be one or the other."

She didn't answer.

"Your boyfriend shouldn't let you come."

She laughed. "Dad, you're not for real. Here's a bit of news: Guy wants to marry me." She stopped talking.

"And?"

"I said no. *Wife!* Smacks of ownership. Territory. *My wife! My husband!* I come close to snarling when I hear those words."

He shook his head and sighed. *Will she ever get married? She's thirty-eight. Still very attractive. Five foot ten. Rich-brown complex-ion. Taut skin. Trim body. Even white teeth.*

"Dad, there's a delicate matter ..." He heard her loud intake of breath.

After she'd been silent for a couple of seconds, he said, "I'm listening … go on, Frida. Ask me anything you want."

"Are you sure, Dad?"

"Yes, I am." But he heard the quaver in his voice.

"Okay. For many years I've felt that you and Mom were always keeping out of each other's way. I mean you hardly ever spoke to each other … Dad?"

"I'm here."

"I know I'm sounding vague, but I don't know how else to say it. You two beamed when Uncle Al and Aunt Beth visited."

Silence. A long one.

"Now, with all the stories of famous men and women changing their genders after decades of marriage, I have images of people going through life unhappy and afraid to say why. And my thoughts always come back to you and Mom … Dad?"

"Yes, Frida. One thing is certain: you won't ever walk in on me wearing a frock and high heels. My dear Frida, I'm quite happy with myself as I am."

"Don't get so defensive. I was only giving you an example."

"Is any of this related to your refusal to marry Guy, to become a *wife?*"

"Ah, Dad. I don't feel any deep passion for him. He's kind-hearted, smart; he respects me, and all that, but I don't feel anything deep for him. Lonely Toronto drove me into his arms. Just like Montreal drove me into Michael's and Demetrius's. But their arms won't hold me *until death do us part*. I mean like you and Mom must have been passionate about each other at one time, but all my years growing up I never saw you two show it. Right now, my passion for Guy is lukewarm. Wedding vows might just turn it cold."

Ouch. He wanted to say that sounded cruel. "Just be honest with Guy. Don't let him think you'll one day say yes. Don't string him along. And, of course, be honest with yourself."

"Coming back to you and Mom, I'm just alerting you that I'll be asking you lots of questions. I have some for Aunty May too. I want her to tell me things about your boyhood. You haven't told me much. Is your silence deliberate?"

"Frida, you've lost me."

"I have! Uncle Al is bubbly and talks non-stop, but never says anything memorable about your childhood. You always said the two of you were inseparable."

He wondered where the conversation was leading.

"Is it because I'm female, Dad? One time I asked Mom to tell me how you both met. I was thirteen at the time. She blushed. I poked her. 'From the date of your wedding and my birthday, I know you got pregnant with me before you and Dad got married.'

"'So! I was twenty-nine when I got pregnant, thirty when I had you. What are you insinuating?' She said it with such anger, I told her to drop it. I should have pushed Mom to tell me more about herself. What I know about her comes from Gran. I'm not going to make that mistake with you, Dad. Then Mom wrote that memoir and spitefully decided that she wasn't going to let anyone read it until twenty-five years had elapsed."

Not a memoir, a journal, but if I tell you, you'll know I've read it.

"For all we know, I might be long dead before then. Sounds to me like a power trip. By the way, have you been plugging in her laptop?"

"Yes."

"Dad, do you know what she's hiding from me? What does she have to be ashamed of? She's already dead. When I come home, I'm going to try the passwords I have. Aunt Beth and Claudia can protest all they want. Aunt Beth's firm: 'Maureen said twenty-five years, and twenty-five years it will be.' Well, I will be firmer: I will not wait twenty-five years; one is already too many. Dad, if I succeed, this must stay between us."

"Of course, it will."

"The dead must not control the living."

"Frida, you know from your studies in genetics that the dead *always* control the living. My genes, Maureen's, handed down from —"

"Let Mom control you from the grave if you want. She won't control me. Bye, Dad. I'll let you know my travel plans."

◆

My dear Frida, you won't be reading Maureen's journal any time soon. I erased the file from the hard drive. He knows it's wrong, and it explains in part his nightmares. *I have the right to spend my last days free from scandal.* Twice he came close to asking Allan to search Beth's things for the flash drive and erase the file. But the request might damage their friendship. Not to mention cause problems with Beth if she finds out. At the very least, he should beg Allan, if Beth dies or becomes disabled, to erase the flash drive before turning it over to Claudia. He hopes to God it isn't uploaded in some cloud storage.

He breathes deeply. *My Frida, all right. I won't want her to be otherwise. Well, with a little honey to reduce the tartness.* He limps to the patio table six feet away, his mind fixed on Frida's observation: *"You two beamed when Uncle Al and Aunt Beth visited."* True. He never lost his desire for Allan, but didn't think it showed to the point where Frida would have noticed.

Beth and Maureen were sisters in all but biology. They were often in the house modifying the clothes they'd bought together. In the years when he and Maureen still lived in Kingstown Park and were poor, Maureen sometimes bought fabric and Beth helped her make dresses from scratch. Maggie had already taught Maureen the basics of dressmaking. During those same years,

Allan, then a junior doctor, was often assigned to work nights, and while he was at work, Beth came to the house to play cribbage with Maureen. When they played Scrabble, Gordon joined in and got soundly beaten. Even when he got the *s*'s, *z*'s, *j*'s, and *q*'s, they knew how to capitalize on his plays and would score twice the points he did. After he and Maureen moved to Cane Garden, whenever Beth and Allan came to the house for supper, Maureen and Beth went off to the alcove in the living room to play, and Gordon and Allan took over the side porch and played dominoes or checkers. The domino and checker games were most interesting when Maureen's colleagues and their spouses were present. After Francine died, they always asked Austin to join them. In her teens, to be polite, Frida stayed around a short while before going off to read, study, or visit friends.

Beth teaches home economics at Girls' High School and loves experimenting with desserts. Always brings one whenever she visits; even now that Maureen's gone. Maureen relied on her to provide the dessert whenever she was entertaining. Sometimes they made it in the kitchen here with Francine and Christine joining in. When it came to cooking, Maureen kept Gordon out of the kitchen, even with Beth's many scoldings. She restricted him to doing the laundry and cleaning the house.

Sometimes, from the porch, he'd watch Maureen, sweat-soaked, working in the garden, and, before he began having trouble with his back, he'd descend the steps and take the fork from her and turn the soil over, or take the shears and complete the trimming of the ixoras. When she was weeding — not his preferred task: too hard on his back — he'd bring her a glass of lemonade or iced tea.

He'd never learned to cook before going to study in Montreal. Nor did he want to. Until the last three years in his mother's house, cooking was with wood in a kitchen separate from the house. The woodsmoke itched his eyes and burned his lungs. In the rainy season, the wood was usually wet — there wasn't enough space in the kitchen to store it, and his father, Ben, never built the shed that Lillian kept asking for — and getting the wood to blaze was a challenge. From about age twelve his sister, May, gradually took over the cooking. Sometimes he heard Lillian telling her, "No man going stay with you if this is what you feed him."

May would answer, "Who tell you I want a man?"

"Don't say that, child. You don't see what going on in Marcella house? That's 'cause no man there."

Marcella lived about two hundred yards to their left. Her two teenage daughters had dropped out of school when they got pregnant.

"If you feed your husband this and he beat you, don't be surprised."

"And you think my hands nailed down?"

Lillian chuckled. "Girl, you will soon find out. Sooner than you want. Life tough for we women, yes. Tough."

He'd listen to them and feel glad he was a boy.

◆

Since Maureen's death, he has supper with Allan and Beth most Saturdays. On Sundays he drives out to Riley, and May stuffs him with goat or chicken stew and macaroni pie, and he brings back containers of food that last for days. He got May to show him how to cook her delicious beef stew. Yesterday when she phoned and asked what he was doing, he told her he was preparing beef stew and rice and peas for Frida's coming. "Why you didn' let me do it?"

"If I don't practise, I'll forget."

◆

He dreads the questions Frida will ask him. What does she want to know about Maureen? If all goes as planned, in twenty-four years, the journal will be available. *Frida, you'll learn more than you want to know. Why didn't Maureen leave me? The reasons in her journal don't convince me.*

Chapter 3

HE FEELS AN URGE TO REREAD THE JOURNAL. HE RE-
turns inside, enters his office, sits at his desk, takes his
glasses from his pajama pocket, puts them on, and turns
his desktop computer on. He keeps all of his flash drives in a small
plastic bin on top of his desk, except the one with the journal. That
one he keeps in a blank envelope in the lower right-hand drawer.
He retrieves it, inserts it, and waits for it to charge.

January 9, 2012
I am officially retired. I haven't worked since Easter. In
September 1965, I began working, straight out of high
school, as an untrained teacher at the Kingstown Anglican
School. Mother had wanted me to stay on in school and
do A levels. That would have meant two more years. I
wanted my own paycheque. A paycheque meant freedom.
The illusions of youth. In 1966 I entered teachers' college
and graduated in 1969. Next it was a B.A. from UWI
Cave Hill, in 1973. I resumed my teaching career, this

time at Girls' High School. Forty-plus years. Now what, Maureen?

To prove I'm retired, I stayed in bed until after nine all of last week, and it looks like I'll be doing so again this week. By seven Gordon was up and gone. He's sitting out on the porch with Ginger probably purring on his lap. Gordon's partly retired too, beginning this morning as well. At the Ministry of Finance, they need his knowledge about the workings of CARICOM. For another year to eighteen months, they'll call on him to groom the economist who'll replace him as the CARICOM expert. His retirement party was on December 29. I couldn't go. There wasn't a retirement party for me. Allan put me on sick leave from April to December. He wanted to put Gordon on sick leave too, but Gordon was afraid of what people would say. He'll be sixty-three on April 10, I'll be sixty-four on February 16.

We had planned to work until we're sixty-five. But Allan says that the less stress we're under, the longer and healthier our lives would be. There's the cost of our drugs and the trips we might have to take to Barbados to check on our health. But Allan assures us that for the time being sending our blood samples is enough.

No more lessons to prepare. No more essays to grade. No more agonizing that I might have taught a lesson poorly and my students would flunk CSEC. It has never happened, but that fear has always haunted me.

Now what? This question kept me awake last night. Lying on his back in bed beside me, Gordon snored like a hog. I think I slept better during the six weeks last year when he slept in Frida's room. When he begins to snore, I push him onto his side. He mumbles but doesn't come awake, and the snoring stops until he again rolls onto his back. Last night I didn't. Sleep had left me.

I'll have more time for gardening. I'll get Beth to teach me to make some of her divine desserts.

And get nausea and indigestion from eating them, right? Besides, where will I find the energy to do it all? I suspect that writing this memoir (or keeping a sporadic journal; I'm not sure what this will turn out to be) will be plenty.

A novel would be more interesting. Then I could change the setting and the names and appearances of the characters and make the characters say what I want. There's freedom in fiction. No wonder so many memoirs turn out to be lies. I'll have to stick to the facts. My objective is to get a better understanding of me.

How did I find myself in this situation? I who was called Sister Goody-Goody by my classmates at St. Joseph's Convent. Mildred used to say that I was holier than the nuns. When she found out that I had a boyfriend, she asked if the world was coming to an end. She recounted it all to Gordon when we stayed with her in New York.

Could Gordon and I have held on working for another year? We could use the extra income to repaint the house. Inside, the walls have turned from white to a pale grey. The outside walls facing Kingstown are covered in a film of soot. The once-upon-a-time white sheer curtains in the living room and master bedroom are the colour of dishwater. On Friday, Gordon said he'd wash them this week. I think they should be changed. They've been there for more than ten years.

We moved into this house when I was forty. If we were going to own a house and enjoy living in it, it was then or never. I was tired of paying rent. For the umpteenth time

I'd showed Gordon the tiles in a pile at one end of the counter. They had fallen off the wall bordering the kitchen sink. For two years, Miss Garrison had been promising to fix the problem. "Two years, Gordon! Next week I'm calling a real estate agent."

"Owning a house brings complications," he said, "but if you must, go ahead."

I almost dropped the plate I was drying. I'd expected his usual spiel about living simply — the only argument he makes on the rare occasions he resists my proposals. Of course, I know him better now. He was trying to keep our marriage simple in case I found out the truth about him and decided to leave him. I won't ask if my suspicion is correct. In his place I, too, would say no.

We found this lot by fluke. What looked like a slope unfit for houses turned out to be a few lots where houses shot up like weeds in the rainy season. Even before our house was finished, another went up to the right of us, the one where Freckles, his sons, and Christine now live. I was terrified that a landslide might take us and the house over the cliff onto the Long Wall houses below and maybe as far down as the Grenadines Wharf. The lots seemed too good to be still vacant. Beth got her brother Frederick, an engineer, to test the soil. He told us there was solid rock a few feet below and, as long as the foundation was embedded in it and a retaining wall built to hold any soil that could loosen, there was nothing to fear. The miracles of engineering. There was room for the house, almost at the edge of the cliff, a front yard, and even a road.

Shouldn't I have read a few memoirs before attempting this? How many have I read? Jamaica Kincaid's *My Brother*. I read it at Allan's urging. Virginia Woolf's *A Room of One's Own*. Lorna Goodison's *From Harvey River*. James Baldwin's *The Fire Next Time*. Four! Just four! Well, you had to work too, and help raise Frida and be a wife and have a life. Oh yes. And Richard Wright's *Black Boy*. Who can forget *Black Boy*! Still, I should be ashamed of myself. Goodison's and Kincaid's are the only ones I've read since leaving Cave Hill. I left university certain that I would read every published West Indian book. I don't think I can name ten contemporary Caribbean writers. Put me in a contest to name African American and Black British writers and if I don't win, I'll at least be a runner-up. Of course, it's because Allan reads their books then passes them on to me, so he'll have someone to discuss them with. Beth's reading is restricted to women's magazines and cookbooks.

Can I write this? I fear I'll be tossing around in an ocean far from land, or be like Odysseus.

Maureen, he knew his destination. It was getting there that was his challenge. Encountering problems and extricating himself from them. And don't forget, Odysseus gestated in Homer's head.

Stop worrying. You're not writing this to be published. Write down everything true that comes into your head. Later, when you think you've poured it all out, go back, revise, reorder, and expunge. See it as brainstorming. Exactly as you advised your students.

What's my destination? Making sense of my life in order to understand how I've come to this pass. Thankfully with words. Treacherous, I'll admit. But no one will drown, not literally. Not even Gordon. If I put all the facts here, I'll let the memoir — or whatever it turns out to be — stay under wraps long enough for him to pass on before it's made public. Everything I've read tells me that our lives will be shortened. Frida will, of course, have to deal with the content. I'll seal the whole and entrust it to Beth who, if she finds her health failing, will be authorized to turn it over to Claudia. Just hope I don't die suddenly, before I can arrange this.

I hear Gordon dragging a lounge chair across the porch's terrazzo surface. He's out there reading *Searchlight*. A glance at it earlier turned me off. *Woman shot while playing cards. Three men charged with murder for dunking a boy in boiling water.* Today I'm in no mood for stories of human depravity.

The noise of Kingstown wafts up the cliff and into the room. Car honks mostly. For twenty-two years we've lived with noise and exhaust pollution and the sea's salt-laden damp. When we travel out to Riley to visit May, I envy the peace and quiet there and wonder if I hadn't been too hasty in choosing to build in Cane Garden. Would have cost less too. But we would have had to commute every day in bumper-to-bumper traffic. The real reason, I know now, was that the house would have been built on Gordon's parents' land. I wanted none of those links …

My destination. Getting the grammar, spelling, and punctuation right — that's my task now. The sense too. And the truth. Yes, I must get that right. There's something called false memory syndrome. These memories/reflections must not be tainted. Feels as serious as taking an oath to tell the truth, the whole truth, and nothing but the truth in a court of law.

What sort of truth am I looking for? What is truth anyway? Pastor Crow, in the Pentecostal church of my childhood, once said that when Pilate asked that question, he was prevaricating, that Pilate knew what he was fated to do, that his role had been determined even before the world was formed. That God had already willed it. That statement began to bother me when I was in teachers' college, about the same time that the cruelty in the world invaded my consciousness. God had created that too. Mother was shocked that I had such thoughts.

"Maureen, the Devil created evil. Not God. Remember the snake that tempted Eve? That was the Devil in the form of a snake. If you give your heart to the Lord, the Holy Spirit will guide you in the paths of truth. What I'm telling you, Maureen, is the gospel truth. Maureen, it's all in the Bible, written by God himself." I sometimes wonder if Mother has truly read the Bible. I've stopped arguing religion with her. It's like trying to stop a leak with water.

Mother's truth fitted her needs. Now I'm hoping to record — or is it discover? — my truth, the TRUTH of my life.

Our human roots do not yield their secrets easily, DNA tests notwithstanding. Still, I must begin this voyage. Embark, Maureen.

I'll start on deck — or with the trunk and leaves — with what I can see. Maybe there'll be enough there. I won't have time to knock about in the dark spaces, won't have to uproot anything that must stay rooted.

My names: Maureen Maria. I got them from my mother and my paternal grandmother. That's what Mother said. Mother insisted on the *M* sound. Wanted us both to be stamped with the same sound. I imagine it's as close as she could come to reattaching the umbilical cord. Maria is easy to understand. Mother's parents were Catholic. Mother got her secondary education at St. Joseph's Convent and chose it over Girls' High School when it was my turn to attend secondary school. By then she had long become Pentecostal. I was six when she joined. Then our house was two small rooms. I overheard everything she and Daddy said to each other. She told him that she had given her heart to the Lord and that things between them had to change.

"Like what so?" he said.

"I can't live a life of fornication and sin."

He did not answer. I wondered what fornication was. I could have asked Daddy. He was easygoing. He used to say to me, "My Everything, come and give your daddy a hug, nuh." Or "What's wrong, Star-in-My-Universe? Where's your light?" And I would break into a big grin, and he would grin too and enclose me in his arms. He let me play with his Rasta locs and ride him piggyback, and he answered all my questions.

Two nights after that fornication talk, I woke in the middle of the night and heard my parents quarrelling. I slept on a settee in the main room. Mother and Daddy slept in the bedroom.

"Stop it! You going wake Maureen," Daddy said.

"Then leave me alone. I gave my heart to the Lord. If you want sex, go find another woman … or marry me."

"But the Lord already got your heart," Daddy said. "I don't think the Lord going hand you over to me without a fight." He chuckled. "Skinny me! I ain't no match for the Lord."

Week after week they quarrelled over fornication and sex and marriage and Daddy's marijuana smoking.

Daddy began forgetting to ask for my hugs and to call me My Everything or Star-in-My-Universe. "Star-in-My-Universe, you shine and my darkness disappears." When Mother worked days, he came to the school at three and got me and was with me when Mother worked evenings and nights. After he left, whenever Mother was at work, I went to Aunty Priscilla's place. She was an elementary school teacher and my father's first cousin. She lived about sixty yards uphill from us, alone in a wooden house twice the size of ours. When, in high school, I learned about the imperative voice, I remembered her — she was already dead, victim of a road accident. "Come, dry the dishes ... put that over there ... go do your homework ... darling, repeat that word again. Spell it. B-o-t-h ... now pronounce it properly. We are in Fairhall. No need for a b-o-a-t." Every sentence, uttered in her high-pitched scratchy voice, her eyes like luminous breadnuts focused on me, her hair in curlers making me think of Medusa.

I waited and waited and waited for Daddy to come back. For Daddy to rescue me. Over the years I've wondered, would I have forgiven him if he'd come back to look for me or had taken me with him?

In the first couple of years — I stopped after that — whenever I asked Mother for him, she said, "Forget about him. Your father is the Devil incarnate."

The first time, I asked, "'The Devil incarnate'? What you mean, Mother?"

"What I mean? I mean he will roast in hell forever."

"What did he do?"

"He walked out on you, left me alone to look after you. Walked out on me too. But I don't count. Men, Maureen — you're only seven, too young to hear this, too

31

young to understand, but I'm telling you just the same — never trust a man. I will never speak to your father again and I will never take up with another man."

"Where's Daddy?"

"He's living with his whore up in Dorsetshire Hill."

"Mother, what's a whore?"

"A woman that does bad things, a woman who gives men diseases, a woman that decent people scorn."

"Is Daddy a whore too?"

"Worse than a whore. A man who takes up with a whore is worse than a whore."

I didn't believe my father was a whore. I wanted him to come home and tell me he wasn't a whore.

The years passed. At first Mother cried often. When I asked her why, she said it was because life was hard. For about a year I was sure I would come home one afternoon from school and Daddy would be sitting on the settee and he would say, *Come, shine for me, Star-of-My-Universe. See, I've come back and I will never leave.* I even wrote a story in which it happens. Eventually I forgot what he looked like. And I wondered if what Mother said about him was true. Some of the men who lived near us beat their wives. When I was twelve, a man two houses up from us was accused of impregnating his daughter. The villagers made an effigy of him, put it on trial, and burned it. People came from all the neighbouring communities to witness it. On the evening of the burning Mother said to me, "I hope you're taking stock. Men just like ram goats and bulldogs. You better say thank God your father not around to do this to you."

My hatred for Daddy gelled around this time. Mother said I should consider him dead.

"But he isn't dead."

"That makes it worse. Then he's worse than dead. A man who turns his back on his children might be alive in his body but he's dead in his soul." By the time I was nine, she'd replaced her silent crying with "I have girded my loins and carrying this burden, Lord, that you put on me." On occasion, she added, "Maureen, gird yours too to help me carry it." One time she stomped the living room floor and shouted, "Though he slay me, yet will I trust him!"

She hid two details from me: First, that the property where we lived — where Mother still lives — belonged to Inez, my father's mother. When Daddy walked out on us, he told Mother she could continue to live there, that he would never return to put her out. Mother was sixty-seven years of age when I found this out. And it was only because Daddy had the land title transferred to my name. Mother said she did not hide it, that it just never came up, but I don't believe her. Second, the week after my marriage, Gordon brought me a bag of golden apples and told me that Clem, my so-called father, had sent them. He added, "Maureen, you are too hard on your father. I don't think everything Maggie told you was the truth."

"Gordon, he left when I was seven. The next time I saw him I was fourteen and I didn't know who he was."

"He used to send money for you at Christmas."

"That's a lie."

"Maybe you should ask your mother."

When I asked Mother, she said yes; that for the first three years he sent five dollars at Christmas and at my birthdays but that she always returned it. "It was a bribe to make you think he loved you. A child has to eat every day, not just at Christmas." I agreed with Mother about the eating part, but I think she should have told me about the money. Besides, that money was mine, not hers.

Another time, Gordon said, "Maureen, you ever wondered how come you are Maureen Cumber and not Maureen Abbot?"

"Cumber is my father's name."

"But he wasn't married to your mother. It's because Clem went with your mother to the registry and insisted that they put his name on your birth certificate."

"So, he wants a medal for *that!* So *what!* Both of my parents' names are on my birth certificate. Big deal. That's how it is nowadays, and should have always been. It doesn't make my father virtuous."

"Appreciate the few good things he did; that's all I'm saying."

I steupsed. Men are always trying make themselves appear better than they are. We women must hold them accountable when they're irresponsible.

•

A few days after my fourteenth birthday, a sunny morning, I was outside with a bunch of girls during recess. This man came on to the premises just as recess was ending. Sister Ignatius, who was on yard duty, spoke to him and escorted him inside. After recess, just as classes resumed, Sister Celestine, the principal, came to get me and escorted me to the office. The strange man was sitting in the corridor outside her office. He grinned when he saw me. Beanpole thin. Stringy neck. Bloodshot eyes. Brown, bulging teeth. Leathery molasses-brown angular face. Afro-Indian brush-cut hair. Sister Celestine invited him into the office, pointed to two chairs across from her desk, and told us to sit.

"Maureen? I …?" the man said.

"Sister, who's he?"

She frowned and made an open-hand gesture to the man, who was still standing.

"Maureen, me is Clem, your father," he said while sitting.

I couldn't stop staring at him. He turned his head away. He was wearing a black T-shirt, and the muscles on his thin arms were clearly outlined. I'd already noted that his dungaree trousers were puckered at the front, and his feet, in flip-flops, were coated with dust.

I wondered what I would do if he tried to hug me. He didn't. Sister Celestine intervened. "Mr. Cumber, Maureen has to return to class." I realized then that I was sweating.

Mother wasn't home when I arrived from school. She was on evening duty. I was already asleep when she came in. That night I dreamed that I met this strange man and tried to run away from him but couldn't move. My screams woke Mother up, and she shook me awake. She merely noted that I was screaming in my sleep. She didn't ask me to tell her what the nightmare was. After Daddy left, Mother and I began to sleep in the same bed, and it continued until she added two rooms to the house the year I began to teach at Kingstown Anglican School.

The day after Daddy's visit, Sister Celestine told me that he'd left one hundred dollars to help pay for my school supplies. Too late, I wanted to tell her. It was when I found out who owned the property that I told Mother about Daddy's visit.

A week after he visited the school, I was in Calliaqua and I saw him transporting crates of soft drinks from a truck into a shop and returning with crates of empty bottles. He stacked them and then got into the truck and drove off. He did not see me, and I did not call out to him.

Sometimes this feels like eons ago. I don't want him to roast in hell. In fact, I don't believe in hell. But I can't forgive him for abandoning me. He's now eighty-three and uses a cane. Two years ago, I drove by him walking up Murray's Road and nixed the temptation to give him a lift. Gordon wants me to reconcile with him. All during Frida's childhood, Gordon took her to visit him. Gordon doesn't understand my feelings for Daddy. I tell him that Daddy betrayed me. He says "betrayal" is a strong word, that his own father was no paragon of virtue, but he wouldn't have kept him from attending his wedding if he'd been alive, or refused to reconcile with him if he'd wanted to. But on some things Gordon is obtuse. His father lived at home, cultivated the land that fed his family, was married to his mother. Okay, he had a mistress. Which married Vincentian man didn't/doesn't? Christine complains to me that Percival is often away with one mistress or another until the wee hours of the morning. She says it no longer upsets her. Though I think it's Percival's violent temper that keeps her silent.

Beth is sure that Allan has a mistress, that he meets with her in the Evesham house. "But, girl, as long as he performs his bedroom chores where I'm concerned, I'm prepared to close my eyes. He hits my G spot nine times out of ten." Lucky her. Gordon never performed his chores as well or as often as I would have liked. If I have a G spot, Gordon has never been able to find it.

Daddy! Daddy! Daddy! Showered me with affection until I was seven and then stopped. Cold. Mother didn't always carry that burden well. Loneliness made her toxic. For the most part she vented it on me. Rarely physically. One afternoon — I think it was a month or so before Daddy's visit to St. Joseph's Convent — Mother came in from work tired and cranky, met me cooking, and screamed at me for some stupid thing. I dropped a plate, and it smashed on the cement floor of our outdoor kitchen. She collared me and began to slap me until she was breathless, all the while screaming, "You hussy! You want to send me to poor home!"

Later in the bedroom I stared at my reflection in the dressing-table mirror, at her fingerprints on my face. The tears came then, and I wondered if Daddy were with us, whether she would have dared to abuse me like that.

Sometimes she surprised me. One evening when I was sixteen, she came home unexpectedly. I'd thought she was working that evening. I had told Vince, my first and only boyfriend before Gordon, that he could visit me. Mother knew about him. Vince, too, attended school in town, at nearby St. Martins. A lunch hour two weeks earlier, she'd seen us walking together along Back Street.

"Anything going on between you two?" It was a rainy late afternoon, and she and I were out in the kitchen preparing supper on the two-burner kerosene stove we used on rainy days. Then we mostly cooked with firewood from the trees on the two lots of land our house was on.

"You mean like sex?"

"Yes."

I shook my head. "Nothing, Mother."

"You're sure?"

"Mother, you're funny ... Mother, everyone isn't like you ..."

"What do you mean?" Her voice, full of terror, keened like an ambulance siren.

"Nothing, Mother. Nothing," I replied, fearful and eyeing the kitchen door.

"Well, it better be nothing. None of your damn freshness."

Two weeks later, Vince and I were sitting on the settee. The door was closed but not locked. The door opened and there was Mother framed in it. Vince got up.

"You sit right back down!"

Vince sat.

"Why you want to run? What you guilty of?"

"We wasn't doing nothing, Miss Maggie."

"I accuse you of doing anything? You are accusing yourself." She advanced toward us.

Vince jumped up, ran into the bedroom, and bolted.

"If you run" — she glowered at me — "I'll beat you to a pulp."

She sat beside me on the settee, took my hand in hers, and began to cry. When her sobbing stopped, she said, "I don't want you to turn out like me. It keeps me awake at nights. I know, I know. Don't I know! Your body urging you to have sex. I've been down that road. I wasn't ready to be a mother when you came, and you are not ready to be a mother. How old Vince is?"

"Seventeen."

"How far he is in school?"

"He's writing O levels this year."

"Well, he won't pass English. 'We wasn't doing nothing.'" She fell silent. "Maureen, why you won't give your heart to the Lord?" She sounded tired. "I know I'm not fit to lecture you about sex before marriage. But because

38

I fell into the flames and got burned doesn't mean that you should too. Maureen, I lost my family. Mommy and Daddy put my clothes on the landing when I told them I was pregnant. They told Angela and Bill not to speak to me. To this day they don't. And if they try now, I'll have a few choice words for them because when I needed them, they weren't there. Your father's mother, Inez Cumber — bless her soul — she was an angel, the opposite of your father. She took me in, in this same house, and shared the little she had with me. She took care of you during the day while I studied nursing. She became my mother. That woman has to be in heaven."

Mother joined my free hand to the other, held them both between hers, and stared into my face for about ten seconds. She released my hands and said, "I want us to pray together. Let's kneel."

We knelt.

"Repeat after me, Maureen ... Dear merciful God ... I am begging you to keep me ... from falling into temptation ... Lord, I know that the flesh is weak ... Lord, I don't want to follow in my mother's footsteps ... Lord, I know that fornication is wrong ... Lord, help me to resist the temptation to do it ... Lord, send the Holy Spirit ... to urge me to get saved ... so I can resist the perils of the flesh. In Jesus's name I beg ... Amen."

Mother fell silent, and we remained on our knees for another ten seconds. Then she tapped me on my shoulders. I opened my eyes and saw tears rolling down her cheeks. She stood, motioned for me to stand, and held me in a suffocating embrace for a long time. She swallowed a few times, and I felt her tears falling on me. She took a deep breath and released me.

39

That night, lying in bed beside her, I whispered in her ear, "Mother, stop worrying about me. I won't let any man make a fool of me."

•

Aunt Angela and Uncle Bill. Mother has pointed them out to me from a distance. Both are paler than Mother. Once Aunt Angela and I were travelling on the same minivan. She was sitting one seat in front of me. If she knew who I was she didn't show it. Mother says she lives in Stubbs with a "coolie" man who beats her "at tea, breakfast, and dinner." I don't know where Uncle Bill is. He must be still alive. If he'd died, Mother would have told me. For all of Mother's hatred of her family, she keeps track of them. One Saturday, while I was still living in Kingstown Park, she called me at home and said I should look at the front page of the *Vincentian*. "That girl in the middle is Angela's last child. She had that one for the coolie man." I heard pride and joy in Mother's voice.

"Mother you shouldn't say 'coolie.'"

"I've been saying 'coolie' all my life. I won't stop now. I am happy for the child." A pause. "And for Angela too. Now I hope that girl don't make a fool of herself. The start of the journey always looks promising ..." She did not finish the sentence.

The girl, Angelica, was flanked by two boys. She had a dimpled smile and two side plaits that came down to her chest. She had placed second of 3,364 students who'd written the secondary school entrance exams.

"You won't have to teach her," Mother said. "I'm sure Angela will send her to Convent." She did. The next time I saw a picture of Angelica it was a cutting Mother had made from the *Vincentian* announcing Angelica's graduation with a doctorate in education from the University of London. I'm certain I'm not the only person Mother has shown it to.

•

I love my mother and I wonder if it's out of loyalty to her that I've spurned her relatives. First, it was on her orders. Now they're strangers, and I have no urge to know them. It saddens me, but I won't do anything about it.

I've long dispelled any doubts I've had about Mother's love for me. Apart from never having my own room while I was growing up, I never felt deprived of material things. She rarely hugged me, but she praised me often and thanked me for any good suggestion I offered. "Maureen, what you think ..." was one her often-repeated sentences. I was only able to appreciate this after Beth told me that she and Frederick grew up in a home where the rule was: children should be seen and not heard. Beth said they were afraid of their parents. Not so with me. Mother and I had long conversations — about teachers, the neighbours, the pastor's sermons, items on the news. When I had to write an essay on a social topic — for example, drug consumption — she gave me suggestions.

At church, I was usually among the best dressed in my age group, in frilly dresses when I was younger, in the current fashion when I was older, and it was all clothing Mother had sewn. The Singer machine, one with a treadle, came down from Inez. She'd taught Mother the basics of dressmaking. Mother often went to the Kingstown Public

Library to borrow ideas from the fashion magazines. She bought patterns sometimes, but almost always altered them. On her days off, I'd come in from school and meet pieces of cut fabric spread out on the table, the settee, and sometimes the floor. People said that she and I looked like sisters. And it was true. A photograph of her at sixteen could easily be mistaken for a photograph of me then.

She found the money for me to go on every school trip: once to Venezuela and once to Martinique. She, on the other hand, had few clothes, three pairs of shoes, and two handbags — one brown, one black. She never spoke about what others had. Of course, it took years of living for me to appreciate her sacrifice on my behalf. In all of it, however, her vitriol for my father never attenuated, but she expressed it less and less as I grew older.

I think of my promise to her that night: "I won't let any man make a fool of me." Has that been true? Has Gordon made a fool of me? How does a woman guarantee that no man will make a fool of her? After Daddy left, Mother made a similar vow and has had a loveless life. I dated Gordon for two years before we had sex. He never pushed it, and I felt he was the perfect gentleman. I was twenty-one when it happened. I had recently graduated from teachers' college and felt it was time. I made him use a condom. Later he suggested I go on the pill. When I came back from Cave Hill, and Mother saw that the relationship had lasted, she said, "He looks decent. It's all right if you bring him home."

In her doctrine, sex outside marriage is sinful. By then I had stopped attending the Pentecostal church. Perhaps she wanted me to understand that her house was also my house. I did not know then that the house belonged to my father. Then again, Mother wasn't totally enslaved to doctrine. When I was ten, Pastor Havelock was standing at the door of the church right after service one Sunday and had seen me hand a copy of *Alice's Adventures in Wonderland* to Josephine. The book had been a birthday gift from Mother. "What book is that?" he asked and stretched his hand for it. "A novel! Young lady, I must have a serious talk with your mother. You shouldn't be reading novels. They are lies. Can't have you feeding your soul such filth." Mother was already on the curb waiting for me. He kept the novel. On our way home, I told Mother what had happened. She said nothing. Three days later, when she came in from work, she plopped down on the settee and motioned for me to sit beside her. She extracted the novel from her bag and handed it to me. "I want you to read. Pastor Havelock is a learned man, but he doesn't know everything … Some of the nuns who taught me had funny ideas about novels too."

When I got pregnant, I told her it was deliberate, that I wanted the child. She said I should have discussed it with Gordon. When Gordon suggested an abortion, she was more shocked than me. "You do that and I will never speak to you again. He is a demon. That boy fooled me. Then again, he's a man. What else can we expect?" And when Gordon accepted to marry me, she said, "It won't last. Go ahead, marry him. Your child will be glad. No one will call it bastard, but that's all that will come from your marriage." When Gordon said that the wedding had to be simple and cost-free or he'd call it off, she mused, "See? He's marrying you like a pauper. That means he's planning to leave you soon. He's saying he got you cheaply. No big loss when the whole shebang crumbles." She was sure Gordon wouldn't come back to St Vincent when he finished his studies.

"Mother, he has to. He must return to work in St Vincent or refund the government."

She replied, "He'll refund the government ... If he comes back, he'll treat you badly to force you to leave him."

Gordon came back and our relationship, though not passionate, has been peaceful — until last year. He cultivated a beautiful relationship with Frida. Read to her, taught her to read before she went to school. Made it clear to me that if I hit Frida, he'd end our marriage. Just after I got back from Cave Hill, he and I were having lunch in Baynes' Restaurant, and a former student from my days at Kingstown Anglican came to our table, told me he'd excelled in GCE, A level, and thanked me for the floggings I had given him. "I think you would have done well even without my beatings," I said. Gordon had already convinced me that beating students was wrong. Today I would like to apologize to every one of those students and beg them not to flog their children — or their students, if they've become teachers. Our prime minister has still not convinced Vincentian teachers to abandon the strap. One, whom the court found guilty of excessive abuse, boasted that she would not pay the fine — would rather go to jail — and quoted several Biblical passages that, she said, authorized her to flog her students. "That same Bible," Gordon said, "authorizes killing disobedient children. Hope she doesn't have a disobedient child — or any children, period."

In the early days, he and Mother clashed over child-rearing, and he said harsh things to her. When it comes to forgiving, Mother is worse than Yahweh. Yahweh gives the odd second chance; Mother doesn't. Her favourite saying is: "Hurt me once, shame on you. Hurt me twice, shame on me." Imagine my surprise when she told me: "Every child would love to have a father like Gordon. But don't tell him I said so." But she remains adamant. "He didn't come back because of you; he came back because of Frida."

Was Mother right? I've asked Gordon this question in all sorts of ways and never been convinced by his answer.

Chapter 4

GORDON SCROLLS DOWN TO FIND ANOTHER ENTRY about Maggie, but the date February 18 stops him. He begins to read:

February 18, 2012

The radio is on in the living room. A male caller is berating the prime minister for his litigiousness. "Matthew Thomas shouldn't pay him a cent." Lynch agrees, saying he and all radio hosts are personas when they're on air and shouldn't be prosecuted for their views. Lynch should ask Gordon about personas. Not sure why Gordon has the radio on this station. He no longer needs to apprise himself of all this political sham. I call out to him on the balcony and tell him to turn the radio off.

I feel energetic today. For almost three weeks I did not want to get out of bed.

My birthday was two days ago. I heard the phone ringing all morning and Gordon telling the callers,

"Maureen can't come to the phone right now." He made me lentil soup for lunch. He brought a folding tray into the bedroom and sat beside me and drank his. Half sitting in bed, propped up with pillows, a tray on my lap, I drank half a bowl. The answering machine took three calls during this time. I told him to unplug the phone. At supper he brought an almond cake with candles to the bedside. He must have bought it at Allan's Bakery. Their cakes are as good as those we make at home. "Don't light the candles," I said, "or you'll have to blow them out yourself." He left the bedroom and returned with a sparkler, put it on the cake, and lit it. I ate a sliver so he wouldn't feel bad. I reminded him to take a few slices for Theo and Austin. Up to a year ago we'd have sent some to Percival's boys. Their dog pooped on our lawn recently. Gordon called out to them to come and clean it, and Everett, Percival's last boy, told him to make soup with it. And when Gordon complained to Percival, his response was: "Loosen up, man. That only mean my boy got a sense o' humour." Christine does not have an easy time with them.

Around seven, Allan and Beth came by without warning. Holding a gift bag, Beth came straight into the bedroom. She helped me sit up and arranged the pillows around me. She went into the adjoining bathroom and returned with a hairbrush. She brushed, then braided my hair, went back to the bathroom and brought a damp washrag and wiped my face. She handed me the gift bag. It contained a bottle of perfume, a copy of Toni Morrison's *Love*, and a birthday card, one without pre-written text. The message was in her handwriting: "Maureen, you are dear to us, our sister in everything but biology. We wish you were well today and want you to get well soon. We are confident that you will be healthy and happy when we celebrate your many future birthdays." I told her thanks. The window was open only a sliver. I motioned to Beth to open it wider. The breeze coming uphill from the harbour felt good. She called out to Allan, "You can come now." I quickly sprayed some of the perfume onto my wrist and inhaled it.

He came in grinning from ear to ear. I don't think he'll ever outgrow those dimples. His paunch is getting bigger, though. Beth should go easy on those desserts.

He leaned over and kissed me. "Happy birthday, Maureen. What are you doing in bed on your birthday?"

"You tell me. You are the doctor. Thanks for the gifts."

"You're welcome. You'll like this Morrison novel. I've already read my own copy."

Gordon entered, bringing one of the dining chairs for Allan.

"Bring a chair for yourself too and the rest of the cake," I told him.

He returned ten minutes later pushing the tea trolley — a gift from Mother — with plates, forks, napkins, glasses, a bottle of wine, and the rest of the cake. We toasted my birthday. Allan winked consent for me to drink my half glass of wine. Gordon looked at him alarmed; Allan gave him a wink too. I drank half of my wine. Gordon took a sip of his and put it on the tray. They left around eight, and I had to admit I felt better afterward.

But that night I dreamed that Claudia, Beth, Allan, Gordon, and I were picnicking at Trinity Falls. The Richmond River came down and swept them downstream. Hearing my screams, Gordon awakened me. I told him the dream.

"What do you make of it?" I eventually asked him.

"I don't know," he said.

I looked at the dial on the clock radio. It was 5:26 a.m. Gordon did not go back to sleep. He went into the living room. I remained in bed but couldn't fall asleep. Instead, I thought about this mask of secrecy that Gordon, Allan, and I have been wearing. I guess if dreams were logical, I, not Beth, would have been among the drowned.

The birthday cards are piled up on the night table. Maybe I'll open them later — if I have the energy. On days when I write, I feel completely drained afterward. In happier times, I would have already called or sent emails to thank my well-wishers. I have over sixty unopened emails. The voice mail has stopped taking messages. I'm going to have to muster up the energy to clear up this backlog, otherwise everyone will think that Death is at my bedside, poised to strike me with his hammer.

Chapter 5

April 8, 2012, Easter Sunday

All that's written for February 22 is the date. I remember now. I came here on the morning of Ash Wednesday to record and reflect on a dream I'd had the night before. Instead, I was overcome by a crying fit and became so depressed that I went back to bed. I'm fairly certain that dream was related to a promise Gordon had made that when we retired, we would travel to Trinidad to see the carnival. I dreamed that we were in Trinidad, and I lost Gordon in the crowd. A man came to help me. I told him I was looking for my husband. I mentioned Gordon's name. The man froze momentarily, then said his name was Trevor and began pushing people out of his way to escape from me.

February 21 was the Mardi Gras. As images from the floats of the Trinidad Carnival flashed on SVG TV, Gordon was sitting on the couch beside me. If he were in Trinidad, he would be witnessing it with Trevor at his side. Thoughts of our marriage as a masquerade came to me as I watched the moving floats. *A Primer of Jungian Psychology*, required reading for Professor Bolton's course and now one of my prized texts, states that we all possess a persona: a public, artificial self, that allows us to function harmoniously with society. It serves us well if it doesn't overwhelm or swallow up the true self. There's hell to pay if it does. At home, at work, on the street, Gordon has had to be a heterosexual. He couldn't possibly still have an authentic self. Now I, too, wear the mask of a heterosexual wife and live a life of lies so the news won't spread that my husband is gay and we both have AIDS. What is this doing to my authentic self?

When, following the AIDS diagnosis and Gordon's admission that he was gay, my anger dissipated, Eliot's "Prufrock" and "Preludes" came back to me — that line about creating a face for the thousand faces that we meet, a face that Gordon can only lose when he's asleep. I suspect that his authentic and fake selves battle for sovereignty when he's asleep. My "infinitely gentle, infinitely suffering [Gordon]." If ever there was a "soul stretched tight," it's his. It's another reason why I shouldn't discuss our situation with anyone. My friends won't understand. Not even Beth, who turns a blind eye to Allan's infidelity. She'll say it's not the same thing. Having sex with men! The parameters aren't the same, Maureen. He has given you AIDS. That's indefensible. Leave the bastard. Yes, even Beth will be angry with me, much like many American women have been with Hillary Clinton for not leaving Bill. Allan has assured me that he won't discuss our situation with her. He invokes professional ethics. In St Vincent, they exist on paper only. But I'll take him at his word and hope he doesn't betray me.

Not sure any of this is what I would have written on February 22. In any event, I was too depressed to be coherent. This is my first trip back here since. Most mornings I haven't felt like getting out of bed. Gordon sometimes succeeded in coaxing me out. When I do, I don't go onto the porch. I don't want the neighbours to see me or talk to me. They know I'm ill. Christine ran into Beth at the supermarket and tried to wheedle information out of her. A week ago, Flossy showed up with a bowl of soup and asked Gordon for me. I heard him say, "She can't come to the door right now."

"She sick or something?"

"No, she isn't sick, just doing something that she can't leave off now."

Since her visit in February, Beth has invited us twice for supper. I said no but urged Gordon to go alone. Of course, he didn't. Beth has visited twice in the interim. I can't remember which days. Came the first time despite my telling her I wasn't having visitors, and she scourged rather than comforted me.

"It's because you retired cold. Yeah, I know you have liver trouble and it leaves you feeling weak. But you retired with no plans for what you'll do afterward."

"I've started to work on a memoir."

"Oh! You never told me."

"I wanted it kept a secret. I thought I'd wait until it's finished, and I won't let anyone read it if it's not to my liking."

"Why don't you ask Allan to prescribe something for you? From a mile away I can see that you are depressed."

"I'll think about it. I feel so miserable; I don't want to get better; I want to die."

"Well, I don't think Allan can help you with that. Day after tomorrow, I'm going to come and pick you up and take you to Indian Bay. You'll come with me even if I have to handcuff you, hand and foot, stuff a washrag in your mouth, and toss you into the car. Just the two of us, so we can talk woman stuff."

Woman stuff. I became alarmed. Did she know?

I went. What day was it? Had to have been a Saturday or Sunday. Saturday. There was a lot of traffic. I relaxed after it became clear that the trip wasn't about Gordon and my illness. I'll admit I felt better afterward. Indian Bay's warm water, the jollity of the children and young people around me, mostly people visiting from abroad, people who'd put their cares on hold and come to enjoy themselves. They distracted me from mine. It helped that I met no one I knew.

Since then, I've been on a roller coaster. Beth calls me every day, sometimes twice, and Gordon knows better than to tell her, "Maureen can't come to the phone." One day three weeks or a month ago — I'm losing track of time — I made the mistake of telling her that if I had the energy, I would get out of bed and hurl myself over this cliff. She was here within thirty minutes. Brought frozen callaloo soup too that she thawed in the microwave and ordered me to drink to the very last drop.

Not sure what she told Allan when she got back home, but the next day he came too. I heard him and Gordon whispering on the porch. He came into the bedroom and, after asking how I was, held a bottle of pills close enough for me to read the name *Zoloft*.

I shook my head. "I won't take them."

"You have to take this, Maureen. No is not an option."

I did not answer. I wanted to say, Allan, dear, pills don't nourish the psyche. Good news does. It makes us euphoric. For almost forty years I watched the glow in my students' eyes when they received good results, especially when they thought they'd failed. And there was my own joy that came from seeing them happy. Pills, my dear Allan, pills cannot provide that. The soul needs another kind of food.

"Maureen, are you with me?"

"Yes. Just thinking that you don't have what will make me well."

"And what will?"

"Good news."

He sighed, looked away, and seemed annoyed. Facing the window, he said, "You'll take the Zoloft or I'll have you admitted for psychiatric observation."

"Talking to me or to the window?"

He turned to look at me.

"You're just trying to scare me into taking pills."

"No. You are being foolhardy and punishing yourself uselessly. I can't let you go on doing this."

"What were you and Gordon talking about? I heard you both whispering."

"About your care."

"Does he think antidepressants can undo what he's done?"

He swallowed his saliva. "Are you going to take these or do I have to have you admitted for observation? You told Beth that you would like to hurl yourself over this cliff."

"Maybe, if you had AIDS, you would too."

That shut him up for a while. When he spoke next his tone was coaxing. "Be reasonable, Maureen. Don't you want to feel good? Don't you want your energy back? We are worried."

"Okay. I'll try them."

Holding a glass of water, Gordon came into the room immediately. He must have been outside the door listening. Allan unscrewed the cap and tapped a pill into it. I sat up. He tossed the pill into my mouth. I took the glass from Gordon and drank.

"You might not feel the effect for a while, but I'm sure you'll feel better in about a week."

He was right, except that Zoloft exacerbated the mild diarrhea I get from Atripla. After ten days he put me on Prozac. It's definitely helping. After all, here I am again writing. My remaining stomach problems are from the ARVs. My appetite has returned somewhat, but I'm still to regain any of the twenty pounds I've lost. Allan is confident that most of my weight will return. I hope it does. My eyes are in deep holes, my face is like a rutted landscape, my neck's wattled. Today I'm accompanying Gordon to May's place for Sunday dinner. It's a week now that I haven't thought of dying.

I must convince Gordon that he should fly to Montreal to attend Frida's graduation. That girl is restless. Finished a master's five years ago in human physiology. Taught for three years, then decided to do another master's, this time in molecular biology.

Simply announced it: "Mom, I'm going back to school."

"But you have an excellent teaching job."

"Excellent isn't how I'll describe it."

"When do you plan to stop studying?"

"When it begins to bore me. Right now, my job is doing so, and that's why I'm leaving it."

"Can you afford it?"

"I live simply. Don't worry. I won't be asking you or Dad for money."

That conversation was two years ago. I would attend her graduation, but I don't want Frida to see me looking like this. I'll delay that encounter for as long as I can. I'm glad that I have been able to persuade Beth, Allan, and Gordon not to tell her about my depression. I don't want it to affect her studies. She knows nothing about the AIDS diagnosis or that other story about hepatic malfunctioning. I refuse to let anyone photograph me. Of course, there's the possibility that she could hear about me from her friends or their parents. No, Frida, I don't want you worrying about me. Am I glad I procrastinated installing Skype.

My dear Frida, because of the field you are in, you are going to want Allan to send samples of my blood for you to analyze. Of course, if you decide to come home for a visit, I won't know what to tell you. I'll cross that bridge when I get there. Frida, you certainly won't find work in St Vincent. There are no chemical industries here. In our chat two days ago, you said you've already had interviews with drug companies, and you are hopeful of finding something in Toronto. You've been a permanent resident in Canada now for close to ten years. You never told me if you followed up on your plan to get citizenship. It would be a lot easier to travel with a Canadian passport. I want to see you established before I'm gone. I wonder if your romance with that Greek fellow is still on. Where boyfriends are concerned, you're something of a rolling stone as well. What do they call it? Serial monogamy. Doesn't sound healthy to me, but, child, it's your life.

I can't live it for you. It looks like I'll be dead before grandchildren come along. Maybe none will. You are heading for thirty-three.

Whatever we say about children hampering our careers, we feel a need to have them. We yearn for them. If they turn out all right, we luxuriate in them. When Mother meets people for the first time, she tells them, "You probably know or heard about my daughter. She's the deputy headmistress of Girls' High School." (I wonder how she feels now that *is* has become *was*.) And I know there's a glint in her eye when she says it. I am her accomplishment. While Frida was growing up, Beth and Allan treated her like the daughter they would have liked to have. I've never asked Beth why they never had any children. You'd expect her to talk about such things with a close friend. Maybe I'm wrong; maybe not everyone feels a need to have children. Then again, I knew if for some reason I hadn't been able take care of Frida, she and Allan would have done so. I'll broach this subject of children with her. Say it in an accusing way? I shouldn't. The reason might be embarrassing, and she might feel forced to lie, the way I must lie to hide my illness and cover Gordon's shame.

Then there's that need for grandchildren. I feel it. Gordon does too. One time it slipped out of his taciturn mouth. "I wonder if Frida will ever become a mother?" Of course, he'd have denied that he yearns to be a grandfather. He wouldn't want it to interfere with the character he calls Gordon, the one that says, "I must never tell people how to live their lives." Now I understand why, during Frida's teenage years, Maggie's most frequent complaint was that she rarely saw her granddaughter.

Tomorrow I'll see if I'm strong enough to give the garden some attention. Weeds are choking it. I suspect Gordon has been forgetting to water it. You'd think he might have made an effort to keep it weed-free. The zinnias flowered and withered, and I was too out of it to bother to collect some seeds. I'm probably going to need help with it from now on. I saw an ad in *Searchlight* from someone offering hourly services as a gardener. Makes me think of Boccaccio's gardener. I might have benefitted from such a gardener in another time. Wonder how Gordon would react if I told him this.

•

I have to do something for Mother's birthday, coming up on May 6. If I don't, she'll get alarmed and know that I am hiding something serious behind my excuses not to see her. How will she respond when she sees me? Unless I get a caterer to do it, it won't be the usual get-together at the house for her and her church buddies and able-bodied ex-colleagues. It might have to be just supper or lunch at one of those tourist restaurants in Villa where it's unlikely that I'll run into anyone who knows me.

I must call her in an hour to wish her a happy Easter. She's in church now, dressed in white and belting out "Up from the Grave He Arose / With a mighty triumph o'er his foes." Now she croaks rather than sings, but insists on being part of the choir. Maybe I should record her singing and play it back for her.

I haven't been to church since last July. I did think about going this morning. Apart from Beth, no one seems to have noticed my absence. But seeing me would set people's tongues wagging.

Religion is one of the subjects I never discuss with Gordon. He has let Allan turn him into an atheist. And they've both turned Frida into one. Until she turned fourteen, she used to love going to church with me. Was even a member of the junior choir.

I remember that when she was around seven or eight, they were practising for a Christmas concert and she said to me, "Mom, there's something wrong with this song." She sang, "'A child, a child, shivers in the cold, let us bring him silver and gold.' Mom, silver and gold! A shivering child needs a blanket."

"With the silver and gold, they could buy blankets."

"But, Mom, it's happening on Christmas Day when all the stores are closed for the holiday."

I conceded that she had a point but told her not to raise it with the choir director.

At age thirteen her talks about God with Allan and Gordon began, and church was no longer cool. Once she decided to specialize in the biological sciences, all hesitation about the Almighty went out the window. "Mom, I deal with molecules and DNA, not superstition." She saw that I was hurt and tried to soften it. "Mom, I mean ... I'm sorry. It came out worse than I meant it." I said to myself, *Maureen, keep your mouth shut if you don't want your feelings hurt*. Maybe if I believed like Mother does, that sinners will roast in hell, I'd see Gordon getting his comeuppance eventually. But the pleasure would be brief. No one deserves to be treated sadistically. I'm happy to be Anglican. It's an enlightened religion. Allan says that all religions that encourage belief in an afterlife are benighted. Maybe out of deference to May, who Gloria, my ex-colleague, tells me, is one of the pillars of the Evesham Methodist Church, Gordon never says anything bad about Methodists. He should. They oppose LGBTQ rights. Recently, a Barbadian journalist covering a demonstration organized by Christian fundamentalists to fight against LGBTQ rights asked a Methodist minister standing bedecked in sacerdotal robes in front of the James Street Methodist Church for her opinion. She sneered, "Scripture does not support it." The interviewer came back with, "Scripture supports stoning adulterers to death."

Her eyebrows went up but she said nothing.

·

May 1, 2012

Labour Day. A holiday. In the U.S. and Canada, they celebrate it in September. All the talk these last few days has been about the sixteen-year-old boy who committed suicide. I think he was way more courageous than I am.

There's so little noise coming up the cliff that it feels eerie. I can even hear the sea slapping the wharf. I stare out the window at the throngs of people lined up on the Grenadines Wharf, waiting to board the Bequia ferry. In better times Gordon, Frida, and I would ourselves be in that line or in the car queue, or planning to leave later for Indian Bay or Mount Wynne.

This face of mine looks like a dried-out potato and makes me afraid to show myself in public. Every day I hop onto the bathroom scale hoping to see signs of the weight gain that will repair my face. The pound that I seem to gain one day disappears the next. So I keep myself at home and don't venture beyond the garden. At Easter, when we went to Riley, I told Gordon to go via Queen's Drive. The views of Arnos Vale on one side of the ridge and Belair and Fountain on the other are spectacular, but my reason was that I felt we were less likely to run into any of my former colleagues. Before, whenever we went to Riley, I asked Gordon to return via La Croix and stopped to spend a few minutes with Gloria. Outside May's gate, on our return, Gordon turned left. "Oh, no," I said. "Reverse. We are taking the same route back." My heart stayed in my hands until we walked into this house.

May became alarmed and held her breath when she saw me. "What happening to you, Maureen? Why you not eating properly?" She turned her stare on Gordon. "You should see to it that Maureen take better care o' sheself." I told her that the liver processes the food we eat, and when it malfunctions, the body can't utilize food properly. I changed the conversation quickly and complimented her on her recently painted living room. The walls are in light blue, the doors and ceiling in white. She got rid of the settee. In its place is an overstuffed cocoa-brown sofa. Not much of an improvement. It looked out of place. It's alarming to see how TV ads are changing people's tastes. No one is going to get me to give up solid mahogany and cushions. I'm glad she hasn't discarded her parents' china closet and dining table. She asked Gordon to come back in the week to set up her new computer. Astonishing. When Gordon was growing up, electricity had not yet come to Riley.

I'm going to have to get over my fear of letting others see me. I cannot keep putting off colleagues and church members who want to visit me. Beth says they think I have terminal cancer; they're not buying the liver ailment story. I'm glad they don't know Gordon is gay. Otherwise, they'd say I have AIDS.

There are friendships I want to hold on to: Gloria's and Claudia's especially. And Beth's and Allan's of course. It was painful to lie to Claudia a third time. She called two days ago to invite Gordon and me to a picnic at Mount Wynne today. The entire faculty of Girls' High School would be there. I told her Gordon and I had to attend a function at Government House.

Joel, her husband, is a civil servant in the ministry of education. A gem of a fellow. Tall, coal-black skin, perfect white teeth, and eyes that sparkle when he smiles. Now he's beginning to get a paunch. I first met him when Claudia brought him to our housewarming party. He'd already proposed marriage. She'd told him she'd think about it and had asked my opinion. She was twenty-three then, had a B.A., and had just come on to the staff to teach history. He was twenty-seven, a junior clerk in the civil service, and had ended his schooling at GCE. O level. I told her to trust her feelings.

Claudia is no heartstopper. She's short, plain, and overweight. Wears her hair in a boy-cut and uses almost no makeup. She was one of my best students. Got distinctions in almost every subject. She was seriously thinking of returning to university to pursue a Ph.D., when Joel proposed marriage. Marriage won out in the end, but she managed to do a master's while raising two children. When we compliment her, she points to Joel and says, "Compliment him. He took care of the children and ran the household the year I was in Trinidad." Now if he turns out to be gay, the little faith I have in humanity will evaporate. Lots of people think Gordon has been a great catch, a model husband, and I won't let them think otherwise.

Until I became sick, my colleagues invited Gordon and me to their homes often. Most times I went alone. There's not much to do in St Vincent beyond going to the beach and eating and visiting friends and colleagues. Here only students read. In the early years of our marriage, I tried to get Gordon interested in books I'd read and liked. It would have created more conversation between us. No luck. Until I heard it mentioned on TV, it had never occurred to me that in the Caribbean, men who're avid readers are suspected of being gay. Allan is a reader. And I'm certain Allan's not gay. All the books I've read in recent years came from him. Until I became ill, most of our conversation has been about books. At home people mostly listen to music or watch rented films. Of course, for most uneducated Vincentian men, life is work — if they have a job — getting drunk, playing cards and dominoes, and wenching. My colleagues and I rely on board games. Gordon likes to play Chinese checkers with me because he wins. Rarely Scrabble. My best Scrabble games are with Allan, though he often beats me. His scientific vocabulary gives him a huge advantage. Gordon likes to play dominoes and checkers with Allan. Never with me. Beth likes cribbage. She always wins. For Mother, playing cards was gambling, so I never mastered any card games. Same for Gordon. His parents never allowed them to socialize with other children. His mother seems to have been a puritanical Methodist. I never warmed to her. While Gordon was away studying, she sent May or came herself with fruits and vegetables every week. And there was that time when I had a bad case of the flu. Very few words passed between Lillian and me. She must have been an upright woman. Without her intervention, Gordon wouldn't have married me. In hindsight that was probably not such a good thing. To hear Gordon tell it, his father was a sex addict. He lost a well-paying, secure job because he was with a mistress when he should have been at work. The few times Gordon mentioned his father, he always added, "I hope I've learned from his mistakes."

When Gordon and I travelled in Canada and the States, I understood in the starkest of ways how sterile — limited? — our lives here were. North America offered such an array of entertainment and educational possibilities: art exhibitions, theatre, cinema, literary events in bookstores and libraries, free concerts in the park. You name it. On the other hand, most of the people we stayed with were too exhausted on their days off to take in any of these activities. So many possibilities for intellectual growth. I've always wanted to become proficient in French and Spanish. And I'm sure I would have gone on to do that M.A. my heart was set upon. In North America, I came to see that my brain had been functioning on default for a long time. It needed coaxing to soak up what I was seeing and liking. I couldn't help wondering how different my life would have been if we'd emigrated. I'm sure I'd have found a teaching position. Maybe Gordon would have had no need to lie to me and society. He said he made the sacrifice for Frida and me. For Frida, yes. Regardless of what happens, I'm glad that when/if Frida finds out about her father it will be after I'm gone. But, if it happens while I'm still around, I'll try to help her understand why Gordon has had to wear this mask for so long. I don't trust Gordon to do it. A knowledge of psychology isn't his forte. His skill is in numbers, not words. I've warned him that if he breaks the news to her, he must never tell her that he wore his mask to spare her the shame of having a gay father or that he gave up living in Canada because of her. Of course, he never said the latter to me; I'm basing it on Mother's intuition. If, on their own, our children understand and acknowledge the sacrifice we make, fine. But we don't need to tell them about it, because if we do, we make them feel they owe us something.

Now that I know Gordon better, I no longer wonder why he rarely wanted to accompany me to my colleagues' homes. Whenever I upbraided him, he said, "You must accept that I'm a loner." Once I lost my temper and told him, "Cut out that loner crap. I'm tired of going places by myself. Why do I have a husband?"

He replied, "Maybe, you need two husbands or a different kind of husband." A different kind of husband.

Allan almost always accompanies Beth. What a dancer he is! Gordon's sense of rhythm is distorted: he dances with carpenter legs; has none of Allan's fluidity and grace. Without Beth and Allan and Claudia and Joel I'd have felt like a wallflower in my colleagues' homes.

Before I began looking like an Egyptian mummy, I accompanied Gordon to all of his functions at Government House or at the prime minister's residence. There's nothing more insufferable than enduring politicians and their spouses for two hours. I always spent the next day recuperating. After a while, I refused to go to those held during the week. Once I told Frida that I hated these functions.

"Why do you go?" she said.

"Because I'm married to your father, and they expect me to attend."

"I wouldn't."

"You don't know that. You haven't come to that bridge yet."

"You mean after all the work by the feminist movement, women still have to do this?"

"That work was done overseas."

"Guess you are right. Here, men are still slapping, boxing, and kicking women, and judges scold them, and they return home and continue where they left off. No man is going to do that to me and get away with it."

Talk is cheap. I hope she isn't hostile to marriage. She seems to like Demetrius, though she hasn't said anything about marriage. She has seen Allan and Beth's marriage up close — an excellent one. Well, there's Allan's mistress. But from the way Beth's handling it, Frida will never know. If Gordon and I handle our current problem well, she'll never know — while he and I are still alive — that her father is gay.

This is turning into something other than a memoir. No matter. If I intend for Frida to read this, I'm going to have to erase a lot. It won't do her much good to know how flawed Gordon is. Or, for that matter, how weak — perhaps trapped — I am. My handling of Gordon's sexuality won't jive with her understanding of what a liberated woman should do. Should I put the password for this laptop in my papers so that if for some reason I am unable to erase this, Gordon could do it before it falls into Frida's hands? No. I don't want Gordon to ever read what's written here. Hope I don't die suddenly.

•

Valencia begins to work for us tomorrow. Now that Gordon runs the household, he knows how much energy it takes. He likes everything to be spanking clean. Thanks to him my car has always been spotless. He cleaned mine on

Saturdays and his on Sundays. I've always opposed having a housekeeper. I feel that if we clean our own dirt, we will create less of it. It's an essay topic I gave my senior students. Over the years I think only four or five explored it at a metaphorical level. After stating the obvious, one student had focused on the consequences of George Bush's war in Iraq. Gordon's other dirt. Well, there's no way to clean that, and I shouldn't call it dirt.

When Beth visited and saw my weakened condition, she spoke to Gordon about getting household help. Thank God, we can afford it. It means that Frida will inherit less. At least she'll get the house. There's under twenty thousand dollars remaining on the mortgage. We've never had to pay tuition for her. Once she got to community college and focused exclusively on science and math, she aced everything. Inherited her math skills from Gordon. He once boasted to me that he got a one in math for O-level GCE and A's for all of his university math courses. I know that initially, Allan, who was a year ahead of him in secondary school, tutored him. Allan told me so while Gordon was away studying. "The math teacher Gordon had at Emmanuel made them memorize theorems. The fellow didn't know the first thing about math. I taught Gordon what I'd learned. He outperformed me after that."

I hope Valencia is good at doing makeup. I have to hide some of these wrinkles when I see Mother in five days. I look like a jumbie. Gordon tried to get me to cater the event. Men are so daft when it comes to understanding women. He couldn't figure out that I don't want Mother's friends and associates seeing me suddenly turned an old woman. They'll probably think, *My God, she looks older than her mother.* Besides, even if we catered it, we'd still have to spend time decorating and organizing. We're talking about up to thirty people, none of them my friends. When I started the tradition ten years ago, I begged Mother to limit it to twelve people. Her response: "I can't invite Brenda and not invite Comsie ... what will ... say? You want me to make enemies?" Mother's pastor usually makes two trips with the church van. The four or five colleagues of hers, now retired, usually arrange their own transport. In previous years, Beth made the cakes, Claudia the sorrel and ginger beer, May came by and seasoned the chicken and goat for me, and Gordon did the rice and peas and cleaned and decorated the house. I ran around and got the ingredients and did the odds and ends. There was usually a lot of food left over. Mother's friends took containers. I sent containers for Francine, Austin, and Theo. It took a lot of willpower to send some for Percival's brats, but I did. Those boys can't help being who they are anymore than an untrained pit bull can avoid wanting to kill. Poor Christine. Freckles and his sons insult her, as Mother would say, for tea, breakfast, and dinner.

When I called and told Mother we'd be going to a restaurant, she was silent for a good ten seconds. When she spoke, she said, "I thought you were calling to spring a surprise on me, to tell me that Frida will come for my birthday. A restaurant! If that is how you want it." I imagined her: thumb supporting her chin, her eyebrows raised halfway up her forehead. "Rosalie was so looking forward to this. She already bought a new dress for the occasion. Now I'm going to have to tell them that you changed the pattern. You're not worried they'll say you and your husband think you're big shots now and don't want humble people in your house?"

"Mother, please."

"So which restaurant you're taking me to?"

"One of those in Villa."

"Villa! You're out of your head! Why you want me to go to a restaurant in Villa? I'm not a tourist. Those people serve crapaud. Frogs' legs, my foot! Just thinking about it make me want to retch. I bet their food taste like straw. On top o' that, you know I don't eat from any and anybody. I have to be sure the people handling my food clean. Many people don't wash their hands after using the toilet."

"Mother, I have to go. We'll pick you up around noon. Wait for us outside the church. Take care."

No one will believe that the first time I proposed celebrating her birthday here in this house, I had to threaten never to speak to her again if she didn't come. I wonder if Mother knows why she so wants to celebrate her birthday in my house. Most of her church sisters — one of the two brothers who used to come is dead, and the other is in a nursing home — are single-parent mothers. Quite a few with children who've turned out be wastrels. A couple are in prison.

She called me back immediately. "Don't you dare shut me up like that! I guess the change is because of this liver ailment of yours. How are you feeling?"

"I'm coming along. My doctor's doing his best. Allan has looked at the drugs he's giving me and thinks they're appropriate."

"Gordon helping you with the housework?"

"Yes. We're getting a helper."

"That's good. Make sure she's older and not very good-looking."

"What do you mean, Mother?"

"You want competition? Don't put temptation in a man's way. He won't refuse it."

I laughed.

"You're laughing. I hope you don't find out when it's too late."

That's my mother. Wisdom forged in the kiln of cynicism. Wonder what she would do if I invited Clem to the restaurant too. Gordon once threatened to bring him to one of Mother's birthday celebrations. Of course, I knew Gordon wouldn't. "How," Gordon asks at times, "do you and your mother feel carrying around all this hatred?"

"Just like you do with your feelings about your father."

"There's a difference. Clem wants to reconcile. He needs your forgiveness. It's not too much to give to a man who wants to die in peace."

"Let him concoct his own peace. You will have to do that too. I don't mean about your father."

He took a loud breath. Maybe I shouldn't have said that. He's a sensitive man. I know now that buried in the silence that has been there from the time we got married is the guilt he has been carrying since he married me. Those who talk too much, Mother used to say to me, betray their secrets. I admit my culpability in this mess that my life has become. If I had not got pregnant, he wouldn't have felt forced to marry me. Mother was right. I should have discussed getting pregnant before I did. Of course, in having me as his girlfriend, he was using me to make Vincentians believe he was heterosexual. What's done is done, Maureen, and can't be undone.

Yet I could have done worse — been forced to raise Frida on my own. I will never tell Gordon that the way he has parented her made me think of the parenting I never got. What if Frida had disappointed him? I know enough children who, despite the best parenting, have disappointed their parents. Some were my students. Now Mother can brag not only about her daughter, the ex-deputy headmistress of Girls' High School, but also about her granddaughter who's about to receive a second master's degree, this time in molecular biology. "Mom, all that remains now is for me to receive the diploma. That will be in June." It makes sense that Maggie wants to parade Frida in front of her church friends. The only kind thing she's ever said about Gordon is that he has been a good father. If the truth about our illness becomes known, the pedestal Mother has me on will be knocked out from under me. How would she handle it? She'd advise me to keep it secret. She'd be angry, but she's no fool, but I won't be able to trust her not to tell Frida. And the uneasy peace that now exists between Mother and Gordon will be shattered forever.

He scrolls down further, through passages describing Valencia's antics, until he gets to what he's looking for.

May 7, 2012

Yesterday, Mother's birthday, I agonized over how I'd look. On Friday, Valencia, bless her heart, dyed my hair a very dark brown. Just before I left the house, she layered my face with something that felt like goo before applying face powder. "Mr. Wiley, he must keep car cool. You no want sweat. Restaurant cool. You no go sweat." We gave Valencia the afternoon off and offered to drop her home on our way to pick Mother up directly from church. She told us to leave her at the market. She obviously doesn't want us to know where she lives.

The restaurant was on the second floor. About fifteen tables. Three White men sat at one. All the others were empty. We sat at a table that gave us a direct view of Young Island. Just below us yachts and catamarans bobbed up and down on the water. Their occupants, weekend visitors from the nearby islands most likely, sat around on the downstairs patio drinking. Mother sat across from me and never lost her frown.

"What's bothering you, Mother?"

"I don't know why you brought me to this place." Ten minutes had elapsed since the waitress came by, and Mother hadn't opened the menu. The waitress — Afro-Indian, twentysomething, prim and proper, in a white blouse and black skirt — smiled. She had already brought us water and asked what we wanted to drink. Mother had pointed to her glass of water. "That is more than enough for me."

Gordon and I, anticipating indigestion, had asked for Perrier. She'd brought it and noted that Mother hadn't opened the menu. Now, from the far end of the restaurant, she was leaning against the bar counter, her arms crossed below the waist, and looking at us intently. "Mother, the waitress wants you to choose. Why you don't open the menu? There are some lovely seafood dishes. There's paella. You love pelau."

"I don't know what all they have chop up in it. I don't have to read the menu. I sure they have barbecue chicken."

Gordon signalled to the waitress.

"Mother, you first."

"I want barbecue chicken. A leg so I'm sure it's chicken you serving me. That with a baked potato and salad. Don't put any guck on my potato."

The waitress picked up the menu and opened it.

"Honey, you don't need to open that. You all have barbecue chicken?"

"Yes."

"You all know how to bake potatoes?"

The waitress broke into a smile. Gordon was smiling too and shaking his head. My lower jaw was almost on my chest.

"I understand," the waitress said and turned to me.

Gordon and I ordered broiled fish and rice — no salad, we have trouble digesting anything that's uncooked — and asked them to put lots of lemon juice on it, but no pepper.

The waitress left and Mother continued to stare at me. "I want to ask you something. You changed professions?"

"Mother, what you mean?"

"Why you have all that putty on your face?"

"Mother, it's just makeup. Does it look good? You haven't said if it looks good."

"Good! You look like a painted lady."

When the waitress came with the cake — we'd ordered it with the reservation — Mother broke into a smile, her first for the afternoon. I held my breath until she took the first forkful and only released it when Mother nodded her approval. If I'm alive next year, I think I'll return to celebrating her birthday in my home.

•

This morning the scale says I've gained three pounds. I've been eating more. Maybe it's the effect of Prozac. One thing leads to another: I feel better, I eat more, I have more energy, and more energy makes me feel better. Of course, I know this feeling of well-being won't last. How do I combat depression on my down days?

Will my life ever resume its routine? You never think that shopping for groceries, talking to neighbours across the fence, picking up the phone and calling someone, cleaning the house, cooking, going to church, meeting a colleague in town to chat — you never think that such banalities are what comprise a healthy life.

Last night, before sleep came, I thought of Allan's threat to have me hospitalized. Was he telling me I'm mad? Yes, I'm mad. Mad as in angry. I am not insane. If he tells me so one more time, I'll say, *Go ahead and call me crazy, Allan, and I will show you what crazy is.* I will call in *Searchlight*, the *News*, the *Vincentian*. I will tell them everything and show them the drugs I'm taking, and after that I will definitely go crazy. Maureen, you're kidding. You'll never do that. Make a spectacle of yourself! Maybe I can get something good out of it: denounce the laws and attitudes that brought us to this. But that part won't interest journalists.

I hope those who read this understand that getting AIDS has nothing to do with being gay or straight.

Yes, I should be clear in my mind about what's angering me. When Allan and I discussed Gordon's homosexuality, he reminded me, as if I needed reminding, that he'd urged us all to see *Brokeback Mountain*. The Christian Council here had wanted it banned. Eight of us went in a party to see it: Allan and Beth, Claudia and Joel, Gloria and Brent (her boyfriend at the time), and Gordon and me. Afterward, we went to Bickles and joined two tables together. The intent was to discuss the film, but all four of us women were silent.

I'm sure we were all wondering if any of the men with us was leading a double life; since then, that fear has prevented us from even discussing it among ourselves. Allan had wanted a discussion badly. In the end, because we were silent, he ended up giving a lecture. He said that studies show that as many as twenty percent of all human beings were bisexual; that in some cases, same-sex desire was weak and could be resisted. In other cases, no. He felt the shapers of public opinion were aware of this, and it was why shame, censure, and laws have been used to keep same-sex lust in check. He looked from me to Beth — we were sitting beside each other across from him — "You remember Sehon Goodridge, your Anglican bishop who died a few years ago, saying on the radio sometime back in the late nineties that if the church accepts homosexuality, husbands would leave their wives and wives would leave their husbands and their children would suffer? That argument isn't as specious as it seems."

I guess Gordon is what they call bisexual. Didn't he have a responsibility to tell me before we got married? In *Brokeback Mountain*, Ennis and Jack didn't tell their wives. When we got home after the film I asked Gordon how he thought Jack had died. I'd wanted to bring it up in the restaurant.

He said, "His in-laws killed him."

"The film doesn't show that."

"Indirectly it does. Remember the look on the wife's face when she met Ennis? Remember the scene that Ennis recalls about his father taking him to see what happens to homosexuals?"

"I get it. Jack leaves to go fishing with his brother-in-law, and after that we hear of his death. The rest is left to our imagination."

They say that what you don't know won't hurt you. Nonsense. We don't see the microbes in food or water but they'll make us sick or kill us just the same. And we never know what diseases lurk in healthy-looking men and women. We never know.

Chapter 6

HE REMEMBERS THE CONVERSATIONS ABOUT *Brokeback Mountain* in the restaurant and later at home. He was tense while Allan spoke, so tense he couldn't scan the faces of the others. Why had they all been so silent? Were the women wondering if their husbands were closeted gays? He would have never spoken to anyone about the film, let alone urge them to see it and discuss it. Allan should be renamed Mr. Confident.

His legs feel wooden. He thinks of ejecting the flash drive, but there's more of the journal that he wants to read. He gets up and walks out to the side porch. He leans against the railing for a couple of minutes, then goes to sit at the patio table. There are things in the journal that Frida should know. *How was Maggie able to read me so well? At least she feels that I've been a good father. Maureen never told me this. Now I wonder what will May tell Frida about me? The childhood squabbles with our father?* Gordon never confided in May. It wasn't cool for brothers to confide in sisters. Besides, people always repeat what they'd been told. May sometimes spoke to him about this boy or other — or man, usually married — who wanted to bed her, and ended the stories with a headshake and a guffaw. Lillian hounded her about marriage. "Don't be foolish, girl. You must have a man in your life, otherwise people going walk all over you."

"Mama, the women I see need protection from the men — them that you say should protect them."

Lillian would reply, "You go on talking stupidness. One day you going wake up and find it too late. You want to die a lonely old maid?"

He knows now what loneliness is. Never suspected such loneliness existed. Not even in Montreal. There he was too busy studying to feel it. He's sure May feels lonely. Shortly after Lillian died, May had considered adopting a child, but Gordon heard no more about it.

◆

Frida, it was hard to return home after those three-plus years in Montreal; but each time I thought of remaining, I remembered the glow in your eyes — dreamed about it too — your stubby fingers tracing my lips, pulling my beard, tugging at the buttons of my shirt, your screams when we didn't understand your requests or when you wanted me to hold you in my arms, your gurgles of joy as soon as I did. I wanted to be there so you would grow up loved and protected. Your mother and I grew up in homes where our parents held us only when they collared us to rain blows on our backs for some mistake that we — and sometimes they — had made, leaving our backs with welts that later turned to scars. Your mother taught elementary school — Kingstown Anglican School — before going away to university. When KA students met her — she mentions one, but I remember four — they reminded her of the beatings she'd given them, not about the quality of her teaching. Before you were born, I told her, "If you ever hit our child, I'll divorce you and do everything to get custody." Frida, your grandfather abused me physically, and I wasn't going to let that happen to my child.

I wonder if you remember why for years Maggie hadn't visited us. I'd come in one afternoon and met her spanking you. You were around five and she was babysitting you. It took all my willpower not to knock her cold. "You brute!" I screamed, my left hand grabbing the neck of her dress and spinning her around to face me, my right fist balled. I came to my senses and let her go with a shove. She tottered and fell, luckily into an armchair. "Don't come back here. Don't. And if you ever hit my daughter again, there'll be hell to pay. Now get out!"

Three months earlier, I'd come home one afternoon and met you sitting on the living room floor play-acting with your dolls. I sat down on the floor and hugged you. You said, "Dad, what spare the rod and spoil the child means?"

"Who told you that?"

"Gran. She said I was out of place and she slapped me. Then she said that you must bend the tree when it's young and you must never spare the rod and spoil the child."

"Why did she say you were out of place?"

"She said that you are a f-f-del . . ."

"Infidel?"

"Yes. And she is praying to God to change you. And I said, 'My dad told my mom God is a fairy tale.' Then she slapped me and said I was out of place."

"Your grandmother knows that she is not to hit you. The next time she raises her hand to hit you, tell her I said she has no right to. If she doesn't stop, I will prevent her from seeing you."

Maureen was sitting on the sofa, hemming a dress and listening. She gave me hateful looks. "Are you telling Frida to disrespect her grandmother?"

"No, but now I am telling you to tell your mother to keep her beliefs to herself and to keep her hands off my daughter. Your mother is

*full of venom. You heard what she said in this living room last week —
that she would like to see all the bullermen lined up against a wall and
shot. Let her go find Clem and shoot him."*

*"My father isn't a bullerman. You're going to prevent Frida from
spending time with her* grandmother*!" She shook her head in exasperation, dropped her sewing on the sofa, got up in a huff, went into the bedroom, and slammed the door. Later I overheard her telling Frida, "Don't
tell Gran what your dad said. He says stupid things when he's angry."'*

◆

Enough of this for now. Maureen of course defied him and took
Frida to visit Maggie. Fortunately, Frida was the sort of child who
never stoked Maureen's ire. The spanking and slapping probably
continued in secret, but all three conspired to hide it from him.
Should he ask Frida? Maureen's gone. There's no possibility for friction. Maggie's still around and wracked by diabetes and arthritis;
the last person he would want to quarrel with.

Maureen became hot with hate whenever she spoke about her
father. They hadn't spoken for sixty-one years. When Clem ended
up at the Lewis Punnett Care Home, the year before Maureen's
death, Gordon thought she would soften and reconcile with him.
By then he was frail and unable to stand by himself, but his mind
was sharp. *"You* can visit him," she told Gordon. "If I visit him,
I'll end up cursing him out. Gordon, Daddy made his bed, now
he must sleep in it. If you plant dumb cane, you shouldn't expect
to reap sugar cane." Clem attended Maureen's funeral mass. An
employee from the nursing home brought him in a wheelchair to
the Anglican Cathedral.

A replica of Maggie. When Gordon and Maureen moved from
the house they rented in Kingstown Park to this one, they invited Maggie to the housewarming. She didn't come. It took almost a

decade more before she relented. Maggie's verbal abuse never stopped, but Maureen remained devoted to her and always expected Gordon to do the same. "Honour thy father and thy mother," he once told her, "doesn't mean being a doormat for my mother-in-law."

Maggie, now eighty-four, is still living in Fairhall, in the house where she raised Maureen. Now, every couple of weeks, Gordon takes her grocery shopping in Kingstown. If there's something she needs urgently, she phones him, and he gets it and takes it to her. Last week when he dropped in on her, he drew her attention to the light coming through the holes the termites have created in the older, wooden part of her house. She replied that her small government pension barely covered her food, utilities, and medication, and she expected to die before the walls caved in. Then added, "Why you're telling me about the house? My coffin is the only house I care about now. Anyway, it's Frida's house, not mine."

Maureen had willed the house to Frida without a clause ensuring Maggie's right to live in it until death.

"So, Frida," Maggie said after they'd read the will, "that means that if you're broke or I vex you, you can put me on the street?"

"It means no such thing, Gran. You know I will never do that."

"I'm glad to hear it, but words without the legal documents don't reassure me."

Later, after everyone had left, Gordon urged Frida to prepare a notarized document that gave Maggie the right to live in the house until her death. She shook her head. "Dad, it would be a waste of money. Gran knows, you know, I know, everyone knows, that I will never put my grandmother out of her house. It is her house. I've always known it to be her house, and it will continue to be her house until she dies."

Maggie's too cynical about human nature to accept such a promise. He supposes that anyone who has been betrayed a few times earns the right to be.

Maureen told him parts of Maggie's story during the early years of their courtship. Maggie's pregnancy at age sixteen, months before writing the Senior Cambridge examination, traumatized Maggie's parents. They had sacrificed a great deal to send her to secondary school and had been counting on her to finish and get a job so her earnings could pay the school fees of the two younger siblings. In the end, those siblings never made it beyond elementary school and came to hate Maggie deeply. When Clem impregnated Maggie, he was nineteen, an only child living with his single mother, Inez. The year Maggie graduated from nursing school, Inez dropped dead on Indian Bay Beach where she operated a food stand that sold soft drinks and chicken and chips. With the stipend Maggie received while in nursing school and the earnings from the food stand, they had managed somehow. Clem took over the stand after Inez's death, but operated it at a loss. Some days he never bothered to show up. Eventually he gave it up and expected to live off Maggie's salary. Three years later, he walked out on Maggie.

Maureen forgot to mention in her journal that when Clem walked out on them, he told Maggie that he wanted a peaceful life, that he hated nagging and noise, and that living with her was like living in Korea (the Korean War was ongoing). To his credit, Clem did eventually settle down. Got a job driving a drinks delivery truck. He stayed with the new woman, Millicent, until her death. She was childless. Would he have stayed if she'd had children, Gordon wonders. Some fellows don't want to be parents. Allan is one. Fate prevented Gordon from taking that path. Throughout Frida's childhood, whenever Gordon ran into Clem, he gave him ten dollars along with the message, "Tell my granddaughter I send this for her. Don't let her grandmother know. That woman is the diablesse ownself."

Chapter 7

WHEN GORDON TOLD ALLAN THAT FRIDA WAS AR-riving today, he insisted on taking them out for supper on Monday. Allan has managed his life well. Takes care of his needs. Discreetly for the most part. The subject of managing life came up in one of their habitual conversations. In Maureen's lifetime they held them in Basil's Bar around 6:00 p.m. on a Saturday, that interlude between the bustle of day and the bass sounds of night, when Kingstown is briefly asleep.

"Can life be managed?" Allan said, shaking his head slowly. "It's more that life — fate, I mean — manages us. Fate puts a few levers at our disposal but keeps the others out of reach. It controls those at our disposal too. If we humans understood this, there'd be fewer stupid laws and fewer prisons. Look at us, Gordon, at the secret lives we live, because of people's stupid beliefs."

Gordon didn't reply immediately. He tried to think of the levers at his disposal, and each time he identified one, he saw where he didn't fully control it. He nodded. "And we never know what those available levers might put in motion."

Allan sighed. "We never know. A Bahamian fellow I had a fling with when I was at Mona went to the States for additional training. Never finished. Went back to the Bahamas in a coffin. Killed by a jealous lover. 'Fatalitis' is the name I've coined for it."

"Fate's been good to you. You've done a great job managing your life," Gordon said. "Temperament and training are on your side. Now your work in psychiatry must give you further insights, better knowledge."

Allan's eyes puckered and his face crinkled. Next came his cackling laughter. "How little you know human nature, Gord. You let appearances fool you ... Me too, I guess ... all of us. Many doctors smoke. Some gorge on foods that clog their arteries. Some are obese. I urge my patients to exercise, but don't myself. Look at the size of my gut." He pointed to it. "What can I say?" He threw up his hands. "Beth's cooking is bewitching ... as to excessive drinking ..." He glanced at his glass of whisky on the table and shook his head. It was his second drink.

Gordon was sipping Coke. Allan would have been upset if he'd known that he didn't always resist knocking back a shot or two of Sparrow's. Allan's instructions have been, "Absolutely no alcohol. None."

That Saturday they were in a secluded corner of the bar and were the only patrons. Jim, the bartender, was the only other person present. He kept at a discreet distance. It was blustery and raining heavily outside. They could hear it striking the asphalt. Eventually Allan said, "Gordon, in matters of the heart, we are equal. Today your plight is different from mine, perhaps because you've had more opportunities than I to lose control, or perhaps because I've been plain lucky."

Yes, Allan, you've been lucky. He looks down at the line of blooming ixoras and sighs. *Maureen, you've been unluckiest. Day after tomorrow, Frida and I will visit you. I will bring you a bouquet of your deeply loved ixoras. After I got back from Canada, I made it a duty never to forget your birthday. Restricted myself to two pairs of shoes so I could get you a lovely piece of jewellery. Eventually you told me to stop it. You must have intuited why I did it. One time you asked me what I was compensating for. What would have happened if I had told you? I still ponder your long silence after our illness forced me to confess my relationship with Trevor. A list of my failings must have paraded across your mind at that time, aspects of my behaviour that puzzled you. You mention some of them in your memoir/ journal, though you said you wouldn't write about things that were my responsibility to tell Frida. I asked you what they were. And you said, "Gordon, if you don't know now, you will never find out." We stayed silent for several seconds, then you said, "After Frida has read what I've written, she will know that the record is incomplete and will expect you to provide what's missing. Then again, I'm not sure I want you to be alive when she reads it, and I'm thinking of sealing it until we're both dead." How could you never suspect that Allan and I had been lovers or that he, too, leads a double life? Of course, if you'd asked, I would have been forced to lie to you. Allan and I vowed never to out one another.*

Another evening, here on this porch with Allan — his first visit after Maureen's funeral — Gordon was surprised Beth hadn't accompanied him. "How's it Beth's not with you?"

"Beth thinks that men have stuff they're reticent to talk about when women are around."

Gordon's neck muscles began to constrict, and his body stiffened with each stab of pain.

Allan saw the agony in his face, reached across the patio table, and tapped him on the shoulder. "It's all right, Gord. She doesn't suspect anything."

That infernal memoir/journal. What if Beth breaks the terms and reads it? That's too much confidence to put in someone.

Twenty-five years of waiting. Frida protested to Maureen, but Maureen remained firm. Maureen did, in a way, try to prepare her for what she'd read. The day after the funeral, Frida, sitting here on the porch with him, said, "Three weeks ago, Mom said to me, 'You worship your father and for good reason, but you will discover after reading my journal that he is flawed like all humans, maybe more than the average human being. Frida, I expect you to continue loving him, and, if he's still alive, I expect you to give him all the support he needs.'"

They remained silent for almost thirty seconds.

"Will you, Frida?" he asked, trying to hold back tears.

"Goes without saying, Dad." She got up, came to sit on the armrest of his seat, and put her arm around him.

♦

How could Allan be so sure that Beth doesn't know? Allan's a risk-taker. Some thirty years ago, he related to Gordon — word for word — the warning his cousin Alphonse, a captain in the police force, had given him.

"'Cuz, where you been last night?'

"'I went for a drive with a friend to Georgetown.'

"'To Georgetown, eh. Well, I live in St Vincent, and I know Argyle ain't Georgetown. Your arse would be in the slammer today and your name in the papers if the policeman who saw you and your boyfriend didn' know you and me is family. I ain't telling you how to live your life. I just warning you not to bring disgrace on our family. I tell that officer, if you ever mention a word o' what you saw to anybody else, I will fix your business … Allan, I warning you: be careful.'"

Always daring. Had an apartment in town. Has the house in Evesham. No need whatsoever to be having sex on Argyle Beach.

On the other hand, in St Vincent, neighbours keep an eye out to see who comes and goes.

That story was part of the updating that took place between them when Gordon returned from Montreal. In turn, Gordon told him about the relationship with André, but was silent about the countless earlier one-night stands. He'd felt uncomfortable telling Allan even though sex between them had ended when Gordon got married.

For twelve years, from age seventeen to twenty-nine, they had been lovers. Friends in public, lovers in private, with girlfriends as decoys. Their relationship had even survived the seven years that Allan was away studying medicine, first in Jamaica and later in England.

Allan had been back home for five years when Maureen got pregnant. She'd told Gordon she was on the pill. Marriage wasn't something he had thought about. Without thinking deeply about it, he'd somehow assumed that his principal relationship would always be with Allan, and his girlfriends would serve as cover. When he eventually succumbed to marrying, he was sure it would be an even better cover. Gordon and Allan had promised never to let women come between them. Sometimes he wonders if Allan had wanted to end the relationship and used the marriage as an opportunity to do so. Perhaps Allan saw it as betrayal. Maybe he felt the pregnancy was Gordon's fault. Carelessness. To some extent it was. There was no visible rancour on Allan's part; he remained his placid, pleasant self. While in Montreal, Gordon had wondered if he could persuade Allan to immigrate. But Allan saw attempts to mend broken relationships as putting toothpaste back into a tube. Gordon nixed the thought that August when he saw Frida and knew he would have to be a hands-on father.

Allan has been loyal. Few people would risk their careers to prevent a friend's life from becoming swallowed up in scandal. Allan, too, had never intended to get married, but he changed his mind a year after his cousin's warning. By Allan's own choice, his marriage is childless. Frida has been the great beneficiary of this. Allan and Beth dote on her.

Allan is six weeks older than him. Gordon doesn't remember a time when they weren't friends. They grew up in nearby villages: Allan in Evesham. His grandmother's house was about a third of the way toward the top of Ponsomby Hill. Gordon lived in Riley, a village on the hilltop across the valley from Evesham. Their villages were close enough for people to call to each other across the valley. A half-kilometre of steep, unpaved road linked Riley to Evesham. The schools and churches were in Evesham — still are. There was electricity there, and the main road there was paved. Until the mid-seventies, you travelled there to catch the single bus that left at 7:00 a.m. for Kingstown. The rainstorms that lasted from September to November left the Riley road rutted, muddy, and slippery. But there were benefits. Year after year, it was the boys and girls from Riley who won the medals for Evesham Methodist School at the SVG Elementary School track and field competitions. Gordon and Fulton, another boy from Riley, came first and second in 1960. "Strong legs and stamina from climbing Riley hill," their teachers said. Whenever his Evesham classmates told him he lived behind God's back, Gordon pounded his chest, stuck out his tongue, and said, "But is me that make Evesham come first in the one hundred yards; put that in your pipe and choke 'pon it."

Like most Riley folk, Gordon's parents were peasant farmers. During the dry season, when they had several bags of sweet potatoes, eddoes, or tannias to sell, they could cajole Mr. Bullock to drive his bus up the hill and pick up the produce. Not so during the wet season. At such times, Gordon, Lillian, and May — all the village children and women, never the men — made several trips, toting on their heads large bamboo baskets of root vegetables to fill the jute bags left at the junction where the Riley and Evesham roads met. Sometimes they lost their footing and the baskets and their contents went rolling down the hill. A lucky few transported by donkey, but Gordon's family wasn't among them. The most intrepid were those Riley women, Lillian included, who, with baskets laden down with yams, breadfruits, nutmegs, cinnamon — you name it — walked up to Kelbourney, over into Gomea, down to Belair and Fountain, up Arnos Vale hill to Sion Hill, then down to Frenches, and eventually the Kingstown market, pausing on the way to sell to buyers. Just thinking of it makes him wince. It paid for the flour, rice, meat, fish, medicines, and cloth they returned with.

Walking long distances then was the reality for most Vincentians. When he attended school in Mespo, he, too, walked five miles each school day, two and a half miles each way. A few of the Evesham and Riley youngsters walked twice as much to attend Intermediate High School in Kingstown. When he related all this to Frida, she looked at him skeptically. She protested if she had to walk downhill from Cane Garden into Kingstown — less than a mile. On mornings she got into the car with Maureen, who dropped her off at prep school and picked her up on afternoons. Ditto for when she attended Girls' High School where Maureen taught. Her classmates who came from the country all arrived and returned on school buses.

Chapter 8

HIS FIRST MEMORY OF ALLAN IS FROM THEIR METHODIST Sunday school class. The smiling, chubby, round-faced, very black boy sat beside him. The brightness of his dark brown eyes — now they've lost some of their lustre, but back then they were balls of dark amber — and his dimpled cheeks were what first got Gordon's attention. More than once he'd raised his fingers to touch those dimples. Allan wore grey long pants, tartan vests of grey-and-green squares, white long-sleeved shirts, and a black bowtie when he came to church. Every other boy in their Sunday school class wore short pants and short-sleeve shirts.

Somewhere around that time — they were both four — they began attending Teacher Miriam's Prep School and became buddies. Allan lived with his Uncle Bruce and Ma Queenie — some called her Ma Bacchus — his grandmother. Gordon would stare at her, in her broad-brimmed hat that matched her green, gold, or burgundy dress, holding Allan's hand coming down Ponsomby Hill on their way to church.

Allan's mother lived in England. There were times when Allan pushed out his chest and lifted his chin as high as it could go and said, "Me going to England soon, and me coming back in nice pretty clothes, and me going talk nice-nice." One Monday morning he showed up with a copy of *The Tale of Peter Rabbit* (the first book apart from the Bible and the Methodist hymn book that Gordon ever saw), and Teacher Miriam read the story out loud to them. Allan became the star of the class after that, and when he had a falling out with any of his classmates, he'd say, "And when me go a England, me not sending nothing give you."

By the time they were in standard three in regular elementary school, he and Gordon were inseparable. Allan could write with both hands. They loved to watch him close his eyes and simultaneously write regular text with his right hand and a mirror version with his left. He could also wiggle his ears. One time when the teacher called him out for being inattentive, he wiggled his ears at her. She called him to the front of the class and whipped him on his bare legs with the tamarind switch she kept in a corner of the classroom.

By then his Uncle Bruce had gone to live in Boston, and Allan lived alone with Ma Queenie. On Saturdays, if Gordon finished his chores early, he could go over to Evesham and be with Allan, and together they horsed around or read. It was how Gordon came to read all the Mother Goose stories. He thinks he did it over four Saturdays sitting on Ma Queenie's back porch from where he could look out for miles at parts of Riley, Carriere, Cane End, Collins, Richland Park — some of the villages in the Marriaqua Valley. He'd wanted to take the book home, but years earlier, Allan had brought *The Merry Adventures of Robin Hood* to Teacher Miriam's school, and it had got drenched, and Ma Queenie decided that books were no longer to leave the house. Allan read as many as three books per week and would recount the stories to Gordon, who was amazed that he found time to do all that reading. He had no farm chores. Ma Queenie had leased out her land. On mornings before heading off to school Allan fed about a dozen chickens kept in a wire-mesh coop behind the house and made two trips down a steep track to the valley bed to bring back two buckets of drinking and cooking water from a spring down there. For bathing and washing dishes they used rainwater collected in a cement tank. On the Saturdays that Ma Queenie did a big shopping, she took Allan to town to help her carry the shopping bags.

One rainy Saturday while he and Allan were in fourth-year elementary, Gordon met him on the back porch crying. "Me mother sick in England," he told Gordon. He'd already bragged: "Me mother is a big nurse in England, and she been a big teacher before she go to England." After that tearful Saturday, Allan never spoke about going to England, but his church clothes and books continued to come from there. Back then, clothing made abroad stood out. Unlike now, when it's mostly bought off the rack, local seamstresses and tailors made the clothes that almost everyone wore.

The year they both turned eleven and were in standard five, the government increased the number of secondary school scholarships to one hundred. Gordon and Allan were two of the more than 1,300 students who competed for them. Allan got one of the spots, but Gordon failed the English paper. In elementary school, he and Allan were the top students in math, but most of the time Gordon barely passed English. Allan went off to Boys Grammar School, and Gordon went up to standard six. His hope was that he would pass the primary school leaving exam. The few students who did were eligible for training to become primary school teachers, nurses, or police officers.

The Saturday visits stopped. Gordon was sure that Allan now looked down on him. They saw each other in church on Sundays and never said more than hi. But during the first week of the July–August holidays, Allan came over to Riley to visit him early one weekday morning and accompanied him to Carapan to pasture the goats and pick breadfruits to take home to feed the family and the pigs.

While they were walking back from Carapan, Allan put his arm around Gordon's waist and said, "You think I ain't notice that you don't talk to me now. But I not letting you end our friendship. We been buddies since Teacher Miriam school. See. You smiling ... so what is your plan for school?"

A month earlier, Lillian, over the objections of Ben, had taken him to see the principal at Emmanuel High in Mespo; he had passed the entrance exam and had been admitted and would start there in September. He gave Allan the news. Allan stepped ahead of him, turned to face him, dropped the jute sack of breadfruits he was carrying, and gave him a hug that almost strangled him. "I glad. Boy, you don' know how I glad. We must go forward together. When you can find the time, we go study together. I a year ahead o' you, so if you run into difficulty with anything I will help you. I have Spanish and French tapes and a tape recorder that my mother sent me. I getting the top marks in Spanish and French. You can come over the house and listen to them and get good in Spanish and French too."

That hug. A warm feeling had come into Gordon's body and he'd got an erection, but he attached no importance to it until three years later. By then Allan and he were members of the Evesham Methodist Youth Fellowship, and Joan, also a member, had the hots for Allan. At one of their meetings — they met on Wednesday afternoons — Gordon saw that Allan was encouraging her. Toward the end of the evening, Allan asked him something. He doesn't remember what or the answer he gave. Three days later, he went to ask Allan for help with an English assignment. Allan's desk was in his bedroom. When they finished, Allan said, "So what Wednesday been all about?" They were sitting on the edge of Allan's bed.

"What? Nothing."

"*Nothing!* I asked you a question and you answered like if you wanted to bite off my head." His eyes twinkled. He placed a hand on Gordon's thigh. Gordon hesitated, then placed his hand on top of Allan's. They remained like that for several minutes, until Gordon realized that both their hands were sweating. He pulled his hand away and sat up straight — startled. Allan leaned toward him and kissed him on the cheek.

It took a few years for them to be intimate like this again. In the interim, tragedy struck. A fourth of July. Gordon, Allan, and Ma Queenie were in the sitting room. Allan and Gordon had just finished talking about the GCE exams; the results were to be out in a couple of weeks — A level for Allan, and O level for Gordon — and depending on Allan's results, there were tentative plans for him to join his mother in England and continue his studies there. They were listening to commentary about the American Independence Day celebrations on the BBC 7:00 p.m. *World News,* when they heard a car come to a stop on the road outside the house. The house was a few feet in from the road. Ma Queenie pulled the curtain to one side and looked out, went to open the door, and said, "Ginette, girl, what bring you here at this hour?"

Ginette entered. A woman around fifty, slightly overweight. She was wearing house slippers and a loose calico-print dress. Her hair was half in braids and half loose. It was clear that she'd come urgently. Ma Queenie offered her a seat on an armchair. Ginette pointed to the dining table. "Aunty, come. Sit here beside me."

Ma Queenie shrieked and began to totter. Gordon and Allan rushed to support her and guide her to a chair at the dining table.

"Yes," Ginette said. "Two hours ago, ten o'clock London time. At St. Mary's Hospital. Lizbeth phone and ask me to deliver the message."

Gordon pulled Allan into his arms and they both cried. Allan would later learn that the illness his grandmother had mentioned years before was cancer, that it had returned, and that Ma Queenie was prepared for news of the death of her only daughter, Theresa, but had kept the information from him because she didn't want it to affect his studies. Three weeks later, Lizbeth returned to St Vincent with Theresa's ashes. It overshadowed the good news that had come the week before: Allan had aced the A-level exams. Theresa had last seen Allan when he was two. Ma Queenie had already given Allan the details: "Your mother give up a teaching career and run from St Vincent in shame. That scoundrel, your father — he will roast in hell — promise to marry her, set date — everything — and when you hear the shout, two months before you born, he married another woman that he did done breed too." Allan's father lived in Ginger Village, about a mile away. A half-brother, a shy Afro-Indian fellow, was in class with Allan and Gordon, and a half-sister was two grades below. Gordon never saw them interacting.

The relationship between Allan and Joan deepened. She, too, was a student at Emmanuel High in Mespo. She and Gordon wrote and passed O levels the same year that Allan passed A levels, and she and Gordon began working as junior clerks in the civil service at the beginning of September — he at the treasury and she at the Ministry of Communications and Works. By then Gordon had begun to date Joy, a girl from Carriere, who came to the Methodist Church but attended St. Joseph's Convent.

In September, Allan went off to Jamaica to study medicine. The Sunday before he left, he walked over to Riley with Gordon after church. They deliberately slowed their pace to put distance between themselves and the churchgoers. By the time they were at the foot of Riley Hill, the churchgoers had moved on.

Allan said, "Do you dream about me sometimes?"

Gordon didn't answer.

"The answer's in your face and in your smile." Allan's eyes glowed.

"Don't even think about it. We'll get into trouble," Gordon said. "You live close to Ephraim. You told me that one time the villagers surrounded his house and broke down his door after someone saw a man come through the banana field and enter his back door."

Allan nodded, turned his head away, and swallowed loud. "I wish we lived in England."

"How's that?"

"We could you know ... and not worry that we're breaking the law."

"What about Joan?"

"Why? What about Joy?"

Gordon felt sweat dripping from his fingers and running down his face. He had an erection. He thought: this is Sunday; I'm coming from church; this is sinful.

"You think we'll ever get over our fears and ...?" Allan said. "Don't you want to?"

"I'm afraid, and ..."

"And?"

He wanted to say, sinful. "People will mock us and scorn us and even attack us like they do to Ephraim."

"You're right." Allan looked away and swallowed. "I leave for Jamaica next Saturday. You're coming to my going-away party?"

"Will Joan be there?"

"Yes. Stop talking about her. I want you to come and spend Thursday evening with me ... alone. Granny will be at Women's League meeting. Please. Please."

Gordon said nothing. He was afraid. Allan was now around five foot eight, muscular, slightly chubby with a perfect *V* torso, and well-developed thighs. No doubt from those buckets of water he brought up the hill every morning. That smooth, obsidian-black face, lips full and slightly curled, those dimples and glowing eyes.

Gordon dreamed about him often and saw the evidence on his pajamas next morning.

Then he'd sometimes look at himself in the mirror and wonder if Allan found him attractive. He was six foot one and slender. But if not for his muscular thighs, he'd have looked willowy. His face was angular, the colour of raw coffee beans, and his nose aquiline. It bothered him that he had a flat backside. Allan's was the exact opposite. In his dreams Gordon sometimes caressed it.

He did not answer Allan.

"I see ... I'll wait for you and if you don't show up, I'll understand. Stop worrying about Joan. We don't have sex. The only person I want ..." He took a deep breath and turned his face away.

Gordon heard hiccups and turned to see that he was crying. "I'll come on Thursday. I'll come but we will not ..."

"Just come. Just come."

They met that Thursday. They kissed and fondled and masturbated. It left Gordon fearful and guilty and feeling dirty.

Allan went off to Jamaica. He was able to return home, sometimes twice a year — at Christmas and during the summer semester. He had the funds for it. As his mother's dependent, he was entitled to a pension until twenty-one, until twenty-five if he were a full-time student in university, which he was. Allan told him that he'd met gay guys on campus and had had a few fleeting affairs. "It's only in passing. You and I will stay together — here or, better still, in some country that's less hard on gays — until the end of our days. That is, if you want us to." By then Joy had left Gordon and he was dating Maureen. All this he told Allan.

"Just don't get Maureen pregnant, and don't marry her. Play the game, but remember that we belong to each other."

When Allan finished his training and began to work at what's now the Milton Cato Memorial Hospital, he began dating Winnie, a nurse on the staff there. Maureen finished her B.A.

at Cave Hill that same year and began teaching at Girls' High School. Beth entered the picture then, and all five of them would sometimes hang out. When Gordon and Allan needed to be intimate, they met at his grandmother's house. She died two months after Allan's return from studying in England. Eventually Allan got an apartment in town.

Chapter 9

ALLAN HAD BEEN BACK FOR FIVE YEARS WHEN Maureen announced her pregnancy. She whispered it in Gordon's ear as they were entering a restaurant in Ratho Mill where they were having a going-away party for Winnie, who was relocating to California. Gordon was so stunned he didn't remember what was on the menu that evening.

As soon as Allan drove away after dropping him and Maureen off at Maggie's house, Gordon exploded. "You did that to force me to marry you, didn't you?"

"No." She began mounting the stairs to the house.

He reached for her arm and pulled her back. "We have a few things to talk about before you go in. Why you did this? I'm on the list of candidates for study abroad."

"It's an accident."

"I don't believe you. You told me you were on the pill. Otherwise, I would have used condoms."

"The pill isn't foolproof."

"Get an abortion."

"Abortion is murder. Are you mad?"

"And deception — what do you call deception?"

She began to cry.

He realized he was still holding her arm, preventing her from moving. He let it go. "Well, I'm not going to marry you. I'm not ready. I'm not marrying ..." He caught himself before saying *anyone*. She knew he spent more time with Allan than with her. It had on occasion caused friction. She might speculate that something was going on between them. She'd asked him once if there was another woman, if he'd become tired of her.

The yard light came on. Seconds later, the front door opened, and Maggie, already in her nightie, came onto the landing.

Maureen turned to mount the steps. "You're not coming in?"

"Not tonight. I need to clear my head."

He walked out the yard into the narrow road and regretted his decision instantly. He debated whether he should go toward Calliaqua, Fountain, or Fairbaine Pasture. Either way, it was unlikely he'd find transportation at that hour. A long walk lay ahead. He nixed going toward town. Winnie might be with Allan. Even if she weren't, Allan would want to know why he hadn't stayed with Maureen and would give him shit when he found out why. He couldn't take any more of that tonight. He decided to go to his mother's house. It was a clear evening with an almost full moon. He climbed the hill up to the main road at Fairbaine Pasture, continued uphill to Belmont, walked across Ponsomby Ridge to Kelbourney, and then descended into Riley. A few minutes before midnight, he arrived home covered in sweat. He knew where his mother kept a bottle of overproof strong rum that she mixed with cayenne pepper, lemon, and ginger and administered for colds. He got the bottle, poured two ounces into a glass, took it into his bedroom, sat on the edge of the bed, and sipped it. His mind felt numb. The heat from the walk had worn off, and he felt cold.

This was not supposed to happen. He cursed Claude — he had died in Daytona Beach a few years before — a member of Evesham's Youth Fellowship; he had gone to Emmanuel with Gordon, and afterward to teach at Kingstown Anglican where he met Maureen. Since Gordon and he both worked in town, they would on occasion go for a beer at the Cobblestone. On a couple of occasions, Claude brought along Maureen. The second time, a week before Christmas, Allan was home on Christmas break from Mona, and he joined them. Afterward, Allan told him, "Boy, she got the hots for you." He hadn't noticed. Joy had already dumped him for the fellow who eventually became her husband. Gordon needed the mask. He asked her for a date. He'd always felt the relationship would end as easily as it had begun, that she would see he wasn't really passionate about her. But it lasted. He'd never had sex with Joy and with no woman other than Maureen.

He was still living at home for the most part, spending two, sometimes three, nights out. With Maureen, he'd told his mother, but he shared her bed on average once every couple of weeks. His father, Ben, had died two years before, about the same time that Riley got running water, electricity, and a paved road almost to the river. Plans were also afoot to pave the other half up to Kelbourney and on to Gomea. The changes had incited Lillian to add an extra bedroom, an indoor bathroom, and kitchen to the house. She and May shared a bedroom and the other bedroom was his.

For two weeks he did not speak to Maureen or Allan. Allan was the only one among them who had a house phone. Gordon was in the habit of calling him from work almost every day, but to avoid suspicion they'd agreed that Allan shouldn't call him at work. Gordon and Maureen called each other from their workplaces. Those two weeks he told the receptionist at treasury, where he'd been promoted to senior clerk, that when Maureen called him, she should say he was out. She asked if it meant that she now had a chance. He told her to put her name in the hat.

"You and Maureen break up?" Lillian asked him toward the end of the second week.

"Mama, why you ask?"

"Well, you not sleeping out anymore, so I figure something not right between the two o' you. Allan been by today and he leave a letter for you … I find that strange. The two o' you working in town. Why he didn' come by the treasury and give it to you? He could o' phone you too and give it to you on your break or your lunch."

"Mama, please. Just give me the letter."

She handed him the envelope.

He walked outside, stood on the landing, and tore open the envelope.

My dear Gordon,

You have been avoiding me. You have never known how to deliver unpleasant news, and I know you have unpleasant news for me. Let me get to the point. Yesterday Maureen came to see me in my office at the hospital and announced that she was pregnant. She was very upset. She cried for a long time. She'd expected you to be happy about becoming a father, but instead you accused her of deception. Couldn't you have chosen your words more carefully? Couldn't you have taken a few seconds to consider how life-altering all this would be for her? She was so distraught, she even mentioned suicide.

Nor can she understand why you are so non-committal about being a father. She said she wants to be a mother. She described you with some pretty forceful language, with the hope, I suspect, that I would relay it all to you.

I recall that when you and I spoke about managing our relationship to accommodate her and Winnie, the issue of pregnancy came up. I told you that I couldn't be a father, not a biological one at any rate; I'd had a vasectomy before I left England. I never gave you the details. I'd told a fellow intern, who was gay, that you and I had committed ourselves to each other, but that we felt forced to have girlfriends to avoid suspicions about our relationship. He said, "And what if your girlfriend becomes pregnant and demands marriage?" We discussed that possibility, and he advised me to have a vasectomy. Remember when I came home, I suggested that if you wanted to be sure that no accidents came between you and Maureen you should have one too? Well, you didn't. Now the orchestra is playing, and Maureen expects you to dance.

You are in a tight spot, my dear Gordon. And I don't know what advice to give you. I can't help being selfish. I'm on night duty all of this week. I must see you. I'm in as much agony as you. At least we can commiserate together.

Still hoping that we can be each other's forever,
Allan

Much help your letter is, he thought as he pushed it into the envelope and into a back pocket. He walked off the landing, into the yard, and followed the track leading from their house to the Riley road. Just as he got there, he met May returning from the lands at Carapan. On her head a bunch of plantains, in her right hand the rope of their prize stud ram, in her left a machete. Her dog Grover walking behind her, ensuring that the ram kept pace. May entered their gate, and Gordon turned left. For a brief moment he wished he could exchange his life for hers. He scaled the short hill that bordered their property, then descended to the river, skipped the stones, and began to ascend the hill toward Kelbourney, as steep, if not steeper, than the Riley hill.

Midway up the hill he heard, "Aay! Aay! Godson, you ain't hear me call out to you? How you pass me so and don' say howdy?" He looked back and saw Nennie Bradshaw standing at the gate leading to her house. It was the only house between the river and Kelbourney.

"Pardon, my manners, Nennie Bradshaw. I was carried away in my thoughts."

"Boy, is woman you got on your brain, or what? You pass me standing here and didn' even see me. I call out to you and you ain't hear me. Gordon, don' make woman send you to mental home, no."

He chuckled and resumed walking.

Maureen would have been right for him if ... She was easy to get along with. Independent. Intelligent. Attractive: five foot four; slim but not skeletal; round, firm buttocks. Fist-size breasts. Thick, sensuous lips. Café au lait complexion and long, semi-straight hair. He felt no erotic charge when they had sex and he knew why. Allan had about a dozen books on homosexuality and Gordon had read parts of them. He knew why when he and Maureen were having sex, he had to pretend he was with Allan. If he didn't, he lost his erection. Even so, half the time he faked the orgasm, and when he didn't, it was feeble and gave him none of that deep pleasure and emotional release he got when it was with Allan. It had taken quite a while for him to be comfortable with his homosexuality. The books he'd read on the subject and discussed with Allan had helped to free him from thinking that he was a sinful, filthy pervert.

Now he wished he had faked his orgasm every time. In a marriage like this until he died! He'd be better off in prison.

She wouldn't abort. She might tell others that he'd asked her to. They'd spread the news, and in very little time he'd become a pariah. He knew he was trapped. Could he give the child to his mother? May might help too. No, not Lillian. West Indians were just beginning to learn that beating children wasn't necessary, that it was, in fact, damaging. But Lillian called such information nonsense. "A good licking is the best way to straighten out own-way pickney. Talk to them! What you mean, talk to them? They will laugh in front o' your face and behind your back. You have to cut their backside — good and proper." She'd said this one day after listening to a debate on NBC Radio about corporal punishment. She said her mother had beaten her with everything except the kitchen sink, and she had turned out all right.

"Because of it?" he'd asked her and was astounded when she nodded yes. Her views had altered some since, but he still doubted she'd be a good mother.

Nor would he want any child of his to receive the religious indoctrination he and Allan had been subjected to. When Allan returned from Jamaica, he told Gordon that he no longer believed in God. It took Allan a while to convince him. It happened after Gordon had read *Civilization and Its Discontents*; *Why I Am Not a Christian*; *Black Skin, White Masks*; *The Fire Next Time* ... and he, too, came to believe that religion was the opiate of the masses, and that there was a lot that was unholy in the content and history of the Bible.

Lillian asked him why he no longer went to church. He told her, "I no longer believe that stuff."

She froze where she stood in the living room. It took her several seconds before she said, "I didn' hear right. Lemme ask you that question a second time: Gordon, why you stop going to church?"

"You heard me correctly the first time."

She lifted her head to the ceiling. "Lord, what is this world coming to? We must be in the last days in truth." She shook her head frantically. "Boy, God will cut you down! This is blasphemy! Where you get these ideas from?"

"From educated people."

"Educated people! What sort of education can make you turn your back on God? Boy, 'The fool says in his heart there is no God.' This ain't how I raise you."

He began walking toward the door.

"Gordon, where you going? I ain't finish talking to you."

"I have finished listening to you." He left.

She didn't speak to him for a week, not even to return his greetings. Eventually May asked him about it. He repeated their conversation verbatim. She twisted her lips to the left, then to the right, and gave a long series of whaddya-know nods before saying, "Every day I find out more and more about the education I miss out on. But if it make you stop believing in God, I better off without it."

The sound of a car coming up the Gomea road made him aware that the Kelbourney road had ended, that he was in Gomea. Beyond Arnos Vale, a mere sliver of orange sun showed just above the sea's horizon. He hadn't thought to bring a flashlight. He turned to walk back home to avoid the dense darkness of the Kelbourney road, bordered by a cliff with dense overhanging trees. It had spawned many stories of ghosts, diablesses, soucouyants, and jacklanterns that Ben had enjoyed telling them, even making himself a character in them, sometimes forgetting the stories were about places in St Vincent and not Barbados. Gordon's fear, however, was twisting his ankles in the road's ruts.

It was dark when he re-entered the path to their yard, the tall nutmeg trees on both sides making the darkness denser. From the gate, some thirty yards from the house, he saw that the yard light and the living room lights were on. About ten feet from the door, he heard several voices, one of which was Maggie's.

"Men are hound dogs."

May chuckled.

"Some men," Lillian said, "not all."

May chuckled again.

"Mother, we have to be going," Maureen said. "Cousin Bernie is on the flat waiting for us."

"I going talk to that ornery son of mine," Lillian said. "Telling you to throw away your child. What this world coming to? Believe me, I didn' raise him to think that way. Maureen, I will talk to him. He can't just breed you and drop you. It ain't right. I won't stand for it."

At that point, Grover ran out onto the landing and began wagging his tail.

"I think he come," May said.

"Gordon, you arrive just in time," Lillian called out to him.

He entered the house.

"Bring one o' the dining chairs to sit on," Lillian said. Maureen and Maggie were sitting on the two Morris armchairs. May and Lillian were sitting on the settee that used to be Gordon's bed before the house was enlarged.

He placed the chair as far away from them as politeness allowed and sat down.

"Gordon," Lillian said, "Maureen tell me that she in the family way, and you is the father, and you tell she to throw away the child. I is right so far?"

"Go on," he said.

"Throw away the child! Gordon, you can't mean that?"

He said nothing. It was pointless to argue with her. He'd heard enough stories about women whose wombs were said to be grave-yards. Whited sepulchres, they were called. Invariably they were destined for hell and were sure to call lists (recount horrible crimes) on their deathbeds. He knew he was outnumbered. Not even May would be on his side. Once, when he was around sixteen, she'd told him that she felt he and Allan were bulling and they'd better not let people catch them and hang them, meaning that the villagers would make effigies of them, put the effigies on trial, pronounce them guilty, and burn them. He'd taken her comment as an out-burst of the sibling rivalry she usually managed to hide.

"You not saying anything in your own defence?" Lillian continued.

He shook his head.

"Well, I have a lot to say. We is from a decent God-fearing family. You hear? Decent. My parents been poor, but we is decent, and I think I and your father — may his soul rest in peace — raise you to be decent too. You don' have the right to ruin the reputation o' my family and ruin Maureen life."

He wanted to say, *Decent! My father decent! Is that why he died from a stroke in Vera's house?*

"With everyone here as my witness, I saying to you, Gordon, you going to do the right thing and marry Maureen and treat her with respect and dignity. Gordon, I expect you to obey me, 'cause is out of this womb that you come ..." She tapped her stomach. "Maureen, how long the two o' you been together?"

"Eight years. We started dating before I went to study in Barbados."

The truth was that Maureen had invested in keeping the affair going, and she hadn't given him a reason to break it off.

"All-you love affair last through that, and now Gordon, after you get the best o' her, you want to toss her on the rubbish heap? No. No. Not as long I have breath in my body."

He felt like saying, *Ma, you intend to get a potion from the Obeah man for me? Because otherwise, I have no intention — none whatsoever — of becoming bogged down in marriage.*

At that moment a car horn tooted out on Riley Flat.

"That must be Bernie," Maureen said. She got up. Maggie did too. Lillian took the flashlight off a shelf in the dining room, and she and May accompanied them out to Riley Flat.

Gordon was distraught. He needed Allan's arms around him, but there was no way for him to get into town at that hour. If he didn't have to go to work the next day, he would have walked. He heard May's and Lillian's footsteps coming toward the house. He went into his bedroom and closed the door. If they spoke to him, he would not answer. He'd go brush his teeth when he was sure they were in bed.

He heard them enter and pull the door shut.

"Gord, your supper in the oven," May said. "Boy, you can't go to bed on a' empty stomach. Gas going full you up."

Should he answer? He decided not to.

The next morning, he left with a small suitcase of clothes early enough to catch the first bus to town, and headed straight to Allan's apartment. Allan wasn't in. He was probably making his rounds at the hospital.

He stayed with Allan for eight days. On the afternoon of the ninth, he left work an hour early and got to Riley around four, early enough to catch the last minibus back to town if Lillian began pestering him about Maureen. Lillian wasn't home. May told him she was in La Croix attending a funeral.

For the two or so hours before Lillian returned, he and May said nothing to each other. He stayed in his bedroom. When Lillian returned, he heard May telling her that he was in his bedroom. Instantly Lillian began to sing. "Can a woman's tender care / Cease toward the child she bear? / Mine is an unchanging love / Higher than the heights above / Deeper than the deepest sea ..." *Mama*. He laughed to himself. She knew how to get to him.

Around six thirty, May called him for his supper. Lillian was at the dining table. He did not speak to her.

She cleared her throat.

He cleared his.

May chuckled once, then chuckled again. "The two of you like overgrown children. Mama, why you don' just tell Gordon what on your mind?"

He took a deep breath. "Yes, Mama, tell me what you have to tell me. Of course, if you putting me out, I can't leave before tomorrow morning. The buses have stopped running."

"Leave! Like is leave, you want to leave. I ever say anything 'bout leaving? What I say ten days ago, and I saying it again, is, I expect you to do the honourable thing and make Maureen your wife. You is twenty-nine years old, Maureen is thirty. I is fifty-five. Is time for me to have grandchildren." She looked at May.

"Don' look at me. I can't have them by meself."

"Well, you turn down every man that want you."

"Them is your kind o' man, Mama. Like Daddy. I will drown myself before I marry a man like Daddy."

"You dare say that to me! You dare talk about your father like that to me!"

May steupsed and waved her hand dismissively. "Stop, Mama, 'cause if you don't, Gordon ain't the only one who going leave this house."

"May, I not studying you. Not studying you at all." She turned her focus onto Gordon. "Young man, I expect you to marry Maureen."

"Mama, you think that is a good thing, if Gordon don' want to marry her. They going be living like snake and mongoose."

"Not while I alive."

May gave a loud cackling laugh. "You did promise to restore Gordon faith in God ..."

"You stay out o' this conversation. You hear me? You stay out. I talking with my son, not you."

"*My son.* That's not what you been calling him. Sweet-talk him now. As they say, you can't catch flies with vinegar."

She shot May a scorching stare.

"You think that is right, Gordon? To bring disgrace on this girl? She teaching high school. The students going lose respect for she. Put yourself in her place, Gordon. You would like a man to do the same thing to May?"

"Mama, leave me out o' this. I can take care o' myself. You talking like if Maureen is some innocent thirteen-year-old child. She thirty years old. She don't know if you have sex and don't protect yourself, you going get pregnant? Why you blaming Gordon? Blame her."

He decided to rile Lillian. "I was thinking, since she doesn't want to have an abortion, that you and May could raise the child."

"I ain't raising nobody child. Get that outta your mind. You enjoyed the food, now deal with the heartburn," May said.

"I will help to raise my grandchild, yes — if you marry the mother."

"If I don't marry her, it will still be your grandchild."

"I don't want no bastard grandpickney. Do I make myself clear, Gordon?"

"But your father had Hortense. And Dad had Albert before he married you."

"I not responsible for what my father do?"

"And you are not responsible for what I do or don't do."

They fell silent. No one gave ground. Dusk had fallen. May got up, turned on the lights, and went to sit in the living room.

He raised the towel and the plate covering the food May had served him — a large fried jackfish and slices of roast breadfruit and fried plantain. There was a cup of cocoa beside it. But he'd lost his appetite. He put the cover back on the food. "I'll eat it later."

He went into his bedroom and sat down on the hard-backed chair there. Lillian's words came back to him: *Put yourself in her place, Gordon. You would want a man to do the same thing to May?* He could not deny the fundamental decency in them. May was a lot more crass: *You enjoyed the food, now deal with the heartburn.* But Maureen had done this to force his hand, and he felt like punishing her. But what about the child? What about the child?

Chapter 10

THE PHONE IS RINGING INSIDE. GORDON HURRIES IN TO answer it. The screen tells him it's May. She tells him again that they have a meeting with the lawyer on September 13, next Wednesday. They have to transfer their share of their parents' estate into their names. She is making her will as well. She'd reminded him about it two days ago when she came to give his house a deep cleaning. Valencia cleans it once a week. Sort of. She ignores pretty well everything the mop and vacuum won't do.

He returns to sit on the patio. May now lives in a brand-new cement house, in a village now totally transformed from when he was growing up there. It bothers him that she lives alone with two dogs. The house is far back from the road and the nearest neighbour some three hundred yards away. Nowadays St Vincent ranks among the top twenty of the world's most violent countries. Some years ago, when the husband-and-wife supermarket owners were robbed and almost killed at the juncture of the Evesham and Riley roads, he became worried for her safety. Now that the road is paved from Gomea to La Croix, it's easy for the criminals to do their dirty work and get away quickly. May says that robbers go after people like him, people who live in Indian Bay and Cane Garden. She's probably right about that. But there's rape too. So bad that three years ago an article in the *Toronto Star* stated that St Vincent and the Grenadines had the "third-highest rate of recorded rapes after the Bahamas and Swaziland." Riled-up politicians said SVG should stop releasing such statistics, that outsiders were using them to make St Vincent look bad.

He has urged her to sell the Carapan land. He doesn't feel attached to it. It reminds him of sore back muscles — from hours bent weeding — and tired legs — from all those afternoons he toted ground provisions and boxes of bananas and plantains over to Evesham. Initially, his parents had leased Carapan. But Lillian was able to feed and clothe the family with the produce from it while Ben worked at Mount Bentinck. When Carapan estate offered to sell it to them, she had saved enough of her husband's wages to cover most of the cost. For the rest she took out a mortgage on the Riley homestead. "Is because o' Mama sweat that we own Carapan. They sacrifice my schooling to pay for it. Mama ghost going haunt me if I sell it," May replies whenever he raises the subject. She should take a look at all the land in La Croix and Evesham Vale that's returning to forest because their owners are dead or have emigrated.

Ben had been one of half a dozen mechanics who'd come from Barbados to work at the Mt Bentinck sugar factory. He worked on the night shift and stayed out in Georgetown during the week and came back to Riley on weekends. One night in 1956, when one of the grinding wheels malfunctioned, Ben couldn't be found. He lost his job then. After his death, Lillian told Gordon and May that it wasn't the first time he'd left his post to spend time with his mistresses. From 1956, the land was all they lived off. At the time there was a thriving market for bananas and it was mostly what they cultivated.

May complains of painful, swollen knees but says she won't give up farming. "What you want me to do, Gordon? Stay home and go senile?"

"No. Keep the acre nearest to the road, sell everything else, and come live with me."

She gave a cackling laugh. "I won't dignify that with a' answer."

For all he says, he, too, is emotionally attached to the Riley property. The oranges, mangoes, sapotes, avocados, tangerines, breadfruits, breadnuts, golden apples, plumroses that he eats all come from Riley. May prepares baskets of fruits and vegetables for him, and he goes out there and collects them. He gets all his eggs from the chickens she raises. At Christmas, she butchers a pig and gives him a quarter, which he cuts up and packages in two- and three-pound pieces. And Riley is a pleasant place to live. Always cool. Even in the hottest of months. There's always a breeze coming up from the valley or across from Ponsomby during the day, and sweeping down from the Majorca mountains at night. Everywhere in the Marriaqua Valley, mosquitos are a plague. Not so in Riley. Before he lived in Montreal, he used to think it was far from Kingstown. Now he laughs at the absurdity. Four miles via Kelbourney, six via La Croix. Allan, too, cannot bring himself to sell "Granny's house." Still calls it that even though it has long been transferred to his name.

May's seventy-two, four years older than he. Around the time that Gordon began secondary school, Lillian told him that when it had been May's turn to go, they didn't send her, because they were too poor. When Gordon was in secondary two, May and Lillian had quarrelled over it in the kitchen outside where they were preparing the evening meal. Ben was inside the house, about fifteen feet from the kitchen. Earlier that day May had received news that she'd failed the exam she'd written as part of her application to become a pupil nurse in Britain.

"If you all did send me to secondary school, I would o' been accepted without having to write that test," May said.

Gordon was standing beside the rain barrel at the corner of the house, listening.

"Don't blame me and your father for that. What you did want us to do? Rob people to pay your school fees? Darling, you can't get blood from a stone."

"All that money Daddy been giving his mistress could o' more than pay my school fees."

"What money you talking 'bout? He don' have money to give Vera."

"Stop covering up for him."

"Sh! Sh! Not so loud. Your father going hear you."

"Let him hear me." Her voice rose. "I want him to hear."

Ben came onto the landing then and shouted, "Young lady, you's talkin' 'bout muh? Uh don't believe you's talkin' 'bout muh."

"Who else? If the cap fit draw the string."

"Quiet, May! Honour your father and mother like the Bible say," Lillian said.

"Honour *him*!" She gave a staccato laugh.

"Not another word outto yuh!" Ben shouted at her. "This is muh house and as long as you's in it you will honour and respect muh or you will get out. You have uh nerve to blame us. Look at yuh friend Sis. She pass primary school leavin' and get accept into teachin'. Four years now. Why yuh didn' wuk hard loike she?"

"Because you had me weeding land and carrying produce all the time when I shouldo' been studying. Some days you even take me out of school to tote banana. That is why. And 'bout failing Primary School Leaving exam, ain't Gordon fail it too? But look. You all sending him to secondary school 'cause Gordon is a boy. Day in, day out, I weed land in hot sun. Then I have to carry basket upon basket o' load up and down Riley Hill, like if I is some donkey. In pouring rain sometimes, water from the yam scratching me skin and causing rash to break out all over my back. Why? To pay Gordon school fees and buy his books. You all sacrifice me for Gordon." She began to cry and then fell silent.

Ben stood silently on the landing for several seconds, then returned inside the house. When the cooking was over, Lillian took Ben's food inside the house. She, May, and Gordon silently ate theirs sitting on jute sacks spread out on the dirt floor of the kitchen. Ben even slept home that night.

Two weeks later, Gordon was alone at home with Lillian. "We did your sister wrong," she told him. "I see now I should o' push harder for her to go to secondary school, the way I push for you to go. You heard what she say 'bout how hard she working for your benefit?"

Gordon nodded.

"Now you try and do your best in school and make something of yourself so you can help yourself and you sister. Wherever you get to, wherever you go, always remember she help make it happen. Whatever the future bring, don' turn your back on your sister."

"Yes, Mama. I promise you."

He wonders if May remembers that quarrel. In adulthood, their relationship has always been pleasant — she always the dutiful big sister, and he something of a spoiled brother. When still children, they had their moments of complicity: initially they called Lillian Madam-Truth-the-Way-and-Life, before shortening it to Lady Truth. In the years when May had boyfriends, she shared her secrets about them with him. He asked her why she never got married. She said no one ever proposed. For obvious reasons, he couldn't share his secrets with her. If she finds out about his secret life and Maureen's other illness, would she judge him harshly?

When Lady Truth became demented, May took care of her. Not an easy task. The last two years especially. Dementia loosened Lillian's tongue but left her muscles intact. May overlooked the endless stream of *bitch* and *fuck you*, but wasn't always able to dodge the slaps and cuffs, until the doctor prescribed a tranquilizer. And she did it all, sometimes with occasional paid help, while farming their thirteen acres. Gordon feared that she might get sick and urged her to put Lillian in a hospice, but Lillian spared them the trouble. She suffered a massive heart attack on the landing and died on the spot.

Now the road to the land at Carapan is paved. Vehicles go onsite to collect the produce. No one has to tote it beyond the side of the road. Banana cultivation, which sustained them all the years he was in school, has been devastated by black sigatoka disease. Measuring the disease's impact on the Vincentian economy has been one of Gordon's most recent projects. Most of the land that was once under banana cultivation is now abandoned. May seems to be sanguine about it. Now she grows an acre of plantains, which the hucksters buy for resale in Port of Spain, Trinidad and Tobago, but she relies mostly on nutmeg, cinnamon, ginger, peppers, carrots, and turmeric to bring in steady cash. And they seem enough to satisfy her financial needs. Only once did she call on him for monetary help. He paid to replace the roof of her house, which Tomas blew off. He has since insured the house against hurricane damage.

If he'd been more assertive, would he have been able to convince Maureen to build their house in Riley? He thinks not. There was always a coldness between her and May, the cause of which he did not know. When he asked Maureen about it, she said she didn't know what he was talking about. From her journal, he now knows that the tension was deeper than he thought. Riley has flowered into a beautiful village. Unlike Evesham, where the majority of the houses are on small plots, many Riley residents have copious land to build on, and they've used it to their advantage. He thinks of the many nutmeg, breadfruit, golden apple, orange, tangerine, plumrose, and cinnamon trees on their own land. He loves trees. Maureen, who grew up on a property with breadfruit, mango, orange, and avocado trees, did not want trees on their Cane Garden property. She feared the damage they cause during hurricanes. Now that she's no longer around, he should consider planting a few. Drought-resistant ones like neem, acacia, eucalyptus, and flamboyant. Avoid Austin's mistakes; his prized guavas bore fruit for the first time in 2014 and died during last year's drought. His mango, which barely survived, looks scorched, stunted, and starved.

Chapter 11

WHEN GORDON TURNED FIFTY, HE MADE A SOMEWHAT definitive will. There was the fifty percent of everything that by law belonged to Maureen. Half of the remaining fifty percent he bequeathed to May. Now that Maureen's gone, he must update it. But first he must have a serious talk with May before they see the notary on Wednesday. Their paternal relatives are all in Barbados. Maybe their half-brother, Albert, is there too. Most of their mother's family immigrated to Trinidad, the United States, and Canada. His maternal relatives who're still in St Vincent are mostly wastrels. When they phone or come to see him, it's to beg for money. One, a maternal cousin, Phil, half-drunk and looking half-starved, came to Maureen's funeral in a black suit two sizes bigger than him. He said he used to visit his aunt Lillian, but Gordon couldn't remember ever meeting him. A week later, Phil phoned to ask him a favour but refused to say what over the phone. Gordon agreed to meet him at Bickles at 9:00 a.m. a few days later.

He met Phil, who was in flip-flops, lime-green shorts, and a navy blue short-sleeve shirt, smoking outside the restaurant door.

Phil put out his half-finished cigarette, pulled the pack from his shirt pocket, put the half-smoked cigarette in it, and returned the pack to his pocket. The restaurant was less crowded than usual. He asked Phil what he'd like to have. A beer. Gordon joined the queue to the cash. Phil sat at a table just inside the door. Gordon paid and then joined him.

"So, why you want to see me?"

Phil looked away and pulled at his scruffy beard. He glanced at Gordon's face, then staring down at the table, said in a scratchy, raucous voice, "Cousin, me want for build a decent house. Me check with the bank for see if me could'o borrow the money. The man me talk to ask me how much me want, and me tell he 'bout two hundred thousand dollars. He question me 'bout me job, what me own, and things so. He write it all down. Then he say me can get the money, but somebody with twice the amount o' wealth have to stand security." He gave Gordon a prolonged stare. "You is the only family I know in that kind o' position."

He observed Phil's bean-shaped head and face the colour and texture of asphalt; his deep-set, reddish, beady eyes and pouting lips; the deep lines in his face. He didn't answer.

Phil pulled at the fuzz on his chin and kept staring at him. Next, he stared at the table and rubbed the back of his head.

"So," Gordon said, "you think I have money." The repast on the day of Maureen's interment had been in his living room, a large room. It gave a false impression of the house. To have a spacious living room and not increase the cost, they'd opted for four small bedrooms, so he and Maureen would each have an office.

"Ain't you is a big civil servant with university degree?"

"All I own is the house I live in. Half of it belonged to my wife. Now that half belongs to my daughter. It's not mine."

Phil began to fidget. The server called their order and Gordon went to get it: a Hairoun for Phil and coffee for himself. As soon as Gordon put them on the table, Phil said, "I come all the way from Overland early and I ain't had a thing to eat — you can buy me breakfast?"

Gordon swallowed, nodded, pulled out his wallet, and handed Phil a twenty-dollar bill. While Phil was at the cash, Gordon began remembering some of Lillian's stories about Hortense, Phil's mother and her half-sister. He'd seen Hortense a few times in town chatting with Lillian at her market stall. Lillian called her a snake, but never said why.

Phil returned and sat down. "So there ain't no way you can help me?"

"No way," Gordon said, shaking his head. "What work you do?"

"I is a carpenter, but nowadays work scarce."

"So where are you planning to build this house?"

"In Overland. My mother had a wattle and daub there on estate land, and when Cato take power, he give all the people title to the land. I have a two-room board house on it, but woodlice eating it down." He paused. "All round me now is only wall house people building, 'cause even before you finish build a board house, woodlice done start to take it over."

"Are you married?"

He shook his head.

"You have children?"

Phil gave an embarrassed smile. Two incisors kept his top lip from collapsing. "Yes." He reached for the beer bottle and took a swallow.

"How many?"

"Plenty. The women — them don't leave me alone. Them love me can't done." He grinned from ear to ear, deepening the triple folds in his cheeks.

"How many is plenty?"

He pulled again at the fuzz on his chin, rubbed the back of his head, and opened and closed his eyes rapidly. He took a swallow of beer and looked away. It was clear he didn't want to say or hadn't kept count.

"Phil, I'm sorry. I can't help you."

They called Phil for his breakfast then. He came back with it: bacon, eggs, four slices of toast, and hot chocolate. He ate quickly, wiped the bacon grease with the last slice of toast, gulped down the chocolate, and polished off the rest of the beer. He stared at the beer bottle and then at Gordon, who read the gesture but decided not to order another beer for him.

"So that is your *final* decision?"

Gordon nodded.

Phil cuffed his left palm with his right fist, then pounded his thighs. "Shit! ... Okay, let we look at it another way." He frowned at Gordon for a few seconds then dropped his gaze.

"Go on."

"The land at Riley."

"What about it?"

"My mother didn't get none."

Gordon remembered then that he didn't know if Hortense was alive. "Where's your mother now?"

"She in a old folks' home in Brooklyn. Me sister carry she up to New York eleven years ago. That sister — Gwennie — she die last year."

"I'm sorry to hear."

"Every year she promise for send for me. Every year that God send. When she come home for carry Mammie to New York, she say that after she settle Mammie she go work on my immigration papers." He pulled open his right eye with his right forefinger. "People ungrateful, yes. When Gwennie leave to try she luck in America, I sell a cattle I been raising on half share and I give she the hundred dollars I make."

"She didn't repay you?"

He scratched his forehead and gave a guilty smile. "At Christmastime she use to send me twenty American dollars. What twenty dollars can buy? After Christmas that done. Don't you have for eat twelve months a year, Mr. Gordon? When Mammie go up there, she start to send clothes for the children and a shirt and a pants for me. But that stop 'bout five years now. Now Gwennie dead and nobody don't tell me if she leave a will."

"Is Gwennie your only sibling?"

Phil frowned.

"Do you have other brothers and sisters?"

"Yes. Thirteen. Mammie have three girlchild. One in Curaçao. One in Canada. One in Trinidad. After Mammie go to New York, all three o' them stop writing me. The other ten is me father children. They is lawful and they shun us."

Gordon said nothing. He got the picture. Phil had lived with his mother and had lived off the remittances his sisters had been sending. Most likely it was his mother who had been supporting his children. Now his mother was no longer there, and his relatives see him for what he is. It's a familiar story.

"Half o' the Riley land should o' gone to my mother. Her father did die and don't leave no will, and when my mother make her claim your mother say my mother can't prove she is his child and ain't give her nothing."

Gordon knew none of this.

"You should take out a mortgage on the Riley land. You have to make up for the wrong you all do to my mother."

Have to! Gordon gave his triple chuckle, a nervous reaction he has struggled all his life to curb. It happens sometimes at the ministerial meetings and draws looks of reproof from the PM.

"Phil, let's get a few things straight. One, I don't have two hundred thousand dollars. Two, the six acres of land my mother inherited from her parents and have since passed on to us is worth at best seventy-five thousand dollars. Three, my parents bought the remaining seven acres of land that we own. Those seven acres are worth no more than seventy thousand dollars. Even if we were to mortgage all of it, we wouldn't raise two hundred thousand dollars."

Phil's shoulders straightened and his eyes glowed. "I can drop it to one hundred thousand dollars."

"I haven't finished. My sister depends on that land for her living. You haven't told me how many children you have to support — if you are supporting them. The reason is that you know you'll never be able to repay the bank. Have you spoken to May about this?"

Phil shook his head.

"Why don't you ask the government for help?"

"Them won' help me. Them only help their supporters. I is a NDP man."

"Well, there'll be elections soon. You may get your chance."

"The house going fall down before that."

There was silence around him, and Gordon realized that the nearest customers had been listening to their conversation. On his left a woman stared at him, nodded, winked, and gave him a thumbs-up.

For a while he and Phil said nothing. Gordon got up, shook Phil's hand, wished him well, and exited the restaurant. He turned left and began walking toward Bay Street. Halfway there he heard Phil calling out to him. He stopped and let Phil catch up with him. "Mr. Gordon, you can give me fifty dollars? Time hard. Is a month now I ain't work, and my girlfriend ain't have food for the children."

Gordon pulled out his wallet and gave him fifty of the fifty-five dollars he had in it. Instantly he had an inkling he'd done the wrong thing. He watched Phil going the other way and thought, *I should have taken him to the supermarket and given him the equivalent, maybe a bit more, in groceries. My money will be gone in liquor long before Phil gets to a supermarket.*

In an essay that attempted to explain rampant corruption in West Africa, he'd read that relatives pool their money to send bright male family members to study abroad. When the graduates return home, they're expected to get powerful jobs with government or large international corporations and put their relatives in all the posts that become vacant. They are also expected to build large houses so the relatives they cannot place can come and go and live off them. It's not quite as bad in the Caribbean, but every village abounds with wastrels who scorn work and expect their relatives abroad and at home to pay their bills.

From the way Lillian used to speak, there was a time when large extended families took care of each other, but that time is long gone. The most he and May can hope for is that they'll find decent care in a nursing home if they become decrepit. His pension will cover the cost of his care. He's hoping the little money he has saved will be enough to cover May's if it comes to that.

Last week he broached the subject of old age with her. She said, "I don't have to plan for it; I going have a short life. See how young Daddy been when he died? Seventy-four. And Mama, she been only eighty-three. She had me when she twenty-two and you when she twenty-six. After that she miscarry two and the doctor remove her womb when she thirty."

Most of what he knows about their half-brother, Albert, he got from May. She was four when Albert came from Barbados to live with them. Albert was eleven. She liked him. Said he gave her piggyback rides, and when she began going to school, he would hold her hand all the way there. But he used to backchat Lillian, and the last time Lillian called him for a beating, he grabbed a piece of wood and told her, "Na this time, gorblimey. I gon lay wunna flat ef wunna touch me." That weekend when Ben came down from Mount Bentinck, Lillian told him that Albert and she couldn't live in the same house; that Albert would have to go, because she had no intention of leaving the house she'd inherited from her parents. May was seven then and she remembered the Saturday morning that Albert left, wearing a yellow shirt, short khaki pants, and white canvas shoes. He carried a small cardboard suitcase. She'd held on to him and cried. He asked her not to forget him. He promised that when he grew up and began working he'd come back to visit her. She feels that he should get a part of Carapan, if he wants it. But all they know about him is what, Mark, Gordon's cousin, told Gordon in Barbados in 1980 — that Albert was away working on a ship.

Before they get to the notary on Tuesday, he'll raise the issue of estate planning and urge her to put something on paper about how she wants to be cared for if she becomes disabled. He must do the same for himself.

Chapter 12

HE LOOKS OUT OVER KINGSTOWN. A CRUISE SHIP HAS arrived. Every space in the taxi stand is taken. The drivers are in clumps talking and gesturing to each other. He remembers that before he and Maureen became sick, she had convinced him to take her on a cruise. Allan wasn't interested, but Beth had promised to go with them.

He should go make himself some fresh coffee. Or go back to bed and sleep for a few hours. Set the alarm so he'd be up in time to be at Argyle when Frida arrives. In a couple of hours, she'll be landing in Barbados. His car's in the garage. He's supposed to get it on Monday. He hopes Frida calls him from Barbados if the LIAT flight is delayed.

But he doesn't move. Dexter Pottinger's face, painted in the colours of the rainbow, comes back to him. Another Jamaican murdered because he was gay. Three years ago, when Gordon travelled to Montreal to attend the funeral of Fran, the sister of Gordon's Montreal boyfriend, André, the Massimadi Film Festival was on and he saw *The Abominable Crime*, a documentary that featured a woman and her brother, now refugees in Holland, who'd barely escaped being murdered in Jamaica because they're gay. The sister was severely wounded. For a long time after the film ended, Gordon remained frozen in his seat, stricken, while Maurice Tomlinson, a Jamaican gay rights activist, discoursed about LGBTQI persecution in Jamaica.

He recalls the dream he had this morning when he eventually did fall asleep. He wonders whether his anxiety over the questions Frida might ask him had caused this nightmare. When she was sixteen, and he saw how confident she was and knew she could defend herself, he'd hoped Maureen might see how empty their marriage was and divorce him. By then they rarely had sex. He should be truthful: he no longer wanted to have sex with her, and, without discussing it, she understood, and didn't seek it. During the first two years of his relationship with Trevor, he felt a duty to attempt sex with her each time he returned from Trinidad.

Why there hadn't been a divorce was one of the topics she and he talked about when it became clear that she would die within months. She was propped up with pillows in the bed, he was half sitting on the dressing table. "I didn't expect you to come back from Montreal. I was prepared to raise Frida alone, just like my mother raised me," she said with raised eyebrows, and awaited his response. He was silent. She continued, "Any West Indian woman who puts her faith in a man is a fool ... but you came back." She smiled. "I'm glad. Frida loves you, and I know she won't go through life angry like me about a father who turned his back on her. She won't have to hate you the way I've hated Clem." She glanced at the laptop on the bed beside her, then stared at him with such intensity, it alarmed him. Then she chuckled and he relaxed. "I expected you to leave me as soon as Frida was seventeen, as soon as she finished her A levels. Weren't you thinking about it?"

"No. Why didn't *you* leave me?"

She clasped and unclasped her fingers and massaged her palms. "Many, many reasons, Gordon. I'm trying to explore some of them in this thing I'm writing." She made air quotes around "thing" and glanced at her laptop. "I don't know what to call it … Let me ask you a question. Every week we hear about some woman or other who's been severely injured by her partner. For years, Christine took all that physical abuse from Freckles until Austin persuaded her to leave him. I had a neighbour in Fairhall who used to beat his wife almost every day. Why do we women cling to abusive men? Even when we take the men to court, we beg the magistrate to let them go free. Why do we do it?"

"Beth wouldn't."

"Don't be so sure. You mean because she sticks to Andrews, her birth name, and refuses to carry Allan's name, Bacchus?"

"Just my feeling."

"You only know what you would do when the time comes, Gordon. Have we been conditioned to believe our lot is to endure whatever comes?" She sighed. "You know, Gordon, when I got pregnant with Frida, you accused me of deception." She pursed her lips, stared down at the sheets, then at him. "To this day, it still stings. But you were right. I loved you, Gordon, and I wasn't sure that you loved me. You were so damn cold. I learned not to touch you when we were in public. You moved away when I did, and your face twitched. But you didn't run after other women, and that made you exceptional. But you might have been running after men. Were you?"

"No."

"Remember how much I used to question you about your relations with your father? Once you said that I should be glad my father wasn't around, that what you remember most are the scars Ben left on your back…. Now, with the passage of time, I'm sure that you remember more. Good things. You have been a great father to Frida. I loved to watch you and Frida interacting. When you came back from Montreal, she turned you into a toy. Turned you into horse. Sometimes saying, 'Giddy-up!'" She chuckled. "It was Dad-this, Dad-that. I can't say I wasn't jealous sometimes. You were there for Frida, our daughter. I am glad she had a hands-on dad. If it meant setting aside my own needs, well, so be it."

Was she implying that Maggie should have stayed with Clem? In any event, Clem, it seemed, had had enough of Maggie. Gordon didn't think to ask her. He was mindful of her weakened state. That day she was in a positive frame of mind; he didn't want to raise issues that would nix it.

Divorce. She'd touched on something real. A year after he met Trevor, he'd seriously considered asking Maureen for a divorce. But he dismissed the idea for fear of what would happen if — more likely when — it became known that he'd divorced his wife to take up with a man. In any event, Trevor lived in Trinidad. Gordon was forty-eight and Trevor was thirty-six when they met. Trevor is half-Chinese and a good six inches shorter than Gordon. He has a roundish face, flattish nose, hardly any lips to speak of. When they first met, Trevor was working out at a gym daily and had a lean, muscular body. In the later years, he stopped and got a paunch and double chin. His African genes show up in his dark, brown-sugar complexion, his coarse and woolly hair, and his big behind.

They'd met in the bar of a rundown Port of Spain hotel. Allan had told Gordon that it was a secret hangout for gay men.

"Hi, I am Trevor." He extended his hand to Gordon.

Gordon was hunched over the counter and supporting himself with his elbows. He straightened up, shook Trevor's hand, and said, "Reynold. Pleased to meet you."

"A rainy day," Trevor said and turned his head around to stare out the grime-covered glass onto the street. Dusk was falling. "Reynold, you're from St Vincent, right?" Frowning, he stared at Gordon.

Gordon nodded.

"Vincentian girls are pretty. A beautiful one was in class with me at St. Augustine."

Gordon wondered if he was in the wrong bar. "I thought the first prize for female beauty always goes to Trinidad."

"Okay. Let's make St Vincent the runner-up."

Gordon looked at his watch.

"It still early, man. You go to bed with the chickens, or what?"

"No. I had a long day of meetings."

"Here, for a conference?"

Gordon hesitated. "No, to visit relatives."

Trevor frowned and Gordon wondered if his lying was so transparent. "Married?"

Gordon nodded.

"Kids?"

"One. A daughter. Eighteen. Heading off to Mona next month. A degree in the sciences."

"She's leaving home ..."

"Yes, and I am beginning to panic about it."

"Cheer up, Ray. Can I call you Ray?"

"Sure."

Trevor tapped him on the shoulder. "They say at my age, midlife crisis hits. Man, I worry like hell 'bout getting old."

Gordon said nothing. A long silence. Trevor fidgeted. His hands moved constantly — from his thighs to the bar top, to his chin, to scratching his neck. A couple times he gulped his saliva. He drank his beer from the bottle in large gulps. "Another?" Gordon asked.

Trevor nodded.

Gordon took a deep breath and exhaled loud. "You look nervous, man. 'Fraid the missus going beat you when you get in?"

Trevor chuckled. "No missus or mister to beat me or for me to beat ... or hug." He looked into Gordon's eyes then.

Gordon felt a tingling warmth in his fingers. He knew his eyes would be glowing.

Trevor waved his hand around the bar. There were about twelve patrons, men, all middle-aged or older. "See these fellars. They some o' the saddest people on earth."

"How's that?"

"In here, they're all bullermen. Once they go out this door, they turn straight. I wonder when they going break."

"Meaning?"

"When a piece o' wire bend one way and the next constantly, after a time it does break, yes. I tell you something else too. You see how they chummy with one another now? As soon as they hit the sidewalk, they going pretend they don't know one another, yes."

"I take it then that you're gay?"

"Yes. You?"

"Bisexual."

"Real bisexual or bullshit bisexual?"

Gordon didn't answer.

"So you're bullshit bisexual, then."

Gordon didn't answer.

"That means Reynold's not your real name, right?"

He didn't answer Trevor but felt his eyes beginning to flood. He got up quickly, went to the toilet, entered the single cubicle, and waited until he was sure the emotion had passed.

You think you have everything in place, that nothing will go awry, and then someone finds a loose string, pulls it, and you unravel.

He went back to the counter. Trevor was still there. A young, smiling South Asian man was standing beside him. Trevor introduced him as Ranjit. Ranjit exited the bar soon after.

"You come to Trinidad often?"

"Every few months."

"Then, maybe, we can get to know each other better. Here's my card." He retrieved a card from his shirt pocket and handed it to Gordon.

"I don't have a business card." That wasn't true. He got up, extended his hand to Trevor, who shook it. "Got to be going. Have an early day tomorrow." That was true. He had a series of meetings at the CARICOM secretariat starting at nine the next morning.

He asked the waiter to call him a cab and waited at an empty table beside the door the ten or so minutes it took for the cab to arrive. Later, in his room at the Hilton, he looked at the business card. It read "Trevor Anderson, QC. Barrister at Law" and had an address and a telephone number. He wondered if a gay lawyer in St Vincent would give his business card to a stranger, but realized it wouldn't matter. St Vincent was too small for any lawyer, gay or straight, to hide his identity. What was unlikely in St Vincent was having a safe place for gay and bisexual men to hang out. If there were one, the clients would be foreigners and local male prostitutes, the religious right would hold daily demonstrations outside and send letters to the press demanding its closure, and the owners would spend a fortune removing offensive graffiti.

Chapter 13

BACK IN HIS ROOM AT THE HOTEL, HE SAT IN THE ARM-chair at the foot of his bed and reflected on the fact that it had been thirteen years since he'd returned from studying in Montreal, thirteen years without gay sex, thirteen years relegated to watching gay porn that André, his Montreal boyfriend, sent over the first four years. Thirteen years without the arms of a man ever encircling him, without coarse body hair electrifying him. His own body was as hairless as a bottle. Allan and André were hirsute. André more so. His back looked like a shag rug.

The year before meeting Trevor, Gordon had arrived in Montreal salivating, looking forward to ending a twelve-year drought, to being again in André's arms. He was on long leave, and he and Maureen spent two months of it travelling through the U.S. and Canada. They lodged with her friends and relatives, and he rarely got away to be on his own. Because of the huge mortgage they were carrying, he resisted the desire to pick up guys and take them to a hotel. Besides, he was never comfortable with one-night stands. Those thirteen months with André, he'd no longer needed them. Those months were the happiest period of his life. He looked forward to rekindling that happiness as he briskly walked the short distance from the Papineau métro to André's condo on Champlain.

But Gordon found André in a relationship with Bilal. At sixty-three, André was frail and bent, his grey face criss-crossed with wrinkles, blood vessels visible in his face and hairless scalp. Gordon would have passed this decrepit man on the street without recognizing him. What had become of the fifty-year-old, erect, bull-necked, muscular man with bushy eyebrows and a mop of blue-black hair that he'd loved? On the métro later, heading back to Maureen's friends in NDG — they were putting them up for the first few days until Hollis, who had been a member of the Evesham Youth Fellowship, could organize an apartment for them in a housing complex he managed on René-Lévesque — he scolded himself: *What did you expect, you fool? That André wouldn't age? ... But so drastically in thirteen years!*

He'd felt such enormous gratitude for those thirteen months he'd lived with André. Those one-night stands with men who later pretended they didn't know him. A relief when they ended. The intensity of the sexual pleasure surpassed what he'd experienced with Allan. It was because he was more relaxed, had no constricting fears about breaking laws, or feared discoveries that could lead to scandal or extortion. Initially, back in St Vincent, he had a faint hope that Maureen would leave him and that he and Allan would get back together. Allan had not yet married Beth and had said he would marry no one. Gordon had felt no guilt over his infidelity to Maureen. On the contrary, he was happy to be away from her. Not from Frida, though. Thanks to André's generosity and insistence, he was able to talk with her on the phone twice per week. In 1982, long-distance phone calls to the Caribbean were expensive.

When André proposed that he move in, Gordon told him about his marriage and how and why he'd entered into it. André knew four gay men living with their wives and children in Montreal. In two instances, their wives were aware. A fifth, Jean-Marie, lived in Sherbrooke. Every couple of weeks when he came to Montreal to look for sex, he dropped in to see André before heading off to the bars. He had two teenage boys, aged fourteen and sixteen. His wife was a nurse. Not long after Gordon met him, the police raided a gay sauna in Montreal, and Jean-Marie was one of the men the TV cameras captured wearing only a bath towel as they were marched out of the sauna. Their double life perplexed Gordon. Why would Canadian gays need a heterosexual mask? André said it was more complex than that. "Some people find the stigma of homosexuality unbearable. And there are those who're truly bisexual. There's a saying, you know, that Caesar was a husband to many women and a wife to many men."

"I'm definitely not bisexual." He believes that Allan is. He never told André about Allan. When he returned to St Vincent, he told Allan that André had been an occasional lover.

The apartment he shared with André had two bedrooms, one of which was André's office. It was on Doctor Penfield, near Côte-des-Neiges, a short walk uphill from Concordia. André was a partner in a law firm with offices on René-Lévesque. He walked to work.

When Gordon returned to visit him, André was living with his partner, Bilal, a fortyish corpulent South Asian man with a prominent overbite. Except for getting up one time to go to the toilet, André had remained seated on the couch the whole time. It was Bilal who met Gordon at the door.

"Welcome back, G. Where's Frida?" André called out to him while Gordon was slipping off his shoes.

"She's at the Biodôme with her mother." He had faked illness that morning to get out of accompanying them.

"G, you've grown more handsome. Meet Bilal."

Bilal nodded. By then he'd gone to sit at the dining table at the far end of the room.

"Have a seat, G." He pointed to the armchair to the right of the couch he was sitting on. "What would you like to drink?"

"Scotch."

"Bilal, be a gentleman and prepare a Scotch for G. You still take it on the rocks?"

Gordon nodded.

"Bring some munchies too and a drink for yourself and me."

Bilal went toward the kitchen. It was in an alcove off the very large room they were in, a combined living and dining room.

Gordon looked around the walls and saw a few of the paintings he remembered. There were three new ones. Abstracts. Lots of geometric shapes. One was a canvas covered entirely with metallic fractals the size of birch leaves, more reminiscent of a design for fabrics. He didn't know enough about visual art to judge whether the abstracts were good. One of the earlier paintings, that he knew well and liked, featured tall trees — Douglas firs, André had told him. By Jack Shadbolt. It stood by itself on the wall about twenty feet from Gordon. André had bought it a couple of months after Gordon had moved in with him and had spent an hour or so explaining to him why it was a superb painting.

Bilal brought three drinks on a stainless-steel tray — red wine for himself, white wine for André, and Gordon's Scotch. He returned to the kitchen and took out another tray and bowls from a cupboard. From another cupboard he took out bags and filled the bowls. He brought the bowls — pretzels, chips, and mixed nuts — and plunked them clumsily on the coffee table. André raised his eyebrows, but said nothing. Bilal took his drink and returned to sit at the dining table. The couch on which André sat could hold four. There were also two armchairs facing the couch. André gave Bilal a hostile look and glanced at the armchairs. André proposed a toast. Bilal raised his glass but did not come to clink glasses. Gordon began to get up, but André waved him back down.

During the forty or so minutes that Gordon spent at the condo, Bilal did not speak to him, apart from asking if he wanted another drink. Gordon left feeling like an intruder. When he got back to St Vincent, he decided to end his correspondence with André. But two months after his return, André phoned him.

"What happened, G? I've been waiting to hear from you."

"Nothing really. I was caught up readjusting to work. Stuff like that. How are you?"

"Not so good. You must have noticed when you came to visit … I was relying on Bilal to do everything. By the way, I apologize for his rudeness. He knows we were once lovers — I don't keep secrets — and that might have been the reason. You're both from the Caribbean, so you're probably better able to understand what was happening. He told me that in his native Guyana, Blacks and Indians don't get along. When I asked him why he'd been so rude to you, he made that whistling-lip sound people from the Islands make that sounds like they're telling you to fuck off."

"You said you're not so good. What's the matter?"

"Cancer. Terminal. When you visited me, I'd just come off a bout of chemo."

"I'm sorry to hear."

"Should be resolved in about six months. Can I ask you a favour?"

"Go ahead."

"I want you to be at my funeral?"

Gordon gulped his saliva.

"I don't know why. Love is best left unexplained. In any event, you returned to your wife."

"Daughter."

"I guess it's all right for a father to sacrifice a lover for his daughter. One time, you know, I came close to suggesting that you bring Frida to Montreal. You and Fran and I could have raised her."

Gordon said nothing for a while. He did not know what to say. "How's Fran?" She was André's only sibling, five years older. She taught high school biology.

"She's fine. Retired three years ago. Spends her time volunteering at the Montreal General. So, will you come to my funeral?"

"Yes.

"How's Bilal?"

"Grumpy. Has reasons to be. When we became involved six years ago, I wasn't the ghost of a man that I am now. He's forty-one, at the peak of his sexuality. Now not even Viagra can make me function. The nerve controlling all that was severed when they removed my prostate and bladder."

"I'm sorry to hear. Are you sure Bilal will contact me when ...?"

"Fran's in charge of that. She likes you a lot. She's puzzled that our relationship didn't last. I never told her you were married. She'd have scolded me for sleeping with a married man. Told her part of the truth — that you had a contract to return and work in your country. Back to the topic: Fran's my liquidator, and, in my funeral instructions, there's a list of people she must contact. You are one of them. My funeral will be by invitation only."

He lived another fourteen months and, like his father, took his own life. Took a month's supply of morphine in a single dose. In the note he left, he said the cancer was taking too long. Gordon flew back to Montreal for the funeral. Arrived on a Friday evening, attended it on the Saturday — a gathering of twenty-one persons — and flew back to St Vincent on the Sunday. He had to be at a meeting in Trinidad the Tuesday morning, and he was looking forward to being with Trevor. Their relationship had just begun.

Three years later, Fran sent him a cheque for thirty thousand dollars, money André had left him. He placed it in a term-deposit account for Frida and never told her or Maureen about it; he didn't want to concoct a lie about why someone in Montreal had left him money.

Chapter 14

ON OCTOBER 16, IT WILL BE TWENTY YEARS SINCE ANDRÉ died. If he'd stayed on in Montreal, would their relationship have lasted? The little that Maureen wrote about that trip suggests that she wouldn't have been averse to moving to North America. She seemed spellbound by the opportunities there for constant education. But she wrote from the perspective of a visitor. For an immigrant, it would have been different. Since André's death, Gordon has had more dreams about him than when he was alive. The dreams are usually about trips to museums, to the theatre, or hiking in the Laurentians — and sometimes about betrayal.

André grew up in Outremont. His father, Maitre Mathieu Lacasse, was already deceased when Gordon met André.

Penelope, his mother, was English-speaking. Part Greek and part Irish. When Gordon met her, she lived alone in a huge house on Côte-Ste-Catherine Road and had just retired from teaching secretarial studies at the English Catholic school commission. She was a wispy sort of woman, full of nervous tics, and with the sort of face one sees on Roman coins.

The Thanksgiving, Christmas, and Easter that Gordon lived with André were all celebrated at her house. Penelope, hair freshly dyed in gleaming gold, wearing a choker of sapphires with matching earrings, her wrists laden with gold bracelets, paraded between the kitchen and the dining room, giving orders to Bonita, the Filipina servant. Beyond the perfunctory greeting, Penelope never said anything to Gordon on these occasions or when she came to André's place or when they met at Fran's apartment.

The evening of the Valentine's Day that Gordon spent with André, they were lying in bed, their bodies moulded into each other's. They'd got in from supper two hours earlier. "Valentine's Day always brings back painful memories," André said. "My father died on Valentine's Day two years ago." He lapsed into a long silence. "For the last thirteen years of Père's life I didn't spend holidays with them. Never visited the house. Père was one of those men who feel their word is law. When we were children, he made us kneel at New Year's to receive the paternal blessing. At table, after the maid had placed the dishes, we would pass him our plates, and he would spoon the food onto it. If he was late for supper, we were obliged to wait unless he phoned and gave us permission to eat without him. He felt that it was his right to order Maman and us to do whatever he wanted, and we didn't have the right to say no. When I started school, Maman decided to return to work. They quarrelled over it. He tried to dissuade her. I think he felt there was some sort of prestige in having a wife who didn't work. When Maman insisted, he threw a vase at her. Luckily, it missed her.

"When I was thirty-four, the year of Expo 67, and just beginning to enjoy success in my practice, I went to the house with my boyfriend at Thanksgiving. Père didn't answer my greeting when I entered, and he turned his back when I offered to introduce Eric. I should have left then. Maman had already met Eric at Fran's place.

Maman became alarmed when I told her I was bringing him, but I'd said that if Eric couldn't come, I wouldn't either.

"There was a tense silence during the meal. You could even hear the noise of our chewing. While the maid was clearing the table in preparation to serve dessert, I got up to get our jackets and leave. Père, seated at the head of the table, observed my movements. The coat closet was visible from the dining room. He watched me walk to it. 'Leaving?' he said. 'I must have a talk with you before you go.' He got up and beckoned for me to follow him into his office. He did not close the door. 'What's this?' he said quietly. Then loud, 'You dare to bring your man into *my* house!' I turned to leave. My father has a violent temper. One time he didn't like the tone in which I'd spoken to him and boxed me in the temple and knocked me into the wall. I knew that if I didn't leave then there could be trouble. 'I haven't finished talking to you'; his voice was like a thunderclap. 'The next time you come back here come alone or with a woman.'

"I turned to go, but Père held on to me and wouldn't let go. He began to sob — loud sobs. When he was again in control, he said, pleading, 'André, what did Penny and I do wrong? Tell me, what did we do wrong for you to humiliate us so?'

"Gordon, my tears came then, but for a different reason: for the sadness I felt for Père. I saw how trapped my father was in his beliefs and how helpless I was to extricate him. You see, he was convinced that homosexuality was curable. He was pissed too that Fran wasn't married. 'All I have worked and saved for and nary a grandchild to inherit it,' he sometimes complained to Maman.

"He let go of me then and slumped down onto the futon he kept in there. It was a room that was off-limits to everyone — even the maid — unless he invited you in there.

"I left the room then. From their seats in the dining room, Fran, Maman, and Eric stared at me stone-faced. I tapped Eric on the shoulder and signalled that we were leaving.

"The next time I saw my father was at the morgue fourteen years later. Mama had told me two weeks earlier that he'd been diagnosed with dementia and that he'd wanted to see me. I didn't go. Ten days later he went to a notary, rewrote his will, then went into his home office, and put a bullet through his heart." André fell into a long silence. "Père disinherited Fran and me. He left Maman the fifty percent that the law obliged him to, as well as her right to live in the house until she died or sold it. Upon her death or the sale of the house, his half was to go to the law faculty of Université de Montréal. There was also a fifty-thousand-dollar bequest for a certain Lise Compton.

"Maman never allows us to discuss his behaviour with her. I think somebody planted the notion in her head that she should never disagree with her husband's behaviour toward his children." He swallowed several times. "I understand why he disinherited me. But why Fran? When she completed her B.Sc. at McGill and wanted to do graduate work, he told her she should go find a husband and begin having kids. That might be one reason Fran never got married. The occasional boyfriend. Yet when I finished my law degree, he urged me to continue studying, wanted me to get the doctorate he'd started but never completed. I called it quits at the master's. He'd found out by then that I was gay and had given me an ultimatum: 'Undergo therapy and change or I'll stop paying for your education.' I was twenty-seven and still living at home. I said no and moved out.

"Dr. Henri Saint-Onge, Père's boyhood friend from Sept-Îles, was the liquidator for his will. He, too, had come to study in Montreal and had stayed on and set up a dental practice. After Père died, Henri's wife, Gertrude, told Maman and Fran that one time Père had brought Lise Compton to their house, and Père had asked Lise when she was going to give him a son. Lise told him, 'You already have a son.'

"'A son! You mean that *feluette*! You call *that* a son!' Père replied."
A long silence.

"I didn't out myself to my parents. Père had a habit of calling men who crossed him *tapettes*. Gertrude told Maman and Fran that Père came to visit her husband one evening '*et, mes amis, il a brayé sans cesse.*' He bawled and bawled, and drank so much that he had to leave his car in their driveway and Henri had to drive him home. Apparently Guy, a partner in Père's firm, got fed up with Père's constantly calling people *tapettes* and shouted at him in the presence of the secretarial staff that he should clean out his own closet before tackling other people's. 'Go to Le Jardin on Stanley Street on any Saturday night and look for André. I guarantee you'll find him.' Père, you see, kept my McGill graduation photo hanging in the reception area. *My father, who never gave me a compliment*, bragged constantly about me to his colleagues. Guy had a gay son, who'd recognized me from the photograph in the office and told his father he often saw me at Le Jardin.

"Père chose to confront me alone in his office a Sunday after dinner. By then Fran had moved out. He waited until Maman went down into the basement. He was tense. His cheek muscles were ridged, his face florid, his fists clenched, he stank of liquor. I was afraid. He motioned for me to sit on the futon, but he remained standing buttressed by his desk. I am about five centimetres taller than him.

"'André, I've heard a disturbing rumour about you; I want you to confirm that it isn't true. Are you …?' He couldn't say the word. I waited and he, too, waited, his gaze alternating between the wall and me.

"'Am I what, Père?'

"'Do you have a girlfriend?'

"'Père, you're asking me if I'm gay. Right?'

"He snorted and after a long pause said, 'Yes.'

"'You heard right, Père.'

"He steadied himself before pulling out the desk chair and sitting down heavily. His face now grey, his cheeks sagged. We sat without talking for a long time. I listened to his breathing and the frequent gulping of his saliva. I was relieved that he didn't scream at me or get violent. Now I am glad I didn't know he kept a gun in his office.

"'Okay. Go,' he said without looking up.

"I left him in his office. He did not eat supper that evening. He went into the spare bedroom and told Maman not to disturb him. She knew something had happened and asked me what it was. I told her. She hugged me, said she'd suspected, but was afraid to ask me. She took three deep breaths. 'Oh boy, this is the calm before the storm. Brace yourself, André. I wish your father didn't know. Now he'll be putting more pressure on Fran to find a husband.'

"When the storm came, it was quieter than I expected. He called me into his office early the following Sunday, said that he'd made inquiries about therapy for me, and had made an appointment for me to see a psychiatrist.

"'Stop shaking your head,' he shouted at me. 'You want to remain a *tapette*?'

"I walked out of his office and went into my room. He followed me there. 'Unless you agree to change, you cannot stay here, and I will stop supporting you.'

"'Fine,' I said, 'I'll leave now.' I phoned Fran and told her. Then she lived in a one-bedroom apartment on Ridgewood. She said I could sleep on the couch. I had three months left to finish my master's and had already been accepted into the doctoral program. A month before I finished, I got a phone call from a law firm inviting me to apply for a job as a legal researcher. I later found out that Père had got that job for me. Five years later when one of the partners left, Père arranged for me to replace him. I continued to go home for holidays. Eric was the first long-term relationship I had, and that's why I insisted on taking him home. I was hoping that time had softened Père." He stopped talking.

Gordon clasped him tightly. He didn't know what to say.

André got up, left the bedroom, and returned with a drink. "Gordon, in our conversation a few months back, you said you couldn't understand why gays in Quebec would want to hide their sexuality. Now you see why. Just think how different things would have been between Père and me if I'd married a woman and had kids and kept my homosexuality hidden."

That same night, Gordon dreamed that he and Allan were on the seashore somewhere, and he had leaned over and kissed Allan, and he heard Ben's voice shouting from far away, "Gorblimey! Gordon, I gon kill wunna."

Gordon wonders how Ben would have reacted if he'd told him he was gay? Mysterious Ben. On Sundays, the family ate a late breakfast after Lillian, May, and Gordon returned from church. On some Sundays the villagers brought animals to be castrated — pigs, cats, and dogs mostly. Ben and their owners did so under a mango tree about thirty feet from the house. Seeing him do it to a boar once was enough for Gordon. Done without anaesthesia. The howls and squeals were excruciating. Once Gordon dreamed that Ben held him down, flipped open his razor, and said, "Wunna turn, bo." Castrations over, Ben got soap and a bath towel and went down the hill at the back of the house, where their land bordered the Riley River. Ben would bathe in the river, then sit on a boulder there, and smoke his pipe for hours.

◆

In the first six months of Gordon's return from study, the calls from André were so frequent that Maureen began to ask questions. He told her André was someone he'd met at university and they had become friends. But during a call she'd taken in his absence, she'd asked André about their friendship. André told her they'd met in a tavern. It was only after the AIDS diagnosis that she told him about that conversation. He asked her why she hadn't mentioned it before. She replied, "If you go looking for trouble, you will find plenty. I wanted our marriage to last, Gordon. Don't you understand?"

The sunlight has disappeared from the porch. He looks down at the harbour and sees a fast-approaching shower that looks like a milky blur. The first raindrops strike the porch. He heads back to the front, re-enters the house, and goes to sit in the recliner.

Chapter 15

NOW WHEN HE THINKS OF HIS LIFE IN SECTIONS, HE feels that part one ended when he left Montreal. He was thirty-three. Coincidence? In the confirmation class that prepared him to be received into the church, Reverend Kirton told them that Christ was thirty-three when he began his mission. He, Gordon, returned to St Vincent to take up the responsibilities of husband, co-breadwinner, and father. Part two began when he re-integrated into the civil service and began his dull domestic life, and ended with the AIDS diagnosis.

In October 2005, he entered a state of panic from which he never fully recovered. A month earlier he'd been promoted to senior economist. But his quarrels with Trevor had become more frequent, and he suspected that Trevor was tiring of the relationship. Also, the prime minister, indirectly, and another of his ministers, overtly, had expressed a wish to burn gays alive. Gordon worked closely with the PM. His re-election speech excoriated a member of the opposition who was reputed to be gay and included a playing of T.O.K.'s "Chi-Chi Man," a song that advocates burning gays. Around the same time, the minister of National Mobilization, Family, Gender Affairs, Social Mobilization, Persons with Disabilities and Youth said in a public forum that he would like to toss gays onto a flaming pyre.

In 2011, when circumstances forced Gordon to come clean with Maureen, he pointed to the PM's and his minister's statements to help explain why he'd had to stay closeted — for his own security, the security of his family, and his livelihood — and why she shouldn't share the information with anyone, not even Maggie. He reminded her that Maggie once said that she would like to see gays lined up against a wall and shot. Maureen seemed frozen for a few moments, then she nodded.

He'd had an inkling that Maureen would understand. A year after the minister's burning declaration, the naked corpse of Harry Grayson, a consultant to the prime minister, was found in a car. When rumours began to swirl about Grayson's bisexuality, she'd said, "It must be hell to live like that day in, day out, year after year." He remembers, too, her comments about Joe Oxley, who was murdered by Burt Joseph ostensibly because Joe hadn't paid him for sex. "I don't understand it," she'd said, shaking her head. "Why didn't Joe go to live abroad, somewhere where homosexuality is legal?" They were sitting at the dining table, her eyes focused on the newspaper relating the event, or she would have seen his discomfort. He'd had time to turn his head away and get up from the table before she could notice it. Yes, she'd shown compassion and understanding, but often such compassion disappears when the experience is personal.

Did she keep her promise not to tell anyone? She understood very well the stigma attached to HIV. Even now. In St Vincent it's impossible to be treated for HIV and keep the fact a secret. She was the first one to show the symptoms. Ever one to shun doctors, she'd attributed her fatigue and frequent colds to being older than sixty. When rashes showed up on her face, arms, and back, his fears were confirmed. He contacted Allan, who came by and drew a blood sample from her and told her it was to see what substances she might be allergic to. Over at his Edinboro house, Allan took a blood sample from Gordon. Allan knew about the relationship with Trevor, and he feared the worst. He told Gordon he'd send them to Barbados and have them analyzed under fictitious names.

Allan told Maureen she was probably exhausted from overwork and prescribed a month's sick leave. He offered it to Gordon too. Gordon said no. It was less than a year since he'd become the PM's chief advisor on CARICOM. Besides, in small St Vincent, he and his wife being sick at the same time would have raised suspicion. He dragged himself to work each day. No crises came up, and the office staff and the assistant secretary and accountant handled the routine work. Two weeks later the results came, and Maureen learned the truth, though not all the details.

In handling the situation, he was careful not to out Allan. From that day until she died, five and a half years later, it struck Gordon as strange that she never asked him if Allan, too, was gay. And he has wondered if it had anything do with her belief that if you go searching for truth, you might find more than you can handle.

After the confession, the tears, and Maureen's initial depression, a silence he was afraid to break invaded the house. He was glad that Frida was away. She was in Montreal at the time, pursuing a second master's degree, this time in molecular biology. Of course, she noticed it when she came back on holidays, despite their attempts to make things appear normal.

Along with the diagnosis, Allan brought three months' supply of antiretroviral drugs. "Got them from a gay colleague in Barbados. You each owe me two hundred U.S. dollars. This would have cost you nothing if the diagnosis had been made here — not even the symbolic five-dollar-per-prescription fee — thanks to the

Clinton Foundation." Within six weeks, Maureen's rashes went away. Gordon never got the rashes.

She never went back to work. On advice from Allan, that their lives would be healthier if they didn't have to cope with work stress, she announced that she would retire on January 1, 2012, seven weeks before her sixty-fourth birthday. It took Gordon a little longer to make up his mind, but in the end, he, too, retired on January 1, four months before his sixty-third birthday, but he accepted to continue advising the government on matters pertaining to CARICOM. Their plan had been to retire at sixty-five. They'd begun working when the retirement age was fifty-five, but were given the choice to leave at fifty-five, sixty, or even sixty-five. The PM had asked Gordon to continue beyond sixty-five because he was the government's CARICOM expert. He'd accepted eagerly, and, until the diagnosis, had looked forward to the continued frequent visits to Trinidad. The relationship with Trevor was over, but he was hoping he'd meet someone else. Now he curses the day he became a member of the CARICOM team and wishes he had been assigned to another ministry, one that hadn't given him the opportunity to travel to Trinidad or anywhere else for that matter.

Twice per year, Allan sent a tube of their blood to be analyzed in Barbados. Then two years ago, it was the beginning of the end for Maureen. He feels a compulsion to reread Maureen's account of this.

He goes to his office, sits at his desk, removes his glasses from the pocket of his pajama top, puts them on, pulls out the top right-hand drawer, feels for the envelope that contains the drive, doesn't find it, then remembers he left it in the computer. He taps the mouse. It takes a while for the document to open. He scrolls through until he finds Maureen's account of her interaction with Allan at the time of the rashes.

January 15, 2012

After months of feeling perpetually tired, catching one cold after another, and watching my body shrink, on April 15 last year, the Saturday before Easter, rashes broke out all over my body. Until then, I was certain I had cancer and didn't want to find out until the very last moment. Upon seeing the rashes, Gordon felt that I had eaten something that I was allergic to. He phoned Allan. Allan came to the house within hours. He'd known about the fatigue I was having, but I'd ignored his advice to have it checked out. "Tell you what," he said that afternoon, "I've brought syringes. I'll take a blood sample from you and have it analyzed. Don't do anything until you get the results. Maureen, in the meantime, I'm putting you on sick leave." Lucky for me, it all happened over the Easter break. He didn't tell me that he was sending the samples to Barbados. He returned to see us two weeks later, not only with the diagnosis, but with a three-month supply of Atripla — an antiretroviral drug.

What do you do when the man who has been your husband for thirty-two years infects you with HIV? I told Gordon to keep out of my sight. He moved into Frida's bedroom. For the first three or so days, I felt like a stone hurling through darkness and never falling. At times I wondered where I might buy a gun. If there had been one in the house, I would have shot him and myself. It wasn't just infidelity. Every Caribbean woman dreads it, but seems to take it in stride when it comes. Christine has told me more than once that leaving Percival would be like jumping from the frying pan into the fire. "They are all the same, Maureen. They are all bulldogs."

"Not my Gordon," I replied.

"Looks can be deceiving," she replied with raised eyebrows. I wonder now if she suspects anything.

The wrecking of my health. That's unpardonable. It was only when I contemplated the impact killing Gordon and myself would have on Frida and Mother that I sobered up enough to let Gordon speak to me. Ten days had gone by by then. He was tearful, confessed that he was gay, and had been having an affair with a man in Trinidad. But he insisted that he'd been taking all the necessary precautions. I asked him how come he wasn't having any of my health problems. He said that he was; not the colds, but he was chronically tired and was having stomach problems. He just didn't talk about them. He'd thought I had cancer and that I was afraid to have it confirmed until it could no longer be hidden, and so he'd respected my wish. Later Allan provided the details that Gordon was too embarrassed to state: the mechanics of gay sex. He said Gordon told him he'd always used condoms. The likely explanation was that on one occasion the condom broke.

I want to believe Allan's explanation, but he has been Gordon's friend since kindergarten. Whatever he says is calculated to make Gordon appear in the best light. As Mother would say, "Hurt me once, shame on you; hurt me twice, shame on me." Mother is right: never trust a man. As I matured, I found her comment cynical. Neither Gordon nor I ever said any such thing to Frida. We advised her to protect herself. Gordon especially told her that when she begins to have sex, she should make sure her partner wears a condom. He gave her advice he quite possibly did not follow. In any event, if Allan is to be believed, condoms aren't always foolproof. He said that with the heat we experience daily in the Caribbean, if you carry them around in your pocket, they will deteriorate and leak. Why did God — Allan would say nature — make us women so vulnerable? Why?

I began taking Atripla, a combination of four different antiretrovirals, the last week of April. In two weeks, the rashes were gone and my weight loss stopped, but nausea became a problem, so Allan added Gravol. For well over six weeks, I had trouble sleeping and didn't know whether my crippling headaches were from insomnia or Atripla. Slowly my body adjusted, and I've learned to ration how much I eat to lessen the nausea. The last blood analysis, done in November, shows the virus at undetectable levels for the first time.

•

This morning I woke up from a dream that I was at a wedding reception, and none of the men asked me to dance. I stayed awake. Dawn was already breaking, and I reflected on the fact that I hadn't had a real wedding. Some people think that unless you're a virgin, you shouldn't wear white, but I wanted to wear white. On your wedding day, all eyes are turned on you. The entire community comes out to see you. You are queen for a day, complete with bridesmaids and all. When my friend Lydia, already verging on forty, came back from Canada to be married here, she whispered in my ear that she'd already gotten married in the presence of a justice of the peace in Canada.

"So why are you doing it all over?"

"Because if I don't, I will never feel married. And it has to be here with my school friends and family and in the church I attended as a girl growing up." The groom, an Italian ten years her senior, came accompanied by some fifteen members of his family.

I've since read that marriage is a rite of passage and therefore a moment of a major transition, one that requires a ritual that's joyful and reassuring. In a sense, it's as if you're embarking on a journey, and your church, your community, and your family are there to witness the send-off. In India, the wife goes to live with her husband's family and takes with her a dowry. I read, too, that in Europe men searched eagerly for wives who brought a substantial dowry. Of course, in many places it's the groom who provides the dowry, and some see this as the parents selling their daughters into marriage. I experienced none of this. Once Frida asked me if I'd kept my wedding dress. I told her I didn't have one.

"That's weird," she said. "How come?"

"Ask your father."

I wonder what Gordon told her. Did he have the right to impose his will on me like this? Did he do it just because that's what men do: force women to do their bidding? It seemed like such an inauspicious beginning, and yet where decisions are concerned, he leaves them mostly up to me. I get him to do my bidding. He deprived Mother of the role mothers perform in the marriage rite. She could not proclaim proudly — justly so — that she had successfully borne the burden of being both my mother and father. Explains some of her hostility to Gordon. The night before Gordon and I went to the courthouse, she said, "I have a feeling that man is a bully. Maureen, promise me that if he starts abusing you, you will leave him and come back home. I will help you raise your child."

Gordon proved her wrong on all counts that she knows of. On our twenty-fifth wedding anniversary she admitted as much in her toast — that there was already happiness in our marriage and all she could wish us was health. Now I wouldn't dare let her know that Gordon has infected me with HIV. How did he feel those times when Mother spouted her homophobia? However much I'm angry with him, I can't have her saying nasty stuff to him. Sometimes I wonder if her views are from Pentecostal doctrine or if she's basically homophobic and glad that her religion offers cover? She persists in calling Angela's partner the "Coolie man." "Mother, you told me his name is Blair. How would you feel if he calls you nigger?"

"He wouldn't dare."

"'Coolie' is the Asian equivalent of 'nigger.'"

"No, it's not the same. It doesn't bother them."

I shouldn't exculpate Gordon. If only there were someone I could share these feelings with. But I can't. I don't want to be pointed at when I'm on the street as the woman whose husband gave her AIDS. I don't want Frida to be seen as the woman whose father infected her mother with AIDS. And however much I'm angry with Gordon, I don't want him to become a pariah. He is still my husband.

After we resumed speaking to each other and he apologized, he wanted to know if I was going to leave him. I didn't answer right away.

"Maybe I might. Do you want me to leave you?"

"We're both in a terrible situation, and it would be better if we remain together and be there for each other ... as best we can. I hope these drugs we're taking work. I would prefer that you don't expose me, but you might feel better if you do. I don't have the right to tell you how to feel about this."

I'm grateful to Allan for helping me to manage this illness. Physically. Socially too: I shudder to think what might have happened if he weren't here. I've begged him not to tell Beth. Of course, she knows I'm ill. I told her the story that Allan gave me to allay suspicion: my doctor thinks my liver is malfunctioning and so I'm left chronically tired.

What a friend Allan has been! When Gordon was in Montreal, there wasn't a week he didn't drop by. He came to the house and gave Frida her shots. When Gordon returned, she thought for a while that she had two fathers until we got her to call Allan uncle. Around age ten, she began to say Uncle Al. From the outset Beth was Aunt Beth. That never changed. From the time I returned from giving birth in the hospital, Beth became a regular at the house, helping me with housework, driving me to get groceries, dropping me home after work. Sometimes she took Frida and me to her home. Then she lived at her parents' home. A huge house in Clare Valley. It was during this period that she and Allan began dating.

Still and all, I can't help wondering about this closeness between Allan and Gordon. Has Allan, too, been leading a double life? Probably not. Beth is sure it's a woman he takes to the Evesham house. It does seem impossible as well for a man to carry on with another man here and keep it secret.

"Never engaged in gay sex here — not even when you were young?" I asked Gordon.

"No. I was too afraid. I'd seen what happened to Ephraim, a gay man who lived in Evesham. You remember the story in the paper about Fatman, the kid in Mespo who was taunted all the time and who killed himself? I didn't want to grow up and become the sort of outcast that Ephraim was."

"Don't tell me, Gordon, that Trevor was the first and only person you've had sex with."

"No. I had opportunities in Montreal. Nothing serious. Just a couple of times."

If he had said no, I'd have dismissed everything he told me as lies. I resisted asking him about André.

"Were you tempted to stay in Montreal?"

"No. You and Frida were here. I did think, to be honest, of trying to convince you to let us move to Canada, but we both had excellent jobs that we weren't likely to get in Canada. On top of that, Canada is not the best place for a Black child to grow up. White kids that stick out have a hard time too, but hostility and rejection from Whites and pressure from Blacks to conform put huge burdens on Black kids. Four out of ten children in the protection of Ontario youth services are Black. Quebec is almost as bad. I couldn't take that chance with Frida."

Yes, he was probably telling the truth. You can't fool around in St Vincent for long without somebody finding out and spreading the news. Christine knows the names of Percival's mistresses. As soon as Harry Grayson's nude body was found in his car out at Argyle, speculation became rife about which of his boyfriends had done it. Most people had heard that he was "one o' them." They did the limp-wrist gesture and asked, "You think his wife and he pickney-them know he so?" Most felt that the information was too widespread for them not to know. One of those boyfriends was taken into custody. A reporter showed a group of angry people shouting at the courthouse gate, "Wrong person! Wrong person! Let the fellar go." One told the reporter, "This ain't got nothing to do with his boyfriends. Is some political secret Harry been going to spill. They kill Harry to silence him. You ain't see? A single bullet hole. And no blood on the man body. They wash it and put it back in the car. That weak, scrawny boy they arrest can no more do that than I can push down this courthouse. It take plenty people to do that. I tell you all, Harry death got to do with politricks. That money they put up for information is sham. Pure sham." A woman wearing a plaid headtie elbowed him and put a finger on her lips. "You talking too much, Bobby. Them going think you know the truth and kill you next." The reporter kept the microphone in front of Bobby's face, but he said nothing more.

•

Gordon is taking me for a drive out to Riley later. May is preparing Sunday dinner for us. I hope I'll be able to digest it. Truth be told, I don't want to go. I have never felt close to her. I met her for the first time the evening that Mother took me to my mother-in-law's home to plead my case for why Gordon should marry me. The looks May gave me! Hostility doesn't begin to describe them. Since then she has been distant and polite. Never warm. Smiles aplenty for Frida — why not? She's her brother's daughter, has half of her genes. Headshakes and nods for me. She certainly knows that Gordon didn't want to marry me. When Frida came along and Gordon was overseas, Lillian often sent her to help me with the chores; one time when I was sick, she did it for three weeks. If you came to the house and observed us, you would have thought she was mute. Before Gordon and I got married, my ex-colleague Gloria, who is from Evesham and a Methodist, told me that Gordon had dated a girl called Joy who was May's friend. I made the mistake and asked May about her. I was sitting at the kitchen table cutting up vegetables to make soup. She was standing at the sink. She turned around, glared at me, and said slowly as if each word was a knife jab: "Mau-REEN, MIND YO' OWN BUSINESS! I DON' ASK YOU BOUT YO' BOYFRIENDS, DON' ASK ME BOUT GORDON GIRLFRIENDS. DID I MAKE MYSELF CLEAR!" More words in those three sentences than she spoke the entire time she spent with me. After that, I feared that anything I said to her would be the spark to set her off.

Still and all, thanks to her, we rarely have to buy fruits and vegetables. But then again, she has all thirteen acres of the land Gordon's parents owned, and doesn't pay Gordon rent for his portion. She doesn't have any children. Maybe that's why her trigger is always cocked. Wonder whom she'll leave her share of the land to? This isn't something I'm comfortable asking Gordon about. Riley and Carapan are near enough to town. I must remind Gordon that we must update our wills. Frida is now thirty-two. Wonder what she will do with all this jewellery that Gordon has bought me over the years. I hardly wear any of it. I don't even know if Frida is interested in jewellery. I know now that these earrings, brooches, chokers, and bangles are bribes. Gilded guilt.

Yes, I must make a will. If I die before Gordon, there must be no ambiguity that my half of this house belongs to Frida. After all the suffering I am enduring here, I must ensure that when I'm gone, no Trevor, Albert, Harry, or

Conrad move in with Gordon and be the benefactor of my suffering. These days things move with such speed. Who'd have thought gay marriage would be legal in so many countries so soon! Might become legal here too and swallow up all I've laboured and suffered for.

I think I'll end here today.

When he first read this part of the journal he was struck by Maureen's generosity. What would his reaction be if the tables were turned? He thinks that she exaggerates May's indifference and tries to find examples to disprove it. He finds none but is sure there must be some.

Chapter 16

FROM WHERE HE'S SITTING IN THE RECLINER, HE LOOKS across the room at the corner table with a framed eight-by-ten portrait of Maureen and himself. He's wearing a café au lait suit — he hates wearing suits — a white shirt and a dark brown tie. Maureen's wearing a pearl-white dress with a corsage of orange blossoms. It was taken at Allan and Beth's wedding, in the garden beside the pool of the Blue Lagoon Hotel where the wedding reception was held.

How different his and her lives would be if she hadn't become pregnant with Frida? Allan's too. For one thing, he would have stayed in Montreal and persuaded Allan to join him there. Or become André's lifelong partner. Who knows? How would he be feeling now if Frida had turned out to be a different child? She certainly would be different if he'd stuck to his initial decision not to marry Maureen. In the end, his acceptance had come down to parenting Frida. He'd had to choose: his child's welfare or his love affair with Allan — or later, André.

◆

Allan was firm: "No sex between us after you're married. I'll tell you one thing, though." He paused, a long one. They were lying on their backs in Allan's bed, their bodies touching. "All my years growing up, I wondered what it would be like to live with a father. When I saw fathers beating their children, I used to be glad I didn't have one. But one day, I saw Joseph Matthews flanked by his two sons, Bill and Cory, walking along Evesham road. You remember Bill and Cory? Coal-black and bowlegged like their father?"

"Of course."

"Matthews had an arm around each of his sons. I watched until they were out of sight, and I felt a yearning inside me. That was an experience I would never have. I cried. I was twelve."

Gordon wanted to tell him he'd never had any such experience with Ben; that most Vincentian children never experience that degree of affection from their mothers and fathers, but he remained silent. He wondered, too, whether he would have been so demonstrably affectionate with Frida if he hadn't lived in Montreal and witnessed there the warm interactions between parents and children. He was moved by a Mohawk woman's statement that First Nations did not hit children, that she sprinkled a few drops of water on her children when she wanted them to know they were engaging in unacceptable behaviour. In the only literature course he took at university, he read Richard Wright's *Black Boy*, and it helped him to understand that the violent treatment of children in the American South and in the Caribbean had come down from slavery.

That Sunday, after listening to Allan, he tried to assess his own feelings about Ben. The one thing he could confidently say was that Ben provided for his family. After Ben lost his job at Mt Bentinck Sugar Factory, he turned to farming fully and became part of an informal farming co-operative. May's accusation that he gave money to his mistress Vera was probably exaggerated because all the money for the produce from the land went into Lillian's hands. Gordon was present a few times when she gave Ben money to pay for the rum that accompanied the domino games he played at the Riley rum shop. He often grumbled that it was not enough. More likely that Vera gave him money. She was mixed-race and about ten years younger than Lillian. She owned a passenger van and lived alone beside the road linking Carriere to Mespo in a large, two-storey house painted ochre. Gordon passed by it every morning and afternoon on his way to and from Emmanuel High School.

Marcella, their closest neighbour, was a single woman with five daughters ranging in age from twenty-five to fifteen. Men were frequently coming and going to her home. Once Ben told Lillian, "Wunna see wha' going on down there? Wunna find all sort uh fault with muh. But none uh that can happen in muh house while I's alive." Lillian frowned but said nothing. She must have felt he was fishing for compliments. What if she'd said, How would you know what goes on here; you spend your nights at Vera's house?

Once, sometimes twice, per week, depending on the direction of the wind, they heard Mrs. Beach, their neighbour across the stream, screaming from her husband Two-Ton's beatings. In that hill-and-gully thick Barbadian accent that Ben never lost, he'd say to Lillian, "Ef Oi used tuh slap yuh and put yuh in yuh place, or gie yuh uh good lickin loike Two-Ton ..." A few times he raised his hand to do it. One time he was determined to. Lillian and he had been quarrelling over the money she'd received from that week's banana sale. She ran into the kitchen. He ran after her. She grabbed her potholders and lifted the pot of stew for their supper and poised herself to hurl it at him. Whether from fear of being burned or going to bed without dinner, Ben withdrew, but "Ef Uh used tuh slap yuh and put yuh in yuh place ..." continued. Wisely, Lillian never dared him to.

One end-of-term, May brought home her test papers and announced that she'd failed. Ben began taking off his belt to beat her. Lillian told him to leave her alone. "She couldn' go to school for two weeks. She had flu. Leave her alone."

But Lillian wasn't there one time to save Gordon. He had brought home two chocolate bars, one for himself and one for May. He and Allan had been on their way home from school and were running ahead of an approaching rain shower. They came upon Mrs. Robertson frantically trying to save her groundnuts that were spread out on metal sheets to dry. They helped her gather them and waited out the rain at her house. She gave each of them a fifty-cent piece. At the shop on the way up, Gordon spent twenty cents on two chocolate bars and ran home full of excitement. He put the chocolate bars on the dining table. Ben saw him.

"Where yuh goh money from tuh buy these?"

"I get it helping ..."

"Shut up! Yuh infernal liar! Now Uh know who been stealing the change from muh pockets."

"I didn't ..."

"Shut up!" One of his hands was already collaring Gordon so tightly that he couldn't speak; the other hand was pulling the belt from its loops. He gave Gordon six over his back. Gordon collapsed on the floor in front of him. By then Lillian had come into the living room. "Miss Robertson give me that money. I didn't steal Daddy money," Gordon told her between sobbing hiccups. It had happened fast. Over before Lillian, who was outside in the kitchen, could intervene.

"Ben, you is a crazy man. You didn' even give the boy a chance to explain. Wha' wrong with you?" She left May to finish preparing supper and walked over to Evesham. She returned and confirmed his story, but Ben had already left the house. Later Gordon removed his bloodstained shirt and Lillian dabbed the wounds with iodine. The scars are still on his back. Ben never apologized to him. Gordon vowed then — he was around ten — that if he became a father, he would never hit his children. From then until Ben died, Gordon avoided him on every occasion possible and used the fewest of words possible whenever he was forced to converse with him. When Gordon passed GCE, Ben said how proud he was of him and stretched out his arm to hug him. Gordon moved aside and watched him wince. On a couple of occasions, he came close to asking Ben about that beating. Maybe they might have reconciled.

Now he understands that life is full of irremediable mistakes, and it's the lucky few who aren't haunted by them. If he's still alive ten or so years from now, how many of the choices he makes today would he see as irremediable errors then? Ben died from a heart attack one night at Vera's house. Lillian spent the last of her lucid years claiming that Ben had disgraced her and wishing that her mother had not forced her to marry him. Each time she said it, May rolled her eyes.

He should ask May how she feels about Ben. More and more she resembles him. Has his molasses-brown complexion, his oval face, and the frown that joins in a permanent V just above her aquiline nose. She's big-boned and short like Lillian, but has a fat-free body like Ben. Burns up her calories in the hard work of farming.

He wonders if Ben's treatment of Lillian is the reason May has been super cautious about men. Ben occasionally told Lillian to shut up. "Yuh is a woman. Wunna don' know nufffin." He suspects that May has never had sex, but will never ask her. Not something a brother asks a sister. In her twenties, she dated guys off and on, but avoided being with them in secluded places. Once a boyfriend invited her to go to the cinema in Mespo with him. They would have had to walk along stretches of uninhabited road. She said no, and the relationship ended. They all ended when she refused to have sex with them. Some told her they wouldn't buy a pig in a sack, that they had to sample the merchandise to see if it was worth giving up their freedom for. She told Gordon that on her thirty-fifth birthday, she had decided to let the fellow courting her then have his way. But he'd brought no condoms. She mentioned pregnancy to him. He said he would pull out before ejaculating. She said that didn't always work. "Plus, Gordon, I didn't know who he been sleeping with and what diseases he might o' pass on to me. That is what I wanted to tell him, but I stick to the other story. You know what he said to me? 'That is why all-yo woman does get rape. You is lucky yo' mother in the next bedroom.'" He suspects that this incident deepened her suspicion of men.

He has never known her to be without a dog. One evening on her way home from Carapan, a drunk from the Riley rum shop had tried to put his arm around her. Grover sank his teeth into the man's left shank. After that the rum shop denizens never ventured beyond whistling at her.

♦

He stares at the coffee table and sees the letter from Christine that the postman delivered yesterday. You would think that having escaped from that household she would want to leave it behind her. In it she asks for news of Freckles's sons. She writes using a pseudonym in the return address. No telling what Freckles would do if he finds out that Austin, and, to a lesser extent, Maureen, helped Christine escape. Gordon only recently found out that Maureen gave her the text of what she wrote the night Christine slept at their house. He finds it with the search function.

January 6, 2013
Had every intention of going to church this morning. Returning to church was one of my New Year's resolutions.

Couldn't this morning. Christine spent the night here, in Frida's bedroom. I worry that she'll end up in a coffin.

Around 11:00 p.m. Austin phoned us and asked if we think he should call the police. He said Freckles was beating Christine out in the yard, "calling her whore and whatnot." Before he even hung up, we heard someone knocking on our front door. It was she. Gordon pulled her in and closed and locked the door.

Gordon pointed to an armchair. "I'm calling the police. That man is a brute," he said and began walking toward the phone.

Christine shook her head, but Gordon continued. She sprinted toward him and held his hand.

"You can't let him get away with this," I said.

Blood dripped from her swollen lower lip, the front of her dress was bloodstained; her left eye was swollen and half-closed; his fingerprints were all over her face. I went for my camera and took pictures.

"He'll kill me," she said. "Don't you understand? He'll kill me if I leave him or if I ask the police to charge him."

After snapping the pictures, I made her sit at the kitchen table. I got a face towel, a washrag, and a small basin of water and cleaned the blood on her chin. I put ice cubes in another face towel for her to hold on her swollen lip. Gordon brought the bottle of Tylenol and a glass of water.

Right at that moment, we heard a knock at the door. Gordon went to answer it. It was Austin, his face beet red, his eyes wild with anger.

"Girl, why you wasting yo' life and yo' youth with that fucker! Leave the pile o' shit. You ain't got chick nor child. You have yo' profession, you can support yo'self, why you staying with that prick?"

Christine hung her head. "I will. In time."

It's easy for us to say she should leave him. She was right up to a point. Where would she hide in tiny St Vincent? He could easily trace her when she leaves work.

"She fears for her life, Austin," I said.

"Maureen, that is all talk. Is only a coward or a sick man that beat up women. I bet you if he see the police with handcuffs he go start shitting his pants."

"You don't know that, Austin," Gordon said.

"That is why some women end up poisoning their husband or killing them in their sleep, yes."

Gordon pointed to the available armchair. Austin shook his head. "I don't know what sort o' fucking country this is. I call the police. Know what those fuckers said? 'Mind yo own business.'

"'And if he kill she?'

"'We will handle it.'

"Man, I tell you this country is backward. The law le' people do wha' they like."

I stood, tapped Christine on the shoulder, and told her to come with me. "You're not going back there tonight." I took her into the spare bedroom and gave her one of my nightgowns. "Hold on to that bloodstained dress. Don't wash it. You might need it as evidence one day." I told her I had Ativan. She accepted.

When I came out the bedroom, Austin had left.

For a long time, neither Gordon nor I slept that night. Around 4:00 a.m. I looked in on Christine. She was asleep.

Next, I heard Freckles's stomping footsteps on our stairs followed by his ear-splitting knock. It was still dark outside. I shook Gordon awake and told him to go get the door.

"Can I come in?" Freckles's voice.

"No. Get off my property."

"I only give she a little lash. Somebody tell me she been flirting with a doctor at the hospital. I ask she if was true and she ain't answer. I wouldn't'a hit she if she did answer me. Is her fault. Christine, you hearing me. I love you, Christine, I love you."

It sounded to me as if he was crying. Jesus Christ, what sort of a mixed-up man that is!

I heard his footsteps going down the steps. Gordon returned to the bedroom and told me Freckles was standing in the road.

I went to see if Christine had heard him. She was sitting on the edge of the bed. She had turned on the light.

"You have to leave that man."

She was silent.

"Christine, you have to leave that man."

"I will when I can … alive."

"When you change this dress, don't wash it. I will keep it in the freezer here for you"

She's back with him. I hope her plans to leave him come through before the next beating or before he kills her.

Happily, her plans worked out a mere three and a half months later.

April 19, 2013
Caspar London's funeral is tomorrow. I must go. Moving tribute for him in *Searchlight*. A true visionary. Someone who understood how intricately colonialism imprisons our souls. I remember how the police beat him up when he protested Princess Margaret's visit here in 1971. Rest in Peace, Caspar. There's only one person like you in every generation.

Looks like Christine has flown the coop. Freckles knocked on our door this morning and asked if she was here.

"Why?"

"She didn't come home last night. I don't know where she is. All her clothes there. She ain't take nothing."

"I hope you didn't kill her and dispose of the body and now pretending you don't know where she is," Gordon called out to him from the dining room. "Won't put it beyond you."

"Fuck off," he said and left.

"She's safe," I told Gordon. "She asked me for that bloodstained dress and said, 'Won't be long now.' I don't think she's here in St Vincent."

Austin called half an hour later. "You hear the news?"

"Yes."

"I lend she the money and drove she to the airport. That fucker used to make she turn over her pay to him. I tell she to wear a wig and wait for me in Bottom Town right after she come off the night shift. She only had a single carry-on and her purse. I didn' drive in the terminal. Don' repeat this to anybody. I don't want that fucker to kill me."

"Where she went?"

"Canada. And not as no refugee, either. Immigrant. Your girl been working quietly behind the scenes."

The best news I've had in a long time.

Takes just one man like Freckles to frighten women like May away from men. Would Lillian have put up with a Freckles? Maggie definitely not. Sometimes he thinks May is bitter against him and wonders if his gender has anything to do it. Frida once asked him why her grandparents had been unfair to Aunty May.

"How?"

"Well, when it was her turn to go to high school, Granny and Grandad didn't send her. They saved up the money to send you."

"Frida, that might not be the whole story. It might be that they were still paying for the land they had bought with a mortgage."

"So they chose to own land rather than pay for Aunty May's education?"

"I don't know, Frida."

"If I had a brother, would I be second-class?"

"Never!"

She hugged him and planted a kiss on his cheek.

"I would treat you both equally."

"Equally! I want to be your favourite."

"You *are* my favourite. There's no one else."

"Cop-out!"

Chapter 17

MY DEAR, DEAR FRIDA. HE SIGHS WITH PLEASURE. HE REmembers that one Saturday, just before she turned twelve, they both were standing at the seaward end of the side porch, looking at the activity on the quays, and she'd turned to face him and asked, "Why you and Mom named me Frida?"

Six weeks after their marriage, he and Maureen had watched a BBC documentary on the life and work of Frida Kahlo. There was still tension between them. She still chafed that he'd married her reluctantly — more reluctantly than she could have imagined. His first choice always was an abortion, but she was already in the second trimester, and Lillian had become hysterical. May had said to him, "I know you don't love Maureen; you shouldn't marry somebody you don't love; but Mama going have a stroke if you don't marry that woman. Marry her, Gordon, for the sake o' peace between you and Mama. She complaining that you not coming home no more. She think Allan influencing you. 'If I get my hand on that Allan ... that infidel!'" May laughed. "You can always divorce her later, Gordon. Then again you might come to love her. And she look like a good woman. She even have more schooling than you."

"If this child turns out to be a girl, I want to name her Frida," Maureen had said.

Frida's birth erased his smothered anger, cleansed by the magic of the new creature in his life, and created a deep feeling for the woman who'd given birth to his daughter. But he didn't call it love. Maureen made him promise that they would never tell Frida that it was because of her that they'd got married.

He told Frida how she got her name.

"Does that mean that you and Mom want me to be an artist?"

"That would be a pleasure, if that's what you want to become." Her artwork at school was above average. She drew well and understood scale, perspective, and depth. She began taking music lessons every Saturday morning starting at age six. A gift from Maggie. To Gordon's ears, her piano playing was good.

"I want you to be a strong woman like Frida Kahlo. Maybe even stronger. Of course, I wouldn't want you to have her handicap. And if you marry, I would want your husband to be faithful." He smiled at her.

Then he was a trifle anxious. She was on the cusp of adolescence, and he had seen what had happened to many intelligent girls he had gone to school with. Pregnancies. Running away from home. The sort of experience that Maggie had had. By form three, Frida's interest in painting waned but the love of music continued, and she was driven to excel. She wasn't at the top of her class, but she never placed below fifth. What pleased him most was that she was never embarrassed to ask him questions about anything. She shared stories with him about what was happening to her classmates. There was one girl who'd got pregnant and her mother had taken her to Barbados to get an abortion, and the other girls were throwing words at her. He told her she should befriend the girl and tell her classmates to leave her alone. "That's what Frida Kahlo would have done." When next he asked her about it, she said she'd done the first, but couldn't risk having her classmates turning on her. He told her that was fine. Sometimes, we only manage to do half of what we would like.

When at sixteen she began attending community college, he held his breath. She'd gone to an all-girls high school. Community college was co-ed. There she would meet a lot of randy males who had seen their fathers, older brothers, and uncles treat women like discardable toys. He told her so. Maureen objected. They were sitting in the living room: Frida on the piano stool in the far corner, Maureen on the couch, and he in one of the armchairs facing the couch.

"Mom, from the date of your marriage and my birthday, you got pregnant before you and Dad got married."

Maureen blushed and stared at the floor.

Gordon answered for her. "Yes, you're absolutely right. But your mom was thirty and I was twenty-nine. If you've completed your education and can support a child and you allow yourself to get pregnant, I have no problem with that. Adolescents shouldn't be parents. They need all their energy to deal with the challenges of adolescence."

"I don't want you ever to have children out of wedlock. Don't even think about it," Maureen said.

Frida frowned at her and then at him.

He shrugged.

"Did you both plan to have me?" She looked first at him, then at Maureen, whose head was turned away.

Frida gave him a fixed stare. He didn't know what to say. He eventually said, "We could afford you. Just barely, but we could. I was about to go off to Montreal to study."

"You didn't answer my question, Dad."

"Ask Maureen."

"Mom?"

Maureen was silent.

He said, "Let's be frank. I had doubts about getting married. But I'm glad I did. Look at the beautiful and loving daughter that I have."

"Do you agree with abortion, Dad?"

He nodded. "Teenagers aren't ready to be mothers."

"But, Dad, abortion is a crime in St Vincent."

"Yes, but in most advanced countries it isn't."

"Gran believes that abortion is a crime. Do you, Mom?"

"Sometimes I don't know what I believe. But I can tell you something that I would like." She paused.

"What is it, Mom?"

Maureen took a deep breath and looked away. "If you're having sex, insist that your boyfriend wear a condom. There'd be little chance of you getting pregnant and needing an abortion. Better still you won't expose yourself to HIV and other venereal diseases. Many men lead double lives, and you can never be sure that your boyfriend isn't one of them. You can hope but you can never be a hundred percent certain."

"Dad, you know men who lead double lives?"

"Yes."

"Do they include some of your friends?"

"Not friends. Acquaintances."

"Names?"

"Frida, I can't go slandering people."

"Mom, you know any?"

"Yes, one for sure: a man from Fairhall. He was married. He left his wife and went to England. He wrote telling her that he was gay and was ending the marriage. She told the entire village. She had two preteen twin boys. People, old and young, used to ask them if they would grow up to be bullermen too. Today one of those boys is an alcoholic, and I feel that the teasing caused it."

Last year, three days after Maureen's burial, he and Frida were sitting at the seaward end of the porch, chatting about this and that and watching the sun tint the Kingstown harbour yellow just before setting. Their conversation turned to the lies politicians tell. She told him then that when she asked him about the marriage that Saturday several years earlier, she had been trying to see whether he would tell her the truth. He protested that he was no politician. "But you work closely with politicians. You can't avoid their influence." She then related verbatim what Maggie had told her about his and Maureen's marriage:

"'You have your father on a pedestal, but it's thanks to your other grandmother that you're not a bastard. You think the world of Gordon, but let me tell you, he didn't want to marry Maureen. He couldn't come up with a reason. Your father is a selfish man. If I'd been in position to raise you, I would have never let Maureen marry that man. And put this in your head, little miss: if I didn't raise your mother with God-fearing principles, you wouldn't be here.'

"'Gran, what do you mean?'

"'What I mean? I mean Gordon wanted Maureen to commit murder, and damn her soul. Go to jail too, if the law found out. That is if she didn't kill herself first. Bleed to death or develop gangrene.'

"'Gran, what you mean?'

"'Throw you away.'

"'You mean toss me in a rubbish bin?'

"'I mean abort you. Rip you out of her womb before you come to term and kill you. That is what I mean.'"

A long silence ensued between him and Frida. That was Maggie all right. Had a successful daughter and her nursing career, but they were blanketed by Clem's and her parents' wrongs.

"Frida, why you never told me this before?"

"Oh, Dad, you and Gran despised one another. You wanted me to stir up trouble? She told me this almost twenty years ago, so please don't raise it with her now. Besides, I don't want her to get angry with me. I love her with all her faults and strange ideas about hell and heaven. Besides, if I'd told you then, I would have broken my promise to Mom never to tell you anything that would heighten the tension between you and Gran." She chuckled. "Whenever I displeased Gran, she used to say, 'One o' these days I'll cut your backside and go to jail for it if I have to.' At first, I'd tell Mom and she would warn Gran to stop threatening to beat me. After a while I knew it was just Gran's way to express frustration. You two *did not* like one another. I'm glad you've reconciled." She smiled nervously. "I shouldn't have told you any of this, but Mom's no longer with us, so these secrets no longer matter. Be kind now, Dad. Gran's life is miserable enough with diabetes, arthritis, and old age; you won't want to add to her misery."

He nodded. *Diabetes, arthritis, old age, and vitriol.* "You remember what led your grandmother to tell you this?"

"She was telling me how to conduct myself with boys. Stuff you and Mom had already told me. So I told her I knew all that already. Gran came back with 'You have that father of yours on a pedestal, don't you?' And I said, 'Shouldn't I?' And she said, 'I don't.' And I said, 'Why,' and that was when she told me."

He didn't comment.

"Back then, you handled it well, Dad. You told me enough. You're good at withholding information without lying. Mom used to say I copied your habit, though I never really withheld information from her. I only played coy. She should have scolded less and listened more. Her head was full of fears that I was having sex with my boyfriends. I liked it, Dad, that you had confidence in me. You felt I could take care of myself, and I was determined not to disappoint you."

Why would Maggie reveal such information to his sixteen-year-old daughter? Some people go to bizarre extremes to prove others wrong. Maggie believed that children couldn't grow up well behaved and disciplined unless they got an occasional flogging. It must have galled her that Frida proved her wrong. That or she understood that adolescence is when children revolt against their parents and saw this as an opportunity to sow contention between him and Frida. Maybe Maggie wanted Frida to tell him what she'd said and hoped he'd lie and discredit himself in Frida's eyes.

He recalls when Frida said to him late one Saturday afternoon, "Dad, let's walk out to Sion Hill. There's something I want to tell you." She was in her second year of community college. She told him that she had a boyfriend. He was from New Grounds and was following a business profile. She was in the sciences: biology, physics, and chemistry, and getting excellent grades.

"When are we going to meet him?"

"When I'm sure he's serious."

"Do you have a photo of him?"

"No."

That was all she told him. He was glad for the walk with her, for her confidence in him, but he'd found the announcement underwhelming. Of course, he didn't tell her this.

She went through a lot of boyfriends. Usually, they dropped her when she refused to have sex. (May hadn't been shy in advising her how to deal with men.) There was one boy, though, whom she didn't want to leave. He'd given her an ultimatum. She'd come home on a Friday afternoon and stayed in her room and cried and wouldn't tell him or Maureen why. On the Monday, she said she didn't want to go back to school. She told him the story then and asked him if he had treated his girlfriends that way. He smiled, remembering that it was he who'd resisted Allan. "If you think that all this boy wants from you is sex … sex is beautiful when it's done with someone you love and respect and who also loves and respects you."

She said thanks and hugged him.

♦

He still on occasion wonders how different his and Allan's lives would be if Allan hadn't broken off the relationship. There probably wouldn't have been the risks Allan took. Then again, relationships become stale, and men find it a challenge not to be promiscuous. He relives for the umpteenth time the pain he'd felt when Allan ended their relationship. It was a Sunday evening around ten thirty. They'd had sex earlier. Allan was on duty at the hospital beginning at midnight.

"I can't resist Mama anymore and Maureen is showing. If I'm going to marry her, it has to be soon."

Allan was standing in the middle of the room buttoning up his shirt. He frowned and looked across at Gordon sitting on the sofa.

"What do you think, Allan? … Sometimes I feel that if I didn't love you so much, I would run away. Sometimes I wish we could run away together … forgive my childishness." He sighed. "We have a good thing going. No one suspects us. Everyone knows we've been friends since childhood."

Allan paused the buttoning, both hands folded at his navel, but was silent.

Gordon prodded. "We can go on loving each other just as we've been doing; no one will be the wiser."

Another long silence, then Allan spoke, "Let's say, for argument's sake, that you and I continue to be lovers and Maureen were to find out … It wouldn't be pleasant. I've thought through all this. Maybe you'll think I'm weak, but I wouldn't be able to deal with the fallout. I wouldn't risk becoming a pariah … One of the precepts my grandmother instilled in me is 'Never come between a man and his wife.'"

Chapter 18

THE WEDDING TOOK PLACE AT THE COURTHOUSE ON HOLY Thursday 1979. The significance of the date wasn't lost on Maureen. "If this turns out to be a crucifixion, I have no doubt who'll be on the cross," she'd said the night before. (Thirty-two years later, when she got over the shock of the AIDS diagnosis, she said, "You made me undergo a humiliating marriage on a Holy Thursday, and now the symptoms of this deadly disease you've given me show up at Easter.") The wedding wasn't how Maggie or Lillian had wanted it, but Gordon knew his power. She took her vows in a navy blue skirt and a white blouse — clothes she wore to work. She later confirmed his suspicion that she'd done so on purpose. He wore a suit leftover from his churchgoing days. Maggie, Lillian, Beth, and May were the only ones in new clothes. Allan, who was an unwilling witness, did so in a well-worn dark green Terylene suit. Afterward, they had lunch at Olive's Hotel. There were a few toasts, but no real speeches. He was sure they were all thinking some version of: *He's marrying her to take shame out of her eyes, so her child won't be a bastard.* They probably felt like him that the marriage wouldn't last.

There was no honeymoon. Maggie had offered them a weekend in a Bequia hotel. Gordon turned it down. The next day, Good Friday, the volcano erupted. Ash, falling like grey rain all over the island, soon coated everything, and thousands of people had to be evacuated from all the communities in northern St Vincent. Most were given shelter in the schools of southern and central St Vincent. Not an auspicious beginning for their marriage, Gordon felt. He was on two weeks' vacation, but was asked to cancel it and report for work. The independence of St Vincent was being planned for later that year. Until then it was mostly the plantocrats and their stooges who'd opposed independence, but others joined the clamour and were sure that the eruption, especially on Good Friday, was God's warning to Vincentians to abandon independence. To this day some continue to believe this. Especially when they find out that St Vincent can't pay its bills. Vincentians — not just Austin — look at the Cayman Islands and the British Virgin Islands, that benefit from being British overseas departments, and salivate.

Maureen had expected him to live with her at Maggie's house until they could buy their own home. But after a month of Maggie's frowning face and grey frog eyes following him everywhere, he rented a small house in Kingstown Park and told Maureen she could stay with Maggie if she wished, but he was leaving. He regretted the rental decision two months later when he received the scholarship to attend Concordia University. But by then, May, Lillian, and Maggie were paying for the furniture they'd credited to furnish the rented house.

Maureen was due to give birth around mid-August, and there was some doubt whether she would before or after his departure. His flight for Montreal was booked for August 17, so he could register for his courses and attend the orientation sessions for foreign students that began on August 20. On August 1 — Emancipation Day in the Anglophone Caribbean, a holiday — Maggie was visiting them, and she stood in the doorway of the kitchen, her arms akimbo, and shouted across at him in the living room, "What a man! You have a heart of granite. Your wife about to give birth and you book your passage to go away! You can't wait a year? What is your hurry?" He was relieved when Frida came on August 13, a healthy baby weighing seven pounds, four ounces.

◆

In Montreal, his first semester was spent finding his bearings and learning to be on his own. He didn't know how to cook, and his allowance could not cover the cost of eating in restaurants. After two weeks of dry cereal, boiled eggs, toast, apples, oranges, and nuts — from his O-level high school biology course, he knew the necessity of vitamins and their sources — he perused the cookbooks at WH Smith one Saturday and eventually settled on one with simple recipes. Over time he mastered four or five. (During Maureen's illness and since her death, he has returned to that cookbook for the two or three days each week that he has to prepare a meal.) Allan mailed him copies of the *Vincentian*, and he was able to follow Vincentian news, including the independence celebrations on October 27, 1979.

Around the beginning of November, he saw an announcement in the *Concordian* inviting all gay and lesbian students to a meeting in H-110. He was surprised. People could be that open here? Should he attend? What if he were to meet people there who knew him? He'd already run into eight Vincentians, who'd immigrated here and were taking evening classes at the university. All it'd take was for one of them to find out and tell the others. In no time the news would be all over St Vincent. In St Vincent, an announcement for a gay meeting would attract extortioners, evangelicals, and undercover police. The announcement came with a telephone number for those needing information. He lived then in a rooming house across the street from the hall building (the Webster Library now occupies the site). That day his classes finished at 3:15 p.m. He dashed across the road eagerly, bounded up the stairs, and without regaining his breath, phoned the number. "Gay Concordia," a male voice answered.

He hadn't planned what to say.

"Hello ... hello."

"Yes, yes. I ..."

"Go on. How can I help you?"

"I saw ..."

The fellow laughed. "You saw ... Was it something exciting?"

"I mean, I read that you are having a meeting ..."

"... of gays and lesbians in H-110. Would you like to come?"

"Yes, but I'm nervous."

"I see. You sound like you're from the West Indies. My boy-friend is from Barbados."

"Yes, I am."

"Come to the meeting. It's not against the law to be gay in Canada."

"But ... but what if someone who knows me comes to spy and spreads the information back in my country?"

"That's theoretically possible, but highly unlikely. Come to the meeting. There's nothing to fear."

So he went to that first meeting and to many others. He picked up several brochures there: about gay parents, gay counselling, gay tours, gay bars and discos. Even a list of gay doctors. By December, he felt sufficiently confident to attend the Gay and Lesbian New Year Ball at the McGill Student Union Building. That night he had his first Montreal sexual encounter with an engineering student from the Université de Sherbrooke. "In town for a little holiday fun," he'd said. "Are you game?" Of course

Gordon was game. Thereafter he skimped on food to pay for an outing at the Limelight or Le Jardin every Saturday night. It was the rare night that he didn't leave with someone. By the end of his first year, he'd contracted chlamydia, syphilis, and gonorrhea. His doctor was from the list recommended by Gay Concordia. On the questionnaire Gordon had filled out upon becoming his patient, he'd identified himself as bisexual and married. In May, three days before leaving for St Vincent, sores appeared on his penis, and Dr. Allaire insisted that he undergo three months of antibiotic injections. He told Maureen that he'd done poorly in one of his courses and the prof had urged him to retake the course that summer.

After three weeks in St Vincent, he returned to Montreal at the end of August and picked up from where he left off, until he met André and discovered that there were gays who wanted more than a one-night stand.

◆

His permanent return to St Vincent was difficult. He tried hard to contain himself, from fear of scandal, not out of fidelity to Maureen. Ever one to worry about what people would say, she stayed in their sterile marriage rather than risk criticism. She, too, convinced herself that she did it for Frida's sake, was glad Frida got the sort of father she'd always wanted for herself. In his case, it was because he couldn't fathom the thought of Frida's classmates asking her, "Is true your father is a bullerman?" And possibly Frida's coming home and asking him about it. She'd told him about nasty comments her classmates made about a student whose mother had left a marriage and gone to live with her female lover.

But there were times when his sexual attraction to men felt like a pot that was boiling over. For reasons he never understood, when he turned forty, he found he couldn't keep his eyes off attractive men, and got aroused while staring at them. Although his first relationship was with Allan, who was always slightly corpulent, it was usually the twenty-plus, slim, svelte, tall, young men, with coal-black skin and medium-size round butts that got his attention. He stared at them too long, and sometimes they noticed and responded with a wink and a bulge in their flies. There were more men *in society* — Allan's term, picked up in Jamaica, for mask-toting gays — in St Vincent than he could have ever suspected. But these young men lived with their parents, and it wasn't possible in small St Vincent, where everyone knew you, to check into a hotel with a young man and not have the information disseminated by next morning. You set yourself up for extortion too. A Monday morning, one of Allan's colleagues didn't show up for work. Two weeks later, the hospital received his resignation letter sent from London. Doc was married with a daughter who had been Frida's classmate in prep school. Eventually information circulated that Doc had been in a threesome with guys, and a fourth had hidden and taped it, and they were using it to extort Doc.

Joseph, a senior clerk in the ministry, broke through Gordon's shield. Joseph's skin was like polished ebony. When he smiled, his lips parted invitingly, and his eyes flashed. Gordon could not help staring at him longer than he should. Officially he was Gordon's research assistant. For more than a year, nothing happened. Then, one day just before lunch, Joseph came into his office with some documents Gordon had asked him to analyze. He gave them to Gordon but wouldn't leave. With his back to the office door, he stood staring at Gordon and moistened his lips periodically. "The devil finds you wheresoever you be," Lillian used to say. Gordon was mesmerized. He sat there and felt his penis pulsing. He eventually said, "Okay, Joseph. You've smelt me out. I plead guilty … let's not get into trouble."

"I'm only enjoying the smell of your cologne … just kidding," Joseph said.

Silence.

Joseph broke it. "Fine, I made the first move. The next one has to be yours."

More than a month passed. They saw each other every day. Eventually a note came to Gordon along with the documents: *Why have you been avoiding me?* He summoned Joseph to his office and asked him where he lived.

"With my aunt in Paul's Lot, but I have a friend who's willing to let us use his place."

Gordon covered his face with his hands, took a deep breath, and held it for as long as he could. He exhaled and removed his hands. "You told your friend about me!"

"Sort of." After a pause, "I didn't mention your name, though."

Gordon was skeptical. "I won't go to your friend's place."

"You have a place?"

"No."

That weekend Allan and Beth came by for supper. Gordon took Allan outside and told him about Joseph.

"You're right to be careful. He wouldn't blackmail you. He'd want to protect his job and his reputation. But you're right. He might have outed you to his friend. You could use my house in Evesham, but the neighbours will see you. They are always peeping from behind curtains and jalousies. Maybe you could get him to wear a dress and a wig. My guy does that for me."

"Joseph has a beard."

Allan laughed. "Well, if he wants you so badly, he might agree to shave it off. Of course, a month or two later, your mother and May might ask you who's the woman you've been bringing to Evesham, and eventually they'll accuse me of trying to break up your marriage."

"And what about Beth? No one has told her about *your woman*?"

"Not that I know of, though last month she said, 'It's only a matter of time before you older married men start running around. Just keep it out of my sight. Else I will get me a man and bring him to the house and into the same bed you and I sleep in, and give you a big dose of your own medicine.' I wanted to say, if he's sexy, nice-looking, and *in society*, we'd both enjoy him. You know, Gord, it won't surprise me if she knows."

Maybe Allan is bisexual after all. He wishes he were too and could have desired Maureen with the passion that Beth says Allan has. Even so, he misses Maureen now that she's no longer around. She was too uptight. He doesn't remember her having orgasms. Maybe hers were quiet. Though, if she didn't, he couldn't blame her. Not with his tepid lovemaking.

Allan keeps the Evesham house in good repair. He added a carport and replaced the external wood walls with cement. He pays a local man to keep vines from strangling the fruit trees. On public holidays he, too, is often out there trimming with a machete. Sometimes, on his way out to Evesham, he drives up Long Wall and entices Gordon to go along. He keeps a well-stocked bar. After the trimming, cleaning, and harvesting, they sit on the back porch, like they once did in elementary and high school days, and drink — Allan, rum chased with coconut water; Gordon, coconut water or lime squash — play dominoes or checkers, recall old times, and update each other on their escapades. Allan's mostly. Beth rarely goes to Evesham. Maureen never expressed a wish to go. Just before dusk, they load the car with papayas, tangerines, oranges, avocados, golden apples … the fruits available at the time of year, and return to town.

◆

When next Joseph came to see him in his office, Gordon told him that they should forget about a relationship. A month passed during which they barely acknowledged one another. Then Joseph said he was about to go on vacation, that he could spend it in St. Lucia, and Gordon could join him there for a weekend. He stared at Gordon, his eyes aglow with expectation. "Just tell your wife you'll be away on government business."

Gordon was tempted. Those eyes like marbles of amber; that ebony, silk-smooth skin; those lips that curled and uncurled like waves. He envisaged Joseph's lithe body bristling to his lips gently moving over it. He would want it to happen in full light so he could watch him writhe with pleasure. He swallowed and it broke the spell. His hands were sweating. Suddenly he thought about discovery, scandal. Plans go awry. He couldn't risk it. He was conscious that Joseph was staring at him. Without making eye contact, he said, "No, Joseph," shaking his head. "At my age, I want more than sex from a relationship." A feeling of despair came over him, and for several seconds neither spoke. "You should expect more too. Find someone you can have a happy life with."

"That won't be in St Vincent."

Gordon nodded. "You're probably right. It was what I longed for myself. Have you thought of emigrating?"

"Yes, I've tried to go to the States a few times. They won't give me a visa."

Gordon got up from his desk, hugged Joseph from behind, and kissed him on the left cheek. "You are a beautiful man," he whispered. "I hope you meet someone who can appreciate and cherish you. In another place and time, all this would have been fine. Might even have been unnecessary."

Joseph swallowed, brought up his arm, dabbed his eyes, undid Gordon's arms, and left the office.

Two years later, Joseph left for Toronto to marry a girlfriend who'd immigrated there. On Joseph's last working day, Gordon invited him to the Cobblestone for a drink. There were long periods of silence. "You'll have lots of opportunities to lead a double life in Toronto, but remember to always leave home with a condom and to say no to sex without condoms."

"I feel bad and afraid …" Joseph scratched his right cheek.

"You've had sex with her?"

"Kind of … Let's face it, I'm using her."

Gordon said nothing.

"Can I ask you a personal question?"

"Sure. I might not answer it, but ask."

"Are you bisexual or are you a masquerading queer?"

Gordon decided not to answer.

Joseph continued, "You remember that fellow? Marty? He died recently. Was active in NDP politics. Got married, but everyone knew he was gay. The marriage broke up after a few years."

Gordon and Allan had discussed Marty. "What about him?"

"Rumour had it that he couldn't get it up for his wife."

"So?"

"I'm saying that some men can't even masquerade. Did you have anxious moments before you married Maureen?"

"You know my wife's name!"

"Be serious. This is tiny St Vincent. And I have to know who I'm competing with." He smiled and squinted. "I've seen Frida too. Nice-looking girl."

Gordon bit his lip and was silent for a few seconds. *When you have a daughter, you cannot avoid thinking about the pitfalls out there. I wouldn't like Frida to end up in the situation Maureen is in or that your girlfriend will soon be in.* "Here's a bit of advice that I wish someone had given me: unless you are prepared to raise children, don't have them, and don't count on your future wife to take contraceptive measures. I'll tell you something I've discussed with only one other person, a man who was at one time the love of my life: I stayed married only because I had to be present in the raising of my daughter ... Joseph, that's the only piece of wisdom I can share with you. I would like to say to you: don't make a fool of that girl. You understand? I have a daughter. I wouldn't want a man to do that to her. On the other hand, for a gay man, St Vincent is a prison, and this marriage is your key to unlock it. If you go through with it, persuade her not to spend those thousands of dollars done for show at weddings. Threaten to call off the marriage if she doesn't agree. You'll feel better if the breakup comes. But let me beg you to be good to her in every way you can. Express your gratitude. If you leave her, tell her the truth. In Canada, you can do that without becoming a social outcast." He seized Joseph's wrist lying on the table and squeezed it. "Joseph, living a life of lies is soul-destroying. You begin with one lie and you keep on inventing others to conceal it."

Things turned out well for Joseph. They're still in touch, in-itially by letter, now via email. "The night before the wedding," he informed Gordon, "I couldn't sleep. I remembered what you said about Frida, but it was what you didn't say about Maureen — that you felt you'd deceived her — and your life of lies that obsessed me. It was to have been a city-hall wedding. I followed your advice on that. I told Isa I was calling it off and why, and that it would be okay if she got the authorities to deport me. I was totally dependent on her. I didn't have a work visa. For the next two days we didn't speak to one another. She had taken the week off work. We were sup-posed to spend our honeymoon in Niagara Falls. On the Monday morning she came and stood over me — I was lying on the couch where I'd slept the last three nights — and said, 'You should apply for refugee status ... I'll go with you if you like. And I would tell them how life is for gays in St Vincent.' Then she told me that her brother — he's a nurse at St. Michael's Hospital here in Toronto — is gay and had been blackmailed in St Vincent."

Joseph's now a Canadian citizen, a university graduate, a high school math teacher, and married to an Anishinaabe man.

He laughs. A bitter one. He'd given Joseph advice he himself could not follow. But he's glad that someone has benefited from his mistakes. *Mistakes. Can we call them mistakes? Where are the blueprints?*

Chapter 19

H E LIMPS TO THE KITCHEN, REMOVES THE FILTER WITH THIS
morning's coffee grounds, and empties it into the bin under
the kitchen sink. He gets the jar of coffee from the fridge
and takes down the coffee grinder from the cupboard above the stove.
He leaves the coffee brewing and heads off to the bathroom to shower.
Just as he is about to step into the shower cabin, the phone rings. He
listens for the answering machine to call out the number. Allan and
Beth's house number. He lets the machine answer. "Hi, Gord. It's
Beth. You've probably left for the airport, but if you haven't, call me."

He dresses quickly, pours himself a cup of coffee, picks up the
phone from the wall in the kitchen and calls Beth. She tells him
that she knows he's probably busy preparing for Frida's arrival. He
hears distress in her voice.

"What's wrong, Beth?"

She doesn't answer. Her breathing is loud.

"What's wrong?"

"Since yesterday, there's this man with a husky voice calling the
house and asking to speak to Allan, but he won't leave a message.

Then he laughs and hangs up on me. Gordon, he calls on average once per hour. I've called Allan and told him about it. He says he doesn't know who it is. I hope he puts an end to this when he comes in from Union Island this evening. This has the smell of scandal ... What time Frida's arriving?"

"She's coming on LIAT, supposedly around seven."

"That means any time. Let's hope it's before midnight. Thanks for listening to me."

"Any time, Beth. Any time."

He wonders what Allan has got himself into now. Allan's libido sometimes overpowers his reason. He has forgotten his cousin's warning from years ago. It can't be the boyfriend from Sion Hill, who disguises as a woman when he goes with Allan to Evesham. They've been together now for twenty-plus years. Gordon calls him X because Allan has refused to say his name. X was nineteen when he and Allan began dating. Allan was forty-five. He should call Allan.

He tops up his coffee, takes it into the living room, and sits in the recliner. He's tired. The pain in his neck is approaching unbearable. *All this damn deception. Allan, manage your damn life properly! I'm tired. Damn tired.* He pushes the recliner back to its maximum. *I don't care if I fall asleep. Frida, if I don't awaken before you arrive, take a damn cab. Why haven't you called? Cool it, Gordon. Cool it. Breathe in, slowly; breathe out, slowly. Perspective, Gordon. Don't lose it. If you think you are tired, then you'll have to invent another word for how Maureen felt. You could discuss your feelings with Allan. Whom could she discuss hers with?*

He's fairly certain Maureen never found out that he and Allan had been lovers. She'd have said so in her journal. Not that it didn't cross her mind. Before they got married, she must have noticed that he spent more time with Allan than with her, and that he often slept at Allan's place. Winnie was Allan's girlfriend then. Beth was on the fringes, partying with them as Maureen's close and younger friend. He remembers that Beth will be retiring next June. She's taking the sixty option. Gordon met her shortly after she began to teach at Girls' High School. Then she was twenty-two but looked no more than sixteen. Over the years he came to think that she and Maureen had found in one another the sister they'd pined for while growing up. She's five foot nine inches, slightly taller than Allan. At twenty-two, everything about her, except her behind, her personality, and her eyes (they're still big and brilliant), was petite. When Winnie learned that she taught home economics, she said, "You teach home ec? You look like you on a starvation diet." Winnie wouldn't recognize her now. Her body lavishly appreciates her delicious desserts. For about a decade now she has been see-sawing between weight gain and loss, as she begins, stops, resumes, and stops again, exercising.

◆

He'll be dead before the journal falls into Frida's hands. Antiretroviral drugs shorten their users' lives. He'll be ninety-two when Frida reads it, and, if by some miracle, he's still alive and lucid, she wouldn't want to make an old man's life miserable.

Yes, long before Frida reads that journal, I'll be dead. Quickly worn out. I don't sleep enough. Too many nightmares. No drugs to cure nightmares. Glad now I erased the file. Haven't the strength to face any crisis.

Now, my dear Beth, if you and Allan would just leave me alone. Beth, how can you not know that Allan's gay? Or are you just playing along? In that case, play along and just leave me in peace.

There's no doubt you love Allan, as much, if not more, than Maureen loved me. You're both bossy. Maureen's suited me fine. She made most of the decisions and got the credit when they turned out right and the blame when they didn't … Maureen, couldn't you have fallen in love with a decent, honest heterosexual man? A man like Claudia's husband, Joel? You were still very attractive when Frida turned eighteen.

When he got around to asking her why she hadn't left him following the AIDS diagnosis, she smiled, then swallowed. "There's a Carson McCullers story I would like you to read." They were sitting at the dining table. She went to her office and returned with a thick volume. She found the story and handed it to him. He told her he would read it later. She was crestfallen. "I'll read it. I promise you, I'll read it."

She often criticized him for not reading "anything except CARICOM reports and St Vincent's semi-literate newspapers." Sometimes Frida joined in the criticism. When the tumult over J.L. King's *On the Down Low* and E. Lynn Harris's *Invisible Life* spread from the U.S. to the Caribbean, he became engrossed in Harris's books. He read them mostly in his office and on the back porch of Allan's Evesham house. Once, however, Maureen caught him reading *On the Down Low.*

"What's that? Some text about economics?" she asked.

"Sort of." He waited and only let out his breath when he was certain she wasn't coming to the seaward end of the porch, then he went into his office and hid the book.

She complained that she, too, didn't read enough, though he can't remember her without some book or other that she was reading. Toni Morrison and Alice Walker were two of her favourite authors. She'd tried to get him to read *Beloved.* With the exception of Harris's and King's books, he can't say that after university he ever finished any of the books he began reading, unless they were books dealing with gay issues. Most of the books he read before going to university were because Allan had suggested them. A week or two later, Allan questioned him about them. It was too embarrassing to say he hadn't read them.

He read the McCullers story: "A Domestic Dilemma." Heavily annotated with Maureen's comments. Her notes interested him as much as the story, which shows a man not knowing what to do about his wife whom he loves deeply but whose alcoholism endangers the lives of their two children and forces him to hire household help he can ill afford. Without Maureen's comments he would have missed much of the story's meaning. He wouldn't have seen the relevance of the barren wintry landscape.

At breakfast the next morning, he was eager for her to ask him about it. When she didn't, he said, "Don't you want to know if I read the story?"

She laughed. "I know you read it. That triumphant look on your face says it all. I love it when the little child in you pushes aside the adult. It was one of the things that attracted me to you. Good, you read it, and what do you think?"

He couldn't answer right away. He searched for the words but couldn't find any that would state the range of emotions the story had put him through. He said, "If all literature were like this, I think I might have liked it. Thanks for your notes. I remember hearing about foreshadowing; your notes refreshed my memory. I memorized the last sentence of the story. In our marriage, I am like Emily ... 'The immense complexity of love.'" His tears came then. She reached for his hand and her eyes welled up too.

◆

He's too wound up to fall asleep. He looks at the coffee cup on the side table to his right. It's half full. He shouldn't have drunk coffee. He should just call Frida on her cell and put an end to this tense waiting for her to call. He gets up, goes to sit on the couch, and picks up the telephone on the side table beside it. He dials her number and gets voice mail. He remains seated. He thinks about calling

Allan on his cell but nixes it. Allan might tell him bothersome stuff. Bothersome stuff — that's just what might come up with Frida's visit. She has important questions for him. He feels guilty that he erased the file after copying it but knows he would erase the copy in Beth's possession if he got the chance. If Beth dies before the time elapses, the responsibility falls to Claudia. *And if Claudia dies too, before Beth, then what?*

If I could unlive his life. If only. Joseph, you don't know how lucky you are. When Maureen died, Joseph told him it was an opportunity to start over.

"How, Joseph?"

"Come to Canada. You lived in Montreal. You already know the country."

"Montreal isn't all of Canada, Joseph. And what will I do there?"

"There's lots of lonely men your age here. Get hooked up with one."

He did not answer right away. The image of sixty-two-year-old André filled his mind, and he thought of his own body, wracked by the effects of antiretroviral drugs, the arthritic pain in his neck and right knee, the limp he tries to hide when he's with others. "Joseph, in Montreal I saw those old men in the bars prowling for sex or trying to escape from loneliness. More than a few offered me money to go home with them. Even if there was a chance of meeting someone, my pension in EC dollars won't go far, not even in one of those Newfoundland outport hamlets full of moose and abandoned houses. Is that where you're hoping I'll go?"

Joseph chuckled and was silent for a few seconds. "How about the British Virgin Islands? They use EC there. It's legal to be gay there."

"Legal and cool aren't the same thing, Joseph."

"Okay, you win. I was only trying."

"Thanks, Joseph. Too late to start over. Maybe if I were forty-seven instead of sixty-seven."

◆

What a life! Once Frida came along, he didn't even have the option of suicide. Maureen's compassion denied him the punishment he felt he deserved. Of course, it comes when he's asleep. On average once a week he dreams of being caught naked in bed with a man. Sometimes it's Maureen who catches him, sometimes May, sometimes Maggie, sometimes his colleagues at the ministry. Sometimes Allan's the man he's with, sometimes Joseph, sometimes Trevor; sometimes it's some nondescript man who's threatening him with extortion.

He feels he has been unkind to Trevor. They haven't been in touch for six years. The website for his law firm is still in operation. He checked it recently. He should swallow his pride and give Trevor a call.

After the diagnosis, he'd planned to curse out Trevor for infecting him. In the end, they held each other and cried. It was a forlorn Trevor, who had just found out about his own infection a week earlier, that he met. He showed Gordon the lab report. A Trevor who, because he'd used condoms, didn't think he'd passed on the infection to him. Gordon promised that they would stay in touch, but neither contacted the other after that meeting. It's possible that Trevor thinks he got HIV from him. For what it's worth, some HIV-infected persons prefer to see themselves as victims rather than perpetrators. Moot point. Until diagnosed, all infected persons are potential perpetrators. It had taken him three years to understand this, to become this sanguine.

Maybe next week, after Frida leaves, he'll give Trevor a call. Not that Trevor needs his call. He's out to his sister and brother. They support him totally. He can openly access the HIV support group in Trinidad. There's now Euphoria, a gay club, in Trinidad, where Trevor can socialize. In St Vincent, Allan's the only person he can talk to about these issues. These phone calls Beth has been receiving signal trouble. He hopes Allan puts an end to this before it blossoms into a scandal.

Chapter 20

IT'S LATE AFTERNOON OF SEPTEMBER 12, FRIDA'S THIRD DAY in St Vincent. She and Gordon are in a private room in the male surgical ward of the Milton Cato Memorial Hospital. A strong smell of roses comes from the flowers lining the windowsill. Allan is in bed asleep in a half-sitting position. His right arm is in a plaster cast. With the exception of his mouth, nose, and eyes, his head is encased in Styrofoam. An intravenous drip and a cable linked to a monitoring machine are attached to his left arm.

Beth left the room ten minutes earlier to get something to eat. She had been there since Frida dropped her off this morning. Before leaving, she told them that the orthopaedist Dr. Khan had mentioned last night came in from Barbados early this morning, and he confirmed that the blow had fractured Allan's right cheekbone, dislocated his lower jaw, knocked out most of his teeth on the right side, and caused substantial tissue damage to the hard palate. But he was sure that Allan would recover, possibly with slight alterations in his lower jaw and maybe in his speech.

Gordon is momentarily distracted by the pings and numbers on the machine. He replays in his head the video he and Frida had seen on SVG TV the evening before: a cellphone video recorded by Allan's Evesham neighbour, Cuthbert Ryan, whose house is on a slope about fifteen yards above the road directly across from Allan's Evesham house. Cuthbert said he was putting on his pajamas when he heard the sound of glass smashing below the bank. He grabbed his cellphone and ran out onto his landing. The video tells the rest of the story. A car with the rear windshield smashed. A man holding a cricket bat stands on the porch and seems squeezed against the side of the house about a metre from the main door. The door opens and hides the man. Allan, in a green bathrobe, steps out and cautiously looks left; but as he turns to look right, the man steps from behind the door, swings the bat, and delivers a blow, which Allan partially fends off. The fending arm droops. The man swings again. Allan staggers. Falls. The man drops the bat and runs down the Evesham road. For a couple of seconds, the camera stays focused on Allan sprawled on the porch, and there are inaudible comments from neighbours who've now come out of their houses. A female voice (since identified as Rita Bullock's) shouts, "Somebody else in there. A woman. I see a woman go in with him, but she ain't come out." The camera picks up Rita emerging from behind a hibiscus hedge and descending her steps leading to the road.

"Jonah, call the police and tell them send a' ambulance," a female voice from the bank farther uphill says.

"I do it already,'" a male voice says.

Rita, in a floral nightgown, is now on Allan's porch. She enters the house. For a while, silence, then, shouting, "A woman in here; she trying to hide behind the bedroom door." There's a short silence, followed by Rita's exclamation: "Is not no woman ... O Lord, is the man that does play mas with Excelsior." The man, over six feet, dressed like a woman, bolts out the front door and races down the Evesham road. There's a throng of voices outside. Already there's a small crowd and others are coming.

Siren sounds, faint at first, get louder and louder. Next four police officers get out of their jeep. "All yo' get off the premises," the burliest of them shouts. "All yo' going contaminate the evidence. Move!" The crowd, now about twenty, parts into uphill and downhill halves. "Who witness this? Turn them damn phones off."

The newscaster takes over: "*iWitness News* has since identified the man disguised as a woman as Henry Forrester. Indeed, he lives at Sion Hill and is well known for the carnival costumes he designs. The assailant has not been identified. The police think he's hiding somewhere in the area.

"Dr. Bacchus has since been taken to hospital. We have no word on his condition."

It had to be a mistake, Gordon thought. *When did all this happen?* After Frida, Maggie, and Gordon returned from visiting Maureen's grave, Beth and Allan had taken them for supper at the upstairs restaurant at Cobblestone. They'd left the restaurant around seven thirty.

"This is a nightmare," Gordon said, got up from the recliner where he'd been sitting, and began to pace the space from the living room to the kitchen, but the pain in his right knee forced him to sit back down. "Frida," he said, "what has Allan gotten himself into?" Frida came to stand in front of him. She was crying.

"Frida, talk to me. How are we going to handle this?" He crossed the living room over to the kitchen, came back, and crossed again, before plopping down in the recliner, his right hand massaging his knee.

"I hope Uncle Al isn't seriously hurt," Frida said. "Let's call Aunt Beth and go to be with her."

"She's probably at the hospital."

He walked to the phone, but it rang before he could pick it up. Gloria. He let voice mail take it. It rang again. Claudia. He saw

Frida get up and walk unsteadily toward her bedroom. He followed her and watched as she dropped heavily across the bed. He limped back to the living room and dialed Beth and Allan's house number. The voice mail was full. He called Beth's cell. Same message. He decided to go to their house. They drove to Edinboro. They found the house in darkness. He drove to the hospital and parked the car two blocks away. Several journalists milled about outside the gate. They began shouting at him, "Mr. Wiley, Mr. Wiley, you are Dr. Bacchus's friend. Have you an opinion? Do you know who did it? Do you know Forrester? Can you make a statement?" Frida clung to his arm.

"Wiley, that you, man?" Ronald, the gatekeeper, called out from the guardsman hut. He had been a member of the Stubbs Methodist Youth Fellowship at the same time that Allan and Gordon were members of Evesham's. They'd camped together in Bequia and Chateaubelair, gone on hikes to La Soufrière and the Owia Salt Pond, and debated one another on the cultural issues affecting St Vincent. Ronald opened the gate. Two male journalists tried to enter. "Not you. Your name not Wiley." Ronald's arm stretched out to block them. "He in casualty," he said, and gave Gordon directions.

They met Beth sitting stone-faced on a plastic chair in the steaming, crowded room. There were no vacant seats. About a dozen people were standing. There were tracks on Beth's face where her tears had dried. Gordon bent down and hugged her. She squeezed his left arm. Frida bent and kissed her, then stood on her left with a hand on her shoulder. After a couple of seconds, Beth said, "Thanks for coming."

"It's all we can do, Aunt Beth."

This too shall pass, Gordon thought. *I hope it does.*

They remained there in something of a daze. People, some bloody, some smelly, came and went. Around 1:15 a.m., Dr. Khan, a Guyanese man whom Gordon had met at Beth and Allan's house on various occasions, came out to talk to them. "We tekking good care o' him, Beth. He conscious. Of course, he can't speak. The lower jaw and right cheekbone break. The right arm too. Right now, he sedated. We go operate on he this morning soon as Worrell, the orthopaedist, get in from Barbados, in 'bout three hours. You got any questions?"

"What about his brain?" Frida asked.

"No damage as far as we can see."

"Will he be recognizable after surgery?" Frida said.

"I think so ... Go home and try to get some sleep, Beth. Wait, lemme get a sedative for you." Khan left and returned in about five minutes. "I giving you Sonata. Take one when you get home. I give you enough for six nights."

Beth thanked him, then held on to Gordon's arm, and began to sob.

'"Come, spend the night at our place," Gordon said.

As soon as Ronald opened the gate, the reporters turned on their blinding lights, pushed microphones in front of their faces, shouted questions:

"Mr. Wiley, Dr. Bacchus is your friend, what do you think?"

"What condition he's in?"

"Tell us something."

"Mrs. Bacchus, how's your husband?"

"Do you know who did it?"

They followed them all the way to Gordon's car. At Market Square, Gordon breathed deeply when he saw that they were no longer following him; but as he turned to back into his house, he saw the SUV for *iWitness News* parked in his driveway.

"Get off my property," he shouted. "Leave!"

"Can you tell —"

"Just leave! Leave! Get off my property!" he shouted as he rushed at the cameraman pointing his camera at them. An excruciating pain in his right knee stopped him before he'd gone six feet. He wobbled but didn't fall. The cameraman and reporter entered their vehicle and drove off quickly. Across the street and on both sides of him, the neighbours were turning on their lights. Freckles's Rottweiler growled and yanked at its chain.

◆

It's almost noon the next day. Gordon is sitting on one of the two chairs in Allan's hospital room. Allan's asleep. Frida left ten minutes ago and said she would be gone for about an hour. Something about Beth has made Gordon uneasy. This morning, her puffy eyes implied that she hadn't slept, though she seemed asleep when Gordon looked in on her around 3:00 a.m. When she came into the kitchen around seven, she smiled at Frida but barely nodded when Gordon said good morning. He asked how she'd slept and she replied, "Okay." He didn't sleep at all. Scenario after scenario filled his head. The air conditioning was off in the bedroom, but he felt cold. He heard Beth calling the school to say she wouldn't be in. Apart from coffee, she didn't touch the breakfast that Frida made for her. Around 9:00 a.m., Frida drove her home to change her clothes and dropped her off at the hospital afterward. She seemed distant, cold, when a short while ago, she told Gordon that the orthopaedist said Allan would recover, that there would be no serious lasting damage. She left immediately after. She was probably hungry. He's probably reading too much into this.

Valencia, usually chatty, was taciturn when she came to work this morning. When Gordon walked out to his car to begin the drive here, Freckles was standing beside the fence. Gordon said hello. Freckles turned his back and did not answer. To be expected. Gordon is waiting to see how Austin will respond. Those who live in glass houses sometimes throw stones.

He stares at Allan and recalls the stratagems they had in place before they both got married. Those got mucked up by necessity and fate. At least he won't have to face colleagues day in, day out. He should end his consultancy contract with the SVG government. Initially it was for eighteen months, but they've kept renewing it. What will Allan say when his speech is restored? There'll be all the ugly gossip the trial will incite. The news at noon said that Forrester had identified the assailant and said that they knew each other well. What's going on in Beth's head? She will surely ask him if he'd known Allan was gay. What will he tell her? He must be loyal to Allan.

Chapter 21

ALLAN'S EYES ARE OPEN. GORDON WALKS TO THE CENtre of the room.

"Good to see you alive, man. Khan says that when they're finished with you, you'll be as good as new."

Allan lifts his left arm and beckons him to come closer. He takes Gordon's hand in his left hand. Frida walks to the head of the bed and kisses the Styrofoam cast. "Glad, you survived, Uncle Al. I want you around."

Allan pulls his hand from Gordon's and gestures that he wants to write. Frida goes to where her pocketbook is on the floor beside the chair she was sitting on. She pulls out notepaper and a pen. She looks around, then picks up the clipboard with Allan's chart. She tears a sheet from her pad, puts it on the clipboard and holds it up over the bed. Allan lifts his left arm and writes with his eyes closed: *I am dropping all charges.*

Frida straightens up and looks at Gordon in dismay, then turns to stare at Allan. "That's assault, Uncle Al. You can't let him get away with that."

He waves his left hand dismissively.

A long silence. The low hum of the monitor fills the room. Allan signals that he wants to write again. Frida affixes another page to the clipboard. He writes, again closing his eyes, and using his left hand: *Know what happened?*

"Sort of ... a little bit," Gordon says, and gives Frida a look of caution. "That fellow, Cuthbert Ryan, who lives on the bank above the road across from the Evesham house, told the media he heard a commotion and called the police."

Allan signalled again. Frida held the clipboard. He wrote: *Nice try, G. Beth said everything was recorded and shown on TV.*

He feels his anger surging against Beth. There's a time for everything. She shouldn't have told him this. Give the man time to recover. He looks at Frida. She's frowning.

A nurse comes into the room, says hello to Allan, checks the monitor, and installs a full bag of intravenous fluids.

"Are you in pain, Dr. Bacchus?" she asks.

Allan waves his forefinger.

"Alert the nursing station if you are. The buzzer is right beside your left hand."

He gives her a thumbs-up.

The nurse picks up his chart, writes on it, then leaves.

The silence resumes, until Dr. Khan enters the room.

"Hey, Gord. We patched up the young boy good and proper." He winks at Allan.

Gordon thinks he sees Allan's eyes light up.

"We'll have you out o' here in about a week. Right, Allan?"

Allan rotates his hand — maybe.

"Once we get the swelling down, you'll be able to suck food from a straw. You'll leave here slim as a' Olympic runner. Your libido ..." He glances at Frida and stops.

Beth comes into the room then. She says hello to Khan, moves over to Frida, and puts an arm around her, before going to stand on the opposite side of the room.

Yes, there's anger against me too.

Khan leaves then.

The two chairs in the room are on Gordon's side. Frida lifts one to take to Beth.

Beth shakes her head and waves her arm dismissively. "I'm leaving. I don't know why I'm here. You gay men ..." She shakes her head like a bull about to charge, snarls, then takes a deep breath. "I won't be used any longer." She begins walking out of the room. At the door, she says, "I have a hunch why Maureen wanted that journal to stay sealed for twenty-five years. If I have to drink coffee all night long, it will be read by tomorrow morning, and what I discover will be on the evening news. To hell with both of you!"

There's a tense silence in the room. The hum of the monitor is deafening. Finally, Allan signals that he wants to write.

He writes: *The end had to come.*

Gordon thinks of all that Maureen did to protect him. How could Allan be so careless? Involved with two guys at the same time! *Told me about Forrester. Kept the other one a secret. Probably felt I'd accuse him of recklessness. You horny bastard! At sixty-eight you should be past this. What are you trying to prove?* He remembers the warning Allan's cousin gave him decades ago and which had pushed him to marry Beth. That cousin isn't alive to see the warning come true.

Allan signals again that he wants to write:

The truth will set us free. Not pressing any charges. Gord, tell the journalists that.

"Tell them yourself." Gordon hears the anger in his voice.

Allan writes: *Send SVG TV. But be with me when they come.*

"Uncle Al's right," Frida says.

Gordon gives her a withering stare. "I don't want to be here. What difference will it make?"

"Dad, I don't care what you think. Uncle Al's right. Chill, Dad."

He wants to say, *Think before you talk, Frida. You've forgotten where you are, what life in St Vincent is like for gay people?*

He remembers that Valencia should be gone by 6:00 p.m. He checks his watch: 6:22 p.m. He pulls his cellphone from his shirt pocket and calls his house phone. She has a cellphone, but he doesn't have her number saved. He hopes she picks up. Better still that she has put the catch on the lock and left. The voice mail comes on. He phones Austin, who has a key to the house. Theo answers. He gives him the message. Gordon's fingers tremble. Sweat trickles down his side from his armpits. "Allan, I have to go now."

Allan wags a finger at him.

There are no journalists at the hospital gate. Beth must have given them the info they wanted, and they've hurried off to broadcast it. He tells Frida to drive. Before they exit Bay Street, he makes Frida stop so he can pick up copies of the midweek papers. While going up Long Wall, he tells her that he's going to depend on her to contact the media. "I can't do it, Frida. I'll tell you why in due time, and I don't want to be there when Allan meets them."

"Dad, I'm puzzled."

He raises his arm in a plea for silence and turns his head away.

The car comes to a halt at the carport.

The light is on over at Freckles's house. Freckles is sitting on his porch. Gordon says good evening, but Freckles turns his head away.

"Forget that fool," Frida says. "Forget that philandering fool." The last sentence is loud enough for Freckles to hear.

Gordon enters the house, goes into the kitchen, opens the liquor cabinet, grabs a juice glass from the drainboard, and half fills it with whisky. He opens the fridge, takes out a tray of ice cubes, and drops three into the glass. He goes to sit in the recliner and takes a huge swallow. He hears Frida rummaging around in her bedroom.

She comes out from the bedroom and asks for the phone directory. He points to the dining room. "In the drawer of the console table. What are you doing?"

"Calling the police and calling the television station to let them know of Uncle Al's wishes. They can at least call off the search for the fellow. He can come out of hiding."

He shakes his head. "Frida, Allan had surgery today. The TV folks will be there minutes after you put down the phone. They'll do anything for a scoop. You saw them at the hospital gate. Let Allan get a good night's rest. Leave it for tomorrow."

She nods. "You should give Aunt Beth a call. She has every reason to be angry, you know. She didn't ask for all this attention. The worst she'll do is hang up on you."

He contemplates her request. Swallows a few times. "You call her, Frida. She expects you to."

But then he hears a rapping at the door. Frida goes to answer it. It's Austin, accompanied by Theo. Gordon feels the weight of fatigue and the pain in his knee and neck as he gets up to meet them. He points to the couch, thanks Austin for dispatching Valencia, and sits in one of the armchairs facing the couch.

"So, pardner," Austin says, "wha' going on?"

"You know as much as me."

"A drink for you, Mr. Nichols?" Frida asks, standing under the arch demarcating the kitchen and living room.

"If you got whisky, gimme a finger with two ice cubes. Bring a juice for Theo."

"Theo, pineapple's okay?"

He nods.

"Gordon, I come to tell you that you and Allan is me good pardners; nothing ain't change between us. I glad you ain't turn your back on he. Is when a man in trouble he does know who his true friends is, yes. What condition he in?"

Gordon tells him.

"Man, I glad to hear he ain't damage worse. And Beth, how she taking it?"

With hand rotations he signals *half and half.*

"You think she going leave him?"

"I don't know."

"We got so much blasted hypocrisy in this country and damn stupid laws that force people to pretend to be what they not."

Frida comes, sets a wooden tray with the drinks on the coffee table, and hands them their drinks. She has a tumbler of juice for herself. She sits in the vacant armchair. Gordon is sitting in the recliner.

"I see they have the fellow who do it in custody. NBC Radio just announce it. A fellow from Belair. Alston Samuel. Twenty-three years old."

"I didn't hear. As you know, we were at the hospital. Been there for most o' the afternoon. Alston Samuel. Can't say I know him." He wonders why Austin brought Theo.

Austin stares at Frida and says, "You young people that travel to big countries got clear heads. You all not like them who stay here and brag how stupid they is while the rest o' the world progressing."

Frida pouts, gestures maybe, then turns to Theo. "What you think about all this, Theo?"

"All what?"

"I mean what happened to Uncle Al."

He frowns and shrugs his shoulders. "I don't know."

"Theo," Austin says, "tell her what your schoolmates did to you today."

Theo twists his lips and shakes his head.

"Painful, huh."

Theo nods.

"That fucker over there" — Austin points in the direction of Freckles's house — "one of his boys and four others surround Theo on the college grounds today chanting, 'Bu'n chi-chi man.'" He puts an arm around Theo.

"Does the principal know?" Frida says.

"Not this time," Theo says. "It happened before. I reported it the first time, and he told them to stop. When they did it a second time, I went to see him, and he looked up at me from his desk and groaned. Then he said he would handle it. Since then they've done it four more times. Most of the students don't join in. They only look on and laugh. A few girls tell them to stop. They call them lesbians."

"Ain't this damn nonsense, Gord! Why the fucking principal don't suspend them? He must be a fucking homophobe too. When the head sick — you remember Walters did say he want to light fire under gay people? You remember Ralph did play 'Chi Chi Man' at a campaign rally like if was the Labour Party anthem? Man, when the fucking head sick, what you expect from the rest o' the body?" He snorts and brings his balled fists together. His face is blood-red, his blue-grey eyes aflame.

"I have to get Theo away from here. Fast. Here ain't no place for gay people."

Theo blushes and hangs his head.

"Gordon, I don't trust those fuckers over there." He indicates Freckles's place with his thumb. "Remember that graffiti on my fence? I have a feeling is one of his boys that do it. Tomorrow I go-ing install cameras at the front and the back o' my house. If you see them up to anything funny, lemme know."

Gordon nods.

Austin snorts, then swallows. "Frida, how 'bout Canada? You think Canada is a good place for Theo?"

"Yes. I think so. Theo, you should get somebody to record the harassment. It will come in useful if you go to Canada and apply for refugee status."

"A girl from my art class recorded it with her cellphone. She sent it to me."

"Don't lose it."

A long silence.

"With your talent in painting, you can get into an art school. Easily," Frida says.

Austin nods.

Great, he has accepted to let Theo study what he wants.

"When I get back, I'll check out some art schools for you. Right off I can think of the Ontario College of Art & Design University. Mr. Nichols, tuition will be a hefty sum."

"I going spend the last penny I have to see my son happy." He stares at Theo. "Even if I have to sell this property and go live in a rented room, I will get you out o' here." He stares into Theo's face and seems to tighten his arm around him. "Thanks, Frida." He looks at her, then returns his stare to Theo. "I want you gone from this infernal place by September next year."

They sit in silence for a while. Austin downs the rest of his drink and gets up to go. Theo follows.

Standing at the door, Frida says, "Courage, Theo. Focus on your studies. Those bullies want you to destroy yourself. Don't let them win."

"I done tell him to keep away from the schoolyard at recess and lunchtime."

"Papa, they harass me on the bus too."

"Tomorrow, I going over to Glen to give the blasted principal a piece o' my mind. I will sue that fucker if anything happen to you."

"Thanks, Frida. Thanks for the information. Papa and I will work on it," Theo says, his voice higher than usual.

They leave.

Once they're out the door, Frida says, "Finally a Vincentian father who accepts his gay son. None of that foolishness about beating it out of him or taking him to see a psychiatrist. I've seen films made as late as last year in which Jamaican fathers threaten to cut their sons' throats if they discover they're gay." She stares at Gordon.

"Yes, Austin's a good father. A good father. A decent man ... Frida, I'm tired. I don't feel like talking more about any of this. Not right now. For a few years now I haven't been well."

"You never told me this."

"I'm telling you now. You had your studies and Maureen's illness to deal with. I'm telling you now so that if I'm not up to your expectations you will cut me some slack."

"What's wrong? I noticed that you limp."

He shrugs and pauses before answering. "The illnesses that come with aging: hypertension ... the works. Allan helps me manage them. No need to worry. Are you serious about helping Theo?"

"Yes. He could even stay with me until he's settled. I just moved into a two-bedroom apartment. The second room is my library, but I can work something out. He has to get out of here. He'll get refugee status. The trouble nowadays is sorting out the true claims from the bogus ones. I'll vouch for him."

"Sure, if you can help him, by all means do." He has doubts about the refugee claim. Theo is only eighteen. It strikes him that Theo is overprotected. Wonders if he could survive on his own in Canada. Hopes Frida knows what she's getting into. But he mustn't dampen her enthusiasm. "I'm going to have a hot shower and hope it will help me fall asleep. Shouldn't have drunk that whisky when I got in." *But I'm still going to take a sleeping pill.*

He glances at the newspapers Frida pushed to one side of the coffee table. A photo of Allan, in the green dressing gown, sprawled on the porch, his head in a pool of blood, takes up two-thirds of the *Vincentian* front page. *Not reading this tonight. What's in there has already happened.*

Chapter 22

I T'S 9:10 A.M. WHEN HE OPENS HIS EYES. INSIDE THE HOUSE
is quiet, but he hears the noise of traffic coming up from
Kingstown. He thinks he fell asleep quickly. He dreamed
that he and Allan were teenagers again and were having sex in his
parents' bedroom in Riley, and May, Lillian, and Ben barged in
on them. Ben said he was going to get his cutlass and kill them.
Somehow Maureen, Beth, and Frida entered the dream and joined
a group of people throwing stones at them. He gets out of bed and
goes to the ensuite bathroom to brush his teeth. Next the kitchen.
There's a cup with a used tea bag on the counter. He remembers
that it's Wednesday, Valencia's day off. Since Maureen's death, she
prefers to be off on Wednesdays and Sundays.

He doesn't feel as groggy as he thought he'd be. Sunlight
streams through the kitchen window. He looks out and sees Frida,
in khaki shorts and a white tank top, pulling up weeds in the garden. He takes the jar of coffee beans from the fridge and the coffee
grinder down from the cupboard. He grinds enough for two cups
in case Frida wants one. He goes to the living room and turns the

radio on, in the middle of an interview with Pastor Daniel Baynes, chairman of Vigilant Conscientious Christians.

"Pastor Baynes, what's your reason for organizing this demonstration?"

"To show that we won't sit back and let sin gain the upper hand in this country. The Bible is crystal clear. The penalty for homosexuality is death. Not just the Old Testament. St. Paul is clear on that."

"So, are you and your followers calling on the government to execute gays?"

"Not me and my followers — God."

"Don't you think this is going too far? The penalty for buggery is ten years in prison. That's not enough for you?"

"No. I worry for my children and grandchildren when the perverts leave jail …"

"Your grandchildren!"

"Yes. You didn't read the document that God put in the hands of Anesia to warn us? They have a secret campaign under way to turn all the youths gay."

"But that document is fake."

"Not at all. Sister Baptiste is a' upright woman. She won't circulate a fake document. I'm calling on Christians from all denominations to come out this Friday at twelve noon and demonstrate in front of the prime minister's residence and demand that Ralph, the government of St Vincent and the Grenadines, the government that I pay my taxes to, uphold the laws of the Almighty and protect our children. The Bible says —"

"Thanks, Pastor Baynes. We've run out of time. We have been talking with Pastor Daniel Baynes, chairman of VCC — Vigilant Conscientious Christians. We welcome your comments."

Gordon turns the radio off and reminds himself to watch the time. He wants to hear the ten o'clock news. He wonders if Frida called the police and the media.

He returns to the kitchen and pours his coffee. He is not surprised about the demonstration. Evangelicals have latched on to gay bashing to lure away Anglicans and Methodists. Not to be outdone, Methodists and Anglicans, too, have turned up the anti-gay rhetoric. Last year, Bentley Holder, the dean at St. George's Anglican Cathedral, sounded like he wanted all gays hanged. Gordon limps to the recliner, puts his coffee cup on the corner table, and sits.

So Baynes wants all gays dead. Suddenly he becomes fearful for Theo. He hopes Austin doesn't get into trouble at the community college today. He won't find allies there or among the police. Maybe he should keep Theo from school until things cool down. You never know what those fools might do if Theo says the wrong thing. They want him to say something nasty to give them an excuse to beat him up. On that, very little has changed since he and Allan were in school.

He hears the door open and turns to see Frida stepping out of her flip-flops. She wipes the sweat from her forehead with her right forefinger. It leaves a smudge of dirt. She should have worn Maureen's gloves.

"Hi, Dad. All refreshed from your sleep?"

He nods. "You?"

"I couldn't sleep."

"Did you call the TV station and the police?"

"Yes, as soon as I got up.

"Dad, things have gotten a little more complicated since last night. Let me go wash my hands first." She goes off to the general bathroom and returns dabbing her forehead with a facecloth.

"Aunt Beth sent me a text. She says she has explosive information … Dad! You're shaking. What's wrong?"

"My heart. It's beating crazy."

"You're still in your pajamas. Go back to bed. Here, let me give you a hand."

"It will pass. I'll just push this recliner back some more. It will calm down. Happens when I'm stressed."

"I wonder if Uncle Al understands the problem he's created for a whole lot o' people."

"Don't blame him. Sex is like food."

"And some people are gluttons, right?"

"Allan has an outsized libido."

Frida frowns. "Really, Dad. How do you know that?"

"We've been close friends since … since preschool." He holds his breath, hoping she won't question him about this.

Silence. His heart and his breathing have settled. He feels more in control. "I wonder what sort of mischief Beth is up to. Diplomacy isn't her strong point."

"Dad, she has every right to be angry. Uncle Al has splashed a lot of mud and some of it has landed on her. Give her time to deal with it."

He glances at the clock above the archway to the dining room: 9:55 a.m. He asks Frida to turn the radio back on to hear the ten o'clock news. She goes to the coffee table and picks up the remote. The radio comes on in the midst of a lecture about diabetic care. He stretches his hand for the remote and puts the radio on WE FM in the middle of Fya Empress's "Ah Ketch It." Next, he clicks to NBC just as the news begins.

"There are new developments to report in Dr. Bacchus's situation. Yesterday we reported that the police had Alston Samuel in custody. We have just learned that he has been released, that Dr. Bacchus won't be pressing charges for assault and battery and property damage.

"Mrs. Bacchus announced this morning that she will be meeting with a lawyer tomorrow to file for divorce. In her words, 'The half has not been told.' Our reporter pressed her further. She said it was all she was saying for the moment.

"José has resumed hurricane strength and may yet make landfall somewhere on the Atlantic coast of the United States ..."

He turns the radio off.

"Dad, get up. Get dressed. We have to go to Uncle Al, right away. What's wrong with Aunt Beth? Couldn't she have waited until Uncle Al's released from hospital? I'll shower and change quickly."

◆

Allan's asleep and alone when they get to the hospital.

Frida whispers to Gordon, "Yesterday, he was still under the effect of the anaesthesia. It's today that he'll feel the full force of the pain."

"I'll see if they'll let me talk to the doctor in charge. It might be Khan." He leaves Frida in the room and walks to the nursing station.

The nurse sitting at the desk — a stringy Black woman, her white nursing cap perched atop a brown jute wig, squints at him.

"Good morning, nurse. Would it be possible for me to speak with the doctor assigned to Dr. Bacchus?"

She tosses her head this way and that before she answers. "He's not available. These are not visiting hours. Come back after lunch."

"I'm family. Is Dr. Khan on duty?"

She frowns then cuts her eyes at him. "Mister, the doctor ... on duty ... is not ... available. Are you hard of hearing?" She straightens up and her nostrils flare.

"My name is Gordon Wiley. Dr. Bacchus was the best man at my wedding. He is my daughter's godfather. I have entertained Dr. Khan at my house on many occasions." The last statement is a lie.

She raises her arms, palms facing him, glares at him, then picks up the phone, and says, "Dr. Khan, a Mr. Gordon Wiley, who says he knows you, is at the nursing station and is demanding to talk to you ... Mister, he's coming." She gets up, cuts her eyes at him, walks down the corridor, and disappears into a room.

He feels a bit guilty pulling rank and bullying the woman. She didn't make the rules and shouldn't be dumped on for enforcing them. He'd apologize to her if she returns before he leaves.

Khan comes and escorts him to his office on the ground floor. He offers Gordon the armchair and sits at his desk. "Life is a bitch, eh, Gord. Just imagine. You manage your life for years and years, and one day it mash up like a paper bag in a rainstarm. All the same, Allan nuh the first man whose tolo get he in hot water, nuh. This would o' been a nine-days wander if was a woman. Them comedian-fellars would o' make a few jokes praising he for his virility and nothing more. I hear some years back the wife o' you-all governor general take off she shoes and beat his mistress on a Kingstown street. I like the calypso you all make 'bout it:

> Me husband is the GG
> Dat don' mean community property
> Keep away from he zizzy
> Else I go beat you
> From here to eternity."

Gordon laughs.

He remembers hearing about the incident when he resumed work after his studies in Montreal, but he doesn't remember jokes about it or the calypso.

Khan sighs. "So I see these backward churches calling on the government to execute gay people. You should o' hear them on a call-in show last night. In fairness, not all o' them wanted to hang gay people. Most wanted the government to send the 'bullerman-them'" — he makes air quotes — "that is the word they use — to jail for ten years. I go like to tell them, be careful what allyou wish

for: Them jail sentences and the death penalty what you all call-
ing for now might well fall on your children and grandchildren.
Nature don' pick and choose which pickney it going turn gay, yes.
Me father come from a family o' five boys. He turned out straight.
Two brothers turned out gay. One went to England and one drown
heself in the Essequibo same day he turn twenty-one."

"Their churches teach them that people choose to be gay,"
Gordon says. "My mother-in-law wants to see all gays lined up
against a wall and shot. She's Pentecostal ... How's Allan?"

"He in a lot o' pain today. To be expected. We waiting for the
swelling to go down so he can take liquid food through a straw. He
can go to the toilet on his own, with a nurse at his side in case o'
vertigo. We sedate him a hour ago."

"You heard Beth's planning to leave him?"

"No!" Khan presses his lips, cups his right fist in his left hand,
and shakes his head. "Shit!"

"She told the media so this morning."

"You think she did know all the time and acting now 'cause it
public?"

"I doubt it."

"Tell meh something, nuh. You fellows, you all heading for
seventy and got more libido than me, in me forties ... you read the
Vincentian yet?"

Gordon shakes his head.

"It quote one o' the onlookers. She say Allan use to carry a different woman there ... two, three times a week. A short one and a
tall one. One hot man. I does be so damn tired when I get home,
after these twelve-hour shifts, I lucky if I get it up for Selena once
a fortnight. You all have some plant here, some kind o' natural
Viagra, that you all not telling outsiders bout? But, Gord, we
boy is something else." He chuckles. "Made them fellows wear
dresses and all that. One inside the house with him. One outside

waiting with a cricket bat. He should o' go inside and turn it into a threesome."

Gordon winces, then forces a smile.

"Come back to Beth. Why she so hurry to divorce the man? Maybe them fellows getting what he don't give she. She could o' at least wait 'til the man could talk."

"It's to punish him. Understandable. But we shouldn't make those kinds of decisions in the heat of the moment. I hope the law-yer tells her that. She knew Allan was having extramarital affairs. She told Maureen about it. But she'd thought it was with a woman. Doc Khan …"

"Omar, man. Just Omar," Khan says, shaking his head.

"Omar, let's just support Allan through all this. I would say Beth should too, but …" He shouldn't go there.

"You have me word, Gord. Selena and I talk 'bout it last night. If he need a place to stay when he leave here, he more than welcome to stay with us until things settle."

"My place too. We've been like this since childhood." He holds up a clasped middle and forefinger.

Khan's brow furrows.

"By the way, the nurse who called you informed me that it wasn't visiting hours."

"I go take care o' that now." He picks up his prescription pad and writes on it. He tears off the page and hands it to Gordon.

The note reads: *I give permission for Mr. Gordon Wiley, who is a close friend of Dr. Bacchus, to visit him at any time.*

"My daughter, Frida. Remember her?"

Khan nods. "She was with you the other night."

"She's in the room with Allan. I have to rejoin her. Write one for her too."

"Al's probably too drowsy for company," he says while writing. "Leave and come back in about two hours."

Gordon re-enters Allan's room. Allan's still asleep. Frida is standing at the foot of the bed. There's fright in her eyes.

He whispers, "What's wrong, Frida?"

"I just got a text from Aunt Beth. She wants to meet with me alone." She stares into space and rotates her hands. "Dad, is she going to tell me stuff about you?"

"Just go and hear what she has to say, and we'll discuss it afterward."

His cell vibrates. He takes it from his shirt pocket and sees it's May's number. He remembers then that they are supposed to be at the lawyer's office at one fifteen. He exits the room and answers.

"Gordon, I leave a message for you and you ain't call me back, and when I try again it say your box full."

He cannot tell her he hasn't listened to his phone messages for the last couple of days. She has to know what's going on.

"Where are you?"

"At Allan's bedside," he whispers.

She swallows her saliva. Silence, then, "Don't forget the lawyer expecting us at one fifteen."

"I'll be there. It's just a short walk from the hospital. See you later."

His body feels rigid. She did not ask how Allan was. He re-enters the room. He wants to tell Frida this, but restrains himself. Allan might overhear the conversation. He begins to pace, but the pain in his right knee forces him to sit.

Frida is frowning and staring at him.

He puts a finger on his lips, points to Allan, and whispers, "We'll talk later."

She nods.

"I have to meet May at the lawyer's office in about an hour," he continues whispering. "We'll be there for a few hours. I guess you'll stay here with Allan. If the nurses ask you to leave, show them this." He gives her Khan's note. "I must go eat something. This tension is chewing up my gut. What can I bring you?"

"A beef roti and a bottle of mauby."

He glances at Allan. "Don't eat it in here."

She rolls her eyes. "Dad, please!"

At the food counter, the line is long. He won't have time to eat here. He orders two rotis and two bottles of mauby to go. By the time he loops back to the hospital and again to Back Street, it's one twenty. From a distance, he sees May anxiously glancing at her cellphone. *Be calm when you meet her, Gordon.*

They mount the stairs to the office of Grafton Hathaway, QC. The receptionist — a pudgy, fifty-something beige-skin woman wearing a blond wig, white blouse, and navy blue skirt — points to a two-seater upholstered in black vinyl and says the lawyer will be with them shortly.

Gordon unwraps his roti and notes the frown on the receptionist's face. Almost an hour later, Hathaway, panting and florid, sweat streaming from his brow, comes into the office. May chose him. Gordon doesn't fully trust him. He's descended from Mount Pleasant Bequia Whites, who not so long ago stoned Blacks who ventured into their village.

Hathaway enters an office door behind the receptionist's desk. He calls them inside ten minutes later. The drawing up of the papers is simple but long. With the exception of two acres of land that May leaves for Albert, their mysterious half-brother, or his heirs, she wills her part of the estate to Frida. They give each other power of attorney over their affairs, with Frida as deputy. It's almost five when they leave Hathaway's office. He accompanies her to the bus terminal. She's uncannily silent.

When he can no longer endure her silence, he says, "It's terrible what has happened to Allan."

"God don't let sin stay in darkness forever. What in darkness have to come out into broad daylight."

How to respond to that? "It's terrible just the same."

"An educated, intelligent man like Allan choose to indulge in that kind o' nastiness. I not sorry for him at all."

Whoa. He says nothing.

"You did know he into that kind o' *duttiness*?"

He doesn't answer.

"No wonder he don' believe in God."

"May, Allan is in hospital with his head encased in Styrofoam and his right arm in a cast!"

"If he been living in one o' those countries where they does hang bullerman he would o' been worrying 'bout more than a busted head and a broken arm. I's one o' those who think bullermen belong in jail."

"May, Allan is my closest friend!"

She stopped, turned, and stared at him stonily, then said, "How come *you* not worried 'bout your reputation?"

"What reputation?"

"So you approve! You approve of his behaviour! You not 'fraid people will tar you with the same brush? Birds of a feather flock together."

"I don't care what people tar me with."

"Well, I is your sister, and I care. People is known by the company they keeps."

"And a friend is a friend in good times and bad. All that happened is Allan got exposed about something that goes on all the time in secret — without the violence and talk and all that."

She snorts.

They arrive at Little Tokyo. A minivan for the Kelbourney–Riley route is about to leave. She boards it, sits, then calls out to him, "When you bringing Frida to visit me?"

He pretends not to hear and walks out to Bay Street, goes into Veira's Supermarket, where it's quieter, and phones Frida to let her know he's on his way. She says Beth's in the room and that Allan's awake.

Seven minutes later, he's at the hospital. Beth is gone. Frida is red-eyed. She has been crying. A manuscript lies on the chair next to the one she's sitting on.

"Where's Beth?" he asks without taking his eyes off the manuscript.

"She left. You missed her by two minutes. She wanted to deliver this to you in person." She points to the manuscript.

"Maureen's memoir/journal?"

Frida nods.

He stares at Allan. Allan makes dismissive gestures with his left hand.

"What did Beth say, Frida?"

"Not a lot. She read two short passages where Mom wrote that you infected her with HIV, and that you had a boyfriend in Trinidad by the name of Trevor."

"She didn't say anything more?"

"No. But there was hate in her eyes and her lips were pulled back in scorn. I've never seen her like that. I wanted to run out the room."

He's silent. Frida begins to cry again.

"Dad, Uncle Al's waving for your attention."

Allan gestures that he wants to write. Frida picks up the clipboard from the trolley with the monitor and affixes a sheet to it. She hands it and a pen to Allan. He writes, *Gordon, escape while you can. Stay away until this dies down.*

Gordon shows the text to Frida.

"Dad, Uncle Al's right. Go to Trinidad. Stay with Trevor or in a hotel. While you're there, get a tourist visa for Canada and come to Toronto."

Allan gives a thumbs-up.

"I'll think about it."

"Dad, you have to act on it right away. Tonight. Aunt Beth said she was going to share this information with the media."

She violated Maureen's wishes. No point telling the media that. Nothing newsworthy in that. A deep feeling of appreciation for Maureen fills him. Too deep to control. Tears come.

When the crying stops, he says, "Beth said nothing at all except to read from the manuscript?"

"Before she read, she called Uncle Al a fucking viper."

Allan signals again. He writes: *You're both exhausted. I'm all right. Go home, have a drink, relax.*

They leave. At the car, Frida gets in on the driver's side.

As they drive past the market, he remembers May's complaint that Frida hasn't visited her yet. Frida will have to go alone. May's statements have left him with a gnawing feeling. He doesn't want to say it, but what he feels is betrayal, disloyalty.

"Frida, you're leaving on Sunday. That leaves you tomorrow, Friday, and Saturday. May asked when were you coming to see her. And you haven't yet visited Maggie. You must visit Clem too. He needs the visit most of all. I suggest you go to see May tomorrow. Phone her when we get in. You and I will visit Clem together. I hope he isn't aware of all this commotion."

Chapter 23

IT'S 11:30 P.M. ON SATURDAY. EARLIER TODAY HE WAS EXCITED when Allan wrote that he'd had his first intake of liquid food earlier. He also lifted his right arm a couple of inches. Now he has a clipboard, paper, and pen at his bedside.

But the elation vanished when Allan wrote: *Made a deal with Beth. Won't contest the divorce. She said if I gave her the house, she won't cause any more trouble for us. I accepted. Gordon, leave SVG. Go to Canada or Trinidad and stay with Trevor.*

"Uncle Al, where would you live?"

The Evesham house.

Frida's reply was a screwed-up face.

They remained for a short while longer. In silence. Frida kissed Allan goodbye and said, "I want to be one of the first people you talk to when this cast comes off your head."

He beckoned Gordon to come closer, held his hand, and squeezed it. Then signalled wait. He wrote in large print: *Bye, Gordon. Please take the plane out tomorrow. Stay in a hotel if you have to. No one should suffer more than he has to* — and held it up so Frida could read it too.

"I agree," Frida said.

Back home, Gordon called Trevor. Trevor listened, offered no commentary, but accepted to lodge him while his application for a tourist visa to Canada was being processed. Online, Gordon booked a flight for the next day, thirty minutes after Frida's. An hour later, he packed a small suitcase. Around 5:00 p.m., he called on Austin, told him he was going away for a few weeks, and asked him to keep an eye on the house for him. Austin offered to drive them to the airport.

◆

Everything feels topsy-turvy. As he opens the cupboard to get the coffee grinder, his head begins to spin. He holds on to the kitchen counter until it passes. He gets the grinder and then the jar of coffee from the fridge and opens the tap to get the water. "None for me," Frida calls from the corridor to her bedroom. He sits at the kitchen table and waits for the coffee to finish brewing. He wants to be fair to Beth. He wants to be angry with Allan. He feels as if he's on a battlefield dodging enemy bullets from all directions. What is Frida thinking? He's afraid to ask her. He knows she's inside reading the journal. She knows the two crucial facts he wanted hidden from her. Tonight she'll be mulling over them. The storm, if there's one, will come in the morning.

The brewing is finished. He pours himself a cup, goes to sit at the dining table, and perfunctorily turns over the pages of the manuscript. Eighty-four printed pages. He looks up and sees Frida frowning at him from the archway between the kitchen and the living room.

"Dad, don't be reading that now, and why are you drinking coffee at this hour? You made the travel arrangements?"

"Yes."

"Good." She points to the manuscript. "Leave that for later. You'll have lots of time. Go have a shower, take another drink, and go to bed."

He doesn't answer.

She comes to the table and reaches for his coffee.

"Leave that alone," he says in a menacing tone.

Frida shakes her arms in exasperation, leaves, and goes into her bedroom.

He gets up, goes into his office, retrieves the flash drive, comes back to the dining room for the coffee, and goes into his bedroom. He puts the cup on the dressing table, sits in the armchair beside it, takes his tablet off the dressing table, puts it in his lap, and inserts the flash drive.

Maggie's homophobia comes into his thoughts. May's. He remembers Allan's tales of woe about Ephraim. He doubts Beth will keep the information secret. She will feel it's unfair that Allan is exposed, and think he should be too, that Vincentians should know he'd infected Maureen with HIV. *Can I live here and face that? Can I look Maggie in the face again? She would believe Maureen died of AIDS, not cancer. Oh, the satisfaction she'll have that she was right all along, that I didn't love Maureen.*

His left knee is stiff and painful. The pain in his neck is throbbing. Maybe if he had been exercising ... In Montreal, there was a gym in André's building, and André had got him into the habit of exercising; he'd promised André he'd continue. If he'd continued, he be less stressed. Seems André had given up too. He thinks of taking two night Tylenols, begins to get up, but pain shoots from his knees down to his ankles. He remains seated and his mind returns to May. *Such a self-righteous ... what's Allan's word? Sanctimonious.*

I wouldn't want her to be part of a jury trying anyone for homosexuality. What will happen to our relationship now? Turn this tablet off. But he doesn't. Instead he scrolls down several pages.

January 15, 2015

I couldn't sleep last night. Everything I ate seemed to be fermenting in my gut. Today I feel like a balloon begging to be pricked. The tragic news we've been subjected to for the last three days is not helping. Seven killed at Rock Gutter. Near Fancy. Went there one time. Had just begun dating Gordon. Allan drove. Four of us were in the car. Allan was with Winnie then. Two things I remember: St. Lucia looking like it was a stone's throw across the sea and the steep ascent of the hill into Fancy. I couldn't understand why anyone would choose to live in such an area. I remember closing my eyes as we descended the hill on our way back and hoped the brakes would hold.

I can't hide my health problems anymore. On Sunday Allan and Beth came by. "Mo, you don't seem well," Allan said.

"I feel all right."

"No, you don't," Beth said. "Your eyes are yellow. You've lost at least ten pounds. That dress is swallowing you."

On Monday Allan phoned me from his office and said he'd made a medical appointment for me in Barbados for January 20, and, depending on the tests, I might have to stay a few days.

"Allan, we don't have any money. It's all frozen at Building & Loan."

"Okay. I'll pay for the ticket."

"I won't let you do that."

"Put your phone on speaker and call Gordon."

Gordon came. Allan repeated what he'd said.

"Maureen, you have to go," Gordon said. "Never mind the money. We'll manage."

"My colleague Barry will arrange housing for you. Barry's gay. It's he I get your meds from. Don't worry about the money. Barry will cover it and I'll reimburse him."

"I'll go with you," Gordon said.

"Yes, Gord, you should. One thing more: all this will be done in your real names."

●

I hope Mother doesn't insist on seeing me. She'll pester me with questions that I don't want to answer. Gordon said that on Saturday, when he took her shopping, she wanted to stop by. He told her I wasn't home. That excuse is wearing thin. Wouldn't surprise me if she shows up here unannounced. She's afraid of spending money — fears running out before she dies — otherwise she would have already come by taxi. If I could manage on my own, I wouldn't let Valencia come either. Nowadays she's unusually quiet and sometimes I see fear in her eyes. I should ask her to tell me what she's thinking. Of course, she could be having her own problems.

Now, I wait for the diagnosis. It's all I can do: wait. Five days to go. And after that I don't know how long the wait will be. Whatever it is, maybe pills will fix it. If not, I hope it will be quick.

●

February 1, 2015

This might be my last entry here. I don't want to be penning maudlin thoughts. Last night I dreamt that Gordon asked me what I would like said in my obituary.

I arrived in Barbados on the evening of January 19, weak to the point of being dizzy from fasting and the "washing out" before a colonoscopy and gastroscopy. Grateful that Gordon was with me. I suddenly began recalling the names of the Barbadian students I was with in university. For years I exchanged Christmas cards with three of them, but eventually the friendships fizzled. In my last card from Elizabeth, she told me that Helen, who'd got a Ph.D. from London and had become a professor in Michigan, had died. That was seven years ago. Now I wonder if Elizabeth is alive. When Gordon and I made the trip to North America, she made us come a day early and overnight with her in her beautiful house in St. Joseph. If I hadn't been in such a pathetic state, I'd have tried to contact her.

We stayed at the Kings Beach Hotel. Those ten days in Barbados … I relied on Gordon to get me where I needed to go. Morphine blunted the pain but kept me woozy.

The crucial moment in Barry's office: a small room with large windows on two sides. It was midmorning and sunny outside. Pale green vertical blinds softened the light inside. My file was open on his desk. The silver chain from his glasses reached down to about six inches below his chin. The glasses amplified the size of his light-brown eyes. Gordon sat on my left.

"Maureen, the cancer has metastasized. Know what that means?" Barry said, rubbing his forehead and looking at me.

After a while Gordon said, "Yes, we do."

"Several organs: liver, stomach, pancreas, for sure."

"Anything we can do?" Gordon said.

"There's chemo. I won't recommend it."

"What do you recommend?" Gordon said.

"Pain control — Allan will supply the drugs you need. Maureen, try to lead as normal a life as possible until the end comes. Distract yourself as much as you can. But talk about your illness if you feel the need to. Eulogizers often say that this or that person never complained, took it all in stride. I'm not sure that's a good thing."

Silence.

"This will get worse, won't it?" Gordon said.

"Yes. You might have to resort to hospice care."

"Never!" I said, speaking for the first time. "I'll die in my own house."

"Then you might need the services of a nurse. Maybe more than one. Gordon, be careful about overexerting yourself."

Until Barry said that, I had forgotten that I was taking meds for HIV. Resentment welled up in me against Gordon and I began to cry. Gordon put his arm around me. It took willpower not to push it off.

"Did ... did ...?" Gordon said.

Barry frowned.

"Did the HIV ..."

"... cause it?" Barry shook his head. "Not that I know of."

He, too, is gay. Probably going out of his way like this to allay Gordon's guilt. I could ask Allan, but he is Gordon's friend. And what difference would it make?

What is it about a diagnosis that suddenly makes you feel worse? I ate solid food — not much of it, and yes, it bloated me — before going to Barbados. Now it just sits in my gut. Two days ago, Gordon began to prepare broths for me. Yesterday he brought me Boost. It's thick and I have trouble swallowing it and it also stays in my gut.

Gordon wants May to come and give Valencia a hand. I said no. Since my return I barely have the energy to wash myself. I've stopped looking in the mirror.

Feeling nauseated now. Will have to come back to this.

•

November 17, 2015

Didn't make it back here all this time. Today's a rare day. My head feels heavy and I can barely keep my eyes open, but I'm lucid. Didn't think I'd still be alive. Alive? Half alive, maybe less.

I reread the first few pages of this journal — it has turned out to be not a memoir after all — and saw where I wrote that I would come "back, revise, reorder, and expunge." I won't have time to finish pouring out, never mind revise.

Frida has taken a week off from work to come and see me. It takes the pressure off May, who came over my objections. She neglects her farming on the days Valencia is off. Gordon has relieved Valencia from cleaning the house and doing the laundry, so she can be with me when I need her. Seeing the state I'm in, she's offered not to take her vacation this year … what a burden I've become to everybody!

Mother, too, wants to help care for me. I said no. She's half crippled from arthritis; she'll only end up exhausting herself, and her bossy personality will further upset me. She comes on Sundays after church, her pastor drives her.

Of course, Gordon has to take her back home. This Sunday she was still here at 8:00 p.m. Claudia and Beth, who came around 11:00 a.m., had long left. I was exhausted and tried to tell her without coming out and saying it. Finally, I whispered to Frida to take her home.

"Frida, you're telling me I'm not welcome?"

"No, Gran. It's just that I can see Mom's exhausted and Dad's tired. Let's go." I heard Frida jangling the keys. Over the phone, Mother complained that we hurried her out of the house and she did not have time for her usual prayer. Mother believes in miracles and thinks that her faith will make me well.

I didn't think this body would have resisted for so long. Barry said soon. Found out from Allan that Barry owns a house in Bequia. He dropped in to see me two weeks ago. Barry Blumenthal, descended from the first Jews who settled in Barbados.

Got to end this now. My eyes are blurring and I need a shot of morphine.

She lived for another ten months, the last two weeks of it in a coma. Valencia looked after her during the day. May continued to come on Valencia's days off. Gordon took over on evenings and during the night. Maggie kept up her offer to help. Gordon said no. The cost of taxis and the walk in from Sion Hill kept her from coming. She berated Gordon for not coming to get her. Clem came to see Maureen twice. She didn't speak to him. Was indifferent to the trouble he put himself through to come. Gordon doesn't understand. Why hold on to such rancour? The second time, Clem, waiting on the side porch in his wheelchair for the attendant, sobbed. Wanted to come a third time, but by then Maureen was in a coma. Wanted Maureen to say that she had forgiven him. Why withhold that tiny relief from a suffering, guilt-ridden old man? Why? For someone who made some of the best observations he'd ever heard about life, usually in her discussions with Claudia and Allan — "The templates for living were designed by people and institutions intent on controlling us for their benefit, for wealth, for pleasure, or just the joy they get from cruelty.... Our journey through life is a record that only we can dimly read, most of it remains obtuse." He will be always proud of her. Did he ever tell her how much he admired her? Forgave him, understood society's role in his wrongs against her, but couldn't forgive Clem.

◆

He feels pain spreading from his knees to his hips and back. He checks the time on the tablet: 3:37 a.m. He grits his teeth, stands, and hobbles to the bathroom to urinate and get Tylenol. He decides on the daytime ones. He doesn't want to go to sleep right away. He limps out to the living room and slumps into the recliner.

◆

He awakens in the middle of a dream from Frida's calling, "Dad, wake up. You'll be late for your flight." In the dream he's at Building & Loan. Someone is telling him that his account is empty.

What flight? Then he remembers. There's bright sunlight in the room. His full bladder forces him to get up instantly. He brings the recliner to the sitting position, presses the armrests with all his might, and cautiously straightens himself out. His right knee is stiff, but not overly painful. The pain in his neck is less acute. He'll have to use his credit card for everything. He mustn't forget to ask Frida if she has Canadian or American money. Preferably American. Trinidadians snub all but American currency.

While exiting the bathroom, he remembers Valencia. He goes to his office, takes notepaper and his chequebook from his attaché case. He sits at his desk and scribbles a note, thanking her for her service, and writes her a cheque for two months' wages. He'll ask Austin to give it to her. An awkward way to end someone's services, he thinks. She looked after Maureen with a devotion he can't find words for, especially those weeks when she was in a coma. He'll find a better way when he comes back. *Am I coming back? Of course, you're coming back. I'm not so sure.* He thinks of May then. He'll have to call her from Trinidad. Maggie too, so she'll make arrangements to get her groceries. *This has all the marks of an elopement.*

He goes to the dining table, picks up the manuscript, and takes it to his office. For a moment he considers shredding it. Instead, he puts it into his filing cabinet, locks it, and takes the keys out from the top drawer of his desk. *I'll be back when the commotion dies down. Won't stay more than two months.*

He meets Frida standing in the dining room. She effuses one of Maureen's perfumes and is wearing Maureen's gold bangles that were a gift from him. She's dressed in grey sneakers, baggy beige jeans, and a dark brown top, clothing that blends well with her dark-brown complexion. He smells coffee brewing and hears it dripping into the pot.

"Go get ready, Dad. We have to be at the airport in an hour."

The phone rings. Frida picks it up.

"Austin?"

She nods.

"We'll be out in five minutes, Mr. Nichols."

Next his car pulls up in the driveway. They take the luggage out to it.

◆

Gordon and Frida are at the airport. They've checked in but haven't yet cleared security. He notices Frida looking anxiously at him. She has less time than he. "Go ahead," he tells her. "Your flight is before mine. I need to sit here and think a few things through. I have to call May, as well."

"But you can think and call her while inside."

"Just go on in, Frida. I'll come in a short while," he says almost in a whisper.

She raises her eyebrows and begins to walk to the security gate. At the gate she turns to stare at him. Her eyebrows are still raised.

He blows her a kiss.

He heads to the LIAT counter and says he'd like to have a refund. The clerk, a thirtyish bespectacled, mixed-race man, tells him to do it online since he bought the ticket online. He steps out the terminal building just as a cab is dropping off passengers. He takes the cab amidst insulting shouts from the regular airport cab drivers.

As he goes to turn the key in the lock at home, his cellphone rings.

"Dad, where are you? I'm about to board. I didn't give you a goodbye hug."

He takes a deep breath. Should he tell her? "Sorry, Frida. I got lost in my thoughts. Wasn't aware of the time. Have a safe flight. Thanks for coming to be with me. I wish your stay could have been a happy one."

"It's all right, Dad. I'll see you in Toronto within a week or two."

"Have a safe flight, Frida."

Austin is at the bottom of the driveway.

"Man, wha' going on?"

Gordon puts a finger on his lips and points in Freckles's direction. He waits on the porch for Austin. They enter the house via the kitchen. They cross over into the living room. He motions for Austin to sit on the sofa. He sits on an armchair and faces Austin.

"So, pardner, enlighten me. Wha' happening?"

He relates the story of his relationship with Allan. He excludes infecting Maureen with HIV and his relationship with Trevor.

For a long time neither speaks.

"You see, Austin, Beth is divorcing him. I can't just up and go to Canada. I want to be here to support him."

Austin swallows, then moistens his lips. "Yes, man, that is the decent thing to do. I am one friend you not going lose."

"Thanks."

There's a long silence.

Austin gets up to go. Gordon walks with him to the door. At the door Austin hugs him. "Keep your courage, pardner. All the foolishness in the papers and on the air will cool down. Be there for your friend, pardner. Be there for him."

Austin exits and Gordon sits back down. There's only the slightest trace of pain in his knee and neck. He doesn't remember taking any Tylenol since he woke up. Maybe he did and forgot.

His cellphone rings. "Dad, I've just landed in Barbados. Is your flight on time?"

"I don't know."

"What you mean you don't know?"

"I am home, Frida."

A long silence.

"Dad, you're sixty-eight and seropositive! You don't need all this stress. What if Aunt Beth changes her mind and gives Mom's journal to the media?"

"If she does, she does. There are some things, Frida, that we shouldn't run away from. Besides, Allan has always been there for me, and now it's my turn to be there for him — regardless of who thinks what or does what. And, Frida, it is time, too, for me to stop pretending to be what I am not."

She sighs, then gulps, and between gulps, she says, "I always knew I could be proud of you. Take care of yourself and Uncle Al."

"I will, Frida." He ends the call.

He walks into the kitchen, notices that they'd left coffee in the pot. He pours the liquid down the sink. He remembers that he should phone Trevor so he won't make a useless trip to the airport. After that he should try to take a nap before going to see Allan.

Acknowledgements

MY SINCERE THANKS TO THE STAFF AT THE ST VINCENT and the Grenadines Archives, particularly Ms. Cashena Allen-Foster, who enthusiastically got me the documents I needed for this novel. I proffer my thanks to the staff at Dundurn Press: Kwame Scott Fraser, my acquiring editor, for his many suggestions and his faith in this novel; to Russell Smith, for his editorial suggestions; to Shannon Whibbs and Erin Pinksen, for their superb editing; to Laura Boyle, for the beautiful cover design; and to Meghan Macdonald, Julia Kim, and all the other members of the Dundurn team. Finally, I thank my partner, Benoit, for the joy and support he has given me for almost two decades.

About the Author

H. Nigel Thomas immigrated to Canada from St Vincent and the Grenadines in 1968. He obtained a B.A. and an M.A. from Concordia University, a Diploma in Education from McGill University, and a Ph.D. from Université de Montréal. He was a mental health worker at Douglas Hospital, an English and French teacher for the Protestant School Board of Greater Montreal, and, from 1988 to 2006, a professor of literature at Université Laval. He is the author of dozens of essays, six novels, three collections of short fiction, two collections of poems, and two academic books. His novels *Spirits in the Dark* (1993) and *No Safeguards* (2015) were shortlisted for the Hugh MacLennan Prize for Fiction. The French translation of *Lives: Whole and Otherwise — Des vies cassées —* was a finalist for the Prix Carbet des lycéens. He is the founder and English-language coordinator of Lectures Logos Readings and the editor of

KOLA Magazine. He is the recipient of many awards; those since 2020 are Laureate, Black History Month — Quebec (2024); the Canada Council for the Arts Molson Prize (2022); Quebec Writers' Federation Judy Mappin Community Award (2021); and the Black Theatre Workshop's Martin Luther King Jr. Achievement Award (2020).